SEAL
of HONOR

a HORNET novel

D1361963

SEAL
of HONOR

a HORNET novel

TONYA BURROWS

This book is a work of fiction. Names, characters, places, and incidents are the product of the author's imagination or are used fictitiously. Any resemblance to actual events, locales, or persons, living or dead, is coincidental.

Copyright © 2013 by Tonya Burrows. All rights reserved, including the right to reproduce, distribute, or transmit in any form or by any means. For information regarding subsidiary rights, please contact the Publisher.

Entangled Publishing, LLC
2614 South Timberline Road
Suite 109
Fort Collins, CO 80525

Visit our website at www.entangledpublishing.com.

Edited by Heather Howland and Sue Winegardner
Cover design by Heather Howland

Print ISBN   978-1-62061-258-3
Ebook ISBN   978-1-62061-259-0

Manufactured in the United States of America

First Edition May 2013

The author acknowledges the copyrighted or trademarked status and trademark owners of the following wordmarks mentioned in this work of fiction: Academy Award; Google Maps; Firefox; X-Acto; Smith & Wesson; Jeep; *Girls Gone Wild*; 4Runner; Microsoft Word; Hannibal Lecter; Sherlock Holmes; SIG Sauer; *Lean On Me*; *Call of Duty*; Harvard; Gameboy; Superman; Mercedes; *Grey's Anatomy*; *House, M.D.*; Twizzlers; Starbucks; Porsche; Apple iPhone; James Bond; Terminator; Dirty Harry.

To the three most influential women in my life:

Grandma Cheri, for all of the support you've given me as I've pursued this crazy dream.

Aunt Cyndi, for always being my #1 fan. I can't express my gratitude enough.

And, Mom, because you've always been my biggest inspiration. You're my hero.

I couldn't have done it without you all. I love you.

The only easy day was yesterday.

\- U.S. Navy SEALs

CHAPTER ONE

BOGOTÁ, COLOMBIA

God help him if he didn't make it to the airport by seven.

Bryson Van Amee checked his watch for the fourth time in as many minutes and frowned. Armando, his usual driver, was as prompt and reliable as the sunrise, and just as cheerful, which was why Bryson—who was not a morning person—always requested him.

Of all the days for him to be late.

Bryson tamped down a hot surge of fear-laced irritation. He had to meet his incoming cargo in Barranquilla and make a three p.m. appointment in Cartagena, and he did *not* want to piss off this particular client. Just thinking about it made him sweat. Yes, he should have known better than to dip his toes into the murky pool of the gray market, but with that first not-quite-legal gun shipment, he had jumped in with both feet. Now, as he sank into the deep abyss of the black market, where all manner of nasty predators lurked, he couldn't find a life vest. No wonder his heart had been acting up over the past several months.

He tapped his foot, checked his watch again, checked the street. A skinny tabby cat perched on the edge of a dumpster in the alley behind him, but there was no other soul around. Even the vendor that sold handmade knickknacks, who always set up his rollaway shop on the low stone wall across the street, hadn't made it out yet.

Bryson normally enjoyed that Colombian attitude of *I'll get there when I get there.* No mad dashes through morning traffic with a Starbucks cup sloshing mocha frappe crap all over his Porsche. For a man used to the impatient get-up-and-go of American cities, visiting the laid-back country of Colombia was always a nice change of pace.

Except when his driver was running late.

Another quick check of the watch, street, watch. Twenty minutes late. Damn, he should have bought Armando a cell phone last time he was in town. At least then, he would have been able to call and find out what the holdup was.

He reached into his pocket for his own phone. He hated to report Armando to the limo company when the man had been so good to him, but he needed another car. Now.

Just as he swiped away the photo of his wife and kids on the iPhone's screen, the phone rang and his sister's grinning face popped up on the display. Audrey.

He considered ignoring her call—but, God, what if she'd gotten herself into a mess again? He thumbed the answer button and her face filled the screen. Make-up free, her golden brown hair pulled back in a sloppy ponytail, she looked so much younger than her twenty-seven years.

"Hi, Brys," she said with a bright smile. She'd always been a disgustingly chipper morning person, even as a baby.

"Something wrong, sweetie?" he asked. "Are you okay? Do you need more money?"

"I'm fine." She rolled her eyes and raised a coffee mug to her mouth.

God, coffee. He'd forgotten to grab a cup in his rush to get out the door and his mouth watered for a taste.

"And I've told you a thousand times," Audrey added after taking a sip, "I don't need or want your money."

The hell she didn't need it. "You can't tell me you're making enough doing caricature sketches for tourists."

"Uh, well, no. I'm not doing caricatures anymore."

Bryson suppressed the groan rumbling inside his chest, took off his square-framed glasses, and rubbed his eyes. He loved his baby sister, he truly did, but dealing with her was tiring and not what he needed this early in the morning when he was stressing out about the missing—

Ah, there it is.

The shiny black limo rounded the corner at the top of the street and cruised to a stop in front of his apartment complex. Instead of short, balding Armando, a tall dark-haired man got out of the driver's seat.

"Señor Van Amee?"

"Just a minute, Audrey," he said before addressing the driver in Spanish, "What happened to Armando?"

"His son is very sick and had to go to the hospital. I apologize for the delay. It took some time to find a replacement," the driver answered, hustled around the car, and opened the back door. He wasn't dressed in a suit, but Armando didn't always wear one either. "I am Jacinto. I'll get you to the airport in no time."

The hairs on the back of his neck prickled. He'd used this limo company for years now and had never seen Jacinto before. "Are you new?"

"Just started, Señor."

Bryson shifted on his feet, checked his watch again. The idea of using a driver he hadn't screened made him itch but, dammit, what other choice did he have? Barring any morning traffic or an incident at the airport, he should still make both his appointments on time if he left right this very second.

He climbed into the limo.

"Audrey, you still there?" Bryson asked as the driver slid behind the wheel and put up the privacy partition. A moment later, the limo started with a purr and pulled away from the curb.

So maybe Jacinto would do just fine as a replacement. Professional, friendly, and discreet—all excellent qualities in a driver. If his background check came up clean, it wouldn't hurt to keep him in mind for the future in case another emergency cropped up with Armando's family.

Bryson made a mental note to find out which hospital Armando's son was at and send a get well gift. Or money if the family needed it.

"I'm here," Audrey said and reappeared on the screen. "Ran for a coffee refill. Are you busy?"

"On my way to a meeting."

"I won't keep you then. I just wanted to make sure you remembered my opening next weekend at *Museo de Arte Contemporaneo*. You said you'd come."

Uh-oh. Her art show in San José, Costa Rica. He'd forgotten all about it. He checked the schedule on his phone. Could possibly move a couple meetings around, but that would take a lot of shuffling just to indulge her and her silly hobbies. "I'm sorry, Audrey, but—"

She set her coffee mug on the table in front of her with a hard *thunk*. "Brys, you promised!"

"Sweetie, I have some very important business deals happening that weekend, none of which I can shove back, and I have to be in L.A. on Sunday morning for…" He shook his head as his train of thought slid away. What was he saying?

Audrey. Paintings. Work.

It was an old argument, one he could have while gagged and blindfolded, and he settled on one of his pat responses since his mind was suddenly, strangely blurry. "If you want to stay in that condo, I need to work and that means meetings."

"Well, guess what?"

No, he really didn't want to guess. She had that petulant look on her face—drawn brows, a poked out lower lip. The same look that had gotten her anything she wanted as a child. The one that told him he would not like the next words out of her mouth.

"Audrey—"

"I don't live in the condo. Never did. I sold it the week after you left and gave the money to a charity. I gave your accountant the receipt for your taxes."

"You *what*?" Oh God, then where was she living? Hopefully not in another beach shack with no indoor plumbing. His parents would roll over in their graves if they knew their precious baby girl enjoyed living one minuscule step up above a homeless person.

"I told you I didn't want it in the first place," she continued. "I was happy in Quepos. I was happy in my little hut. Don't you get that?"

"No, I—" His vision blurred. He blinked a couple times and when that didn't clear away the fuzziness, he pressed his fingers into his eyelids. Boy, was he tired. All of his time zone hopping was catching up to him. Maybe he should ask Jacinto to stop somewhere for a cup of hot, bold Colombian coffee.

On second thought, if he drank some, he wouldn't be able to sleep on the short plane ride to Barranquilla. A nap hadn't been in his original plan—he intended to review contracts on the plane like he always did—but with the way he felt now, a nap was probably the best idea. Last thing he needed was to be sluggish around the people he was meeting this afternoon.

"Are you even listening to me?" Audrey said, and he blinked her blurry face into focus. Had—had she been talking? He opened his mouth to answer, but his tongue wouldn't wrap itself around her name.

Something was wrong. He tried again and only managed to croak out, "Aw-ree."

"Bryson?" Her tone sharpened with worry, but he could no longer make out her features on the little screen. "Are you okay?"

No. No, he was not okay, but when he tried to tell her, the words slurred off his lips and barely made sense to his own ears. Was he having a stroke? He was only forty-three, but it wasn't unheard of. Or an aneurysm? His head pounded and the inside of the limo spun around him. He'd had that scare last summer, a mini heart attack, and his doctors had warned him to slow it down a little. They said if a clot broke off, it could travel to his brain and—

Oh, Christ.

"Bryson!"

"Aw-ree," he gasped and fumbled the phone in hands that felt as clumsy as catchers' mitts. It landed hard on the floor. He scrambled after it, clutched it like a lifeline. "Eh nee…elp."

Jacinto. He had to get the driver's attention.

Gasping, dizzy, Bryson crawled across the soft leather seat and pounded a weak fist on the partition. The tinted window slid down, and at first, he thought he was hallucinating. Huge bug eyes stared back at him. Some sort of insect now drove the car and—no, not an insect. Jacinto was wearing a gas mask.

Shit.

He collapsed face-first on the seat and turned his head to the side, staring through hazy eyes at the mini fridge across the car. He reached out a hand. Maybe there was something in there… Something he could use to break out the window… Something…

"*Tranquilo,*" Jacinto said, his voice warped by the mask, but still as friendly as ever. Like he was talking about a *fútbol* game. Or the traffic. Or the weather. "Let it happen, Señor Van Amee. Go to sleep now. I won't hurt you. You're worth too much money."

DOMINICAL, COSTA RICA

Audrey watched her computer screen in horror as her brother's face went slack and his eyelids fluttered closed. The phone slipped out of his hand and sent her on a jarring ride to the floor of a limo. Or what she assumed to be a limo. She leaned closer to the screen, saw a curved ceiling, part of a black seat, and the toe of Bryson's

Italian loafer.

"Brys?"

Scrambling. A thump. The picture wobbled and she caught disjoined glimpses of his face, a mini-fridge, the seat, his face again.

"Aw-ree, eh nee...elp"

Her heart thundered blood through her ears and she barely heard his mumbled whisper. She leaned closer. "What? What's wrong?"

His face slipped away and the picture tumbled into another jerky freefall. White shirt sleeve. Gold watch. White shirt sleeve. He must be crawling across the seat, still hanging onto the phone. And then—

Audrey leapt to her feet, her coffee splashing out of its mug, her chair crashing backward. Vaguely, she registered it knocking into her easel across the kitchen, heard the half-finished painting she'd been working on last night crash to the floor. But she didn't give a damn. Her whole world centered on the computer screen, where a tinted partition slid down and a man in a gas mask told her brother that he was worth too much money.

The screen blanked.

No. Audrey shook her head in denial and turned around in a slow circle. Her kitchen, with its eclectic mix of art and cooking supplies, looked exactly the same as it had when she woke up an hour ago. The coffee pot hissed as the last of the new pot brewed. Her dolphin-shaped cookie jar, which chirped like the dolphins that hung out by her dock when opened, grinned at her from the countertop. Sheet-wrapped paintings waited propped against the wall for their upcoming trip to San José.

All the same. And yet, she must have just stepped into a

Twilight Zone episode.

She refocused on the computer screen. Skype had ended the call and now rested on her homepage with her list of contacts. Bryson's name sat at the top of the list.

She straightened her chair, sat down, and tried to call him. The ringtone buzzed. And buzzed. And buzzed.

No answer. Would she like to retry the call?

She blinked back the tears burning her eyes and jabbed yes.

CHAPTER TWO

Gabe Bristow never thought he'd live to see his own retirement party. Never thought he'd have a retirement party if he *did* live that long, but this black tie soiree was so typical of his mother. If Catherine Bristow couldn't find an excuse to entertain, she made one up. Wedding? Throw a party. Funeral? Throw a party. Global disaster? Throw a party in the bomb shelter. Personal disaster? Throw a party and invite the who's who of D.C. politics.

This forced medical retirement definitely qualified as a personal disaster in Gabe's book, so of course, every Tom, Dick, and Jane on Capitol Hill were arriving downstairs in their best monkey suits and gowns.

Standing in front of a mirror in his boyhood bedroom, Gabe straightened his cuffs and then just stared at his reflection. Man, he always figured the next time he wore all of his medals, he'd be in a casket wrapped in an American flag. He'd have preferred it that way. This whole retirement thing felt wrong on so many different levels.

"Oooh, bro, lookin' good. I do love a man in uniform."

Gabe lifted his gaze to see Rafael, his youngest brother, propped in the doorway, wearing a hot pink vest over a black shirt, black trousers with a pink satin stripe down the outer seams, and a pink and white striped tie. He carried a black wool jacket over his shoulder and wore a pair of dark shades against the afternoon sunshine. One bright pink highlight streaked his dark hair over his left eye.

Their parents would have a conniption when they saw Raffi today. God love him.

"You're trying to give the Admiral a heart attack, aren't you?"

Raffi waggled his brows. "That's the idea. Why else do you think I act so *fabulous* when he's around?" He stepped into the room and performed a quick turn, topped off with a fanciful flourish of his arms. "Like?"

"No, it looks ridiculous. And you're not doing yourself any favors by perpetuating this"—Gabe waved a hand to indicate the pink monstrosity of a tux—"stereotype whenever you come home."

"But it's so much fun to see that vein throb next to Dad's eye."

"Raf, c'mon, man. Drop the act. I know exactly how much his prejudice hurts you, and beating him over the head with a rainbow stick every time you see him won't make it any easier for him to accept you."

"I don't want that man's acceptance." His tone said he'd rather lick a platoon of combat boots clean than admit he needed anything from the Admiral. He pointed an accusing finger. "And neither should you."

"Stubborn," Gabe muttered.

"Hard ass." Raffi plopped down on the edge of the bed with a long-suffering sigh. "Dad raised his little sailor so well. It's sad."

"Hey, I like—" No. Past tense. He had to use past tense now. Gabe paused, drew a breath, and corrected himself, "*Liked* being on the teams."

"Okay, you liked it. Though God knows why anyone would like being a SEAL." Raffi propped his chin in his hand and lifted his brows in question. "So…you're going into private soldiering, then?"

"*Soldiering*? Are you trying to insult me?"

"Soldiering, or sailor…ing?" He waved a hand. "You know what I mean. Are you going into the private sector?"

Gabe stifled a groan. This again. He'd already told his best friend and former SEAL teammate, Travis Quinn, that he was not going merc. Several times. In fact, just about every day since the car accident that ended both of their careers last year. "Lemme guess. Quinn talked to you."

"Mm-hmm. A minute ago, downstairs. And let me just say, it's a damn shame that guy's straight."

This time Gabe did groan. "Raffi, man, I love you, but please don't talk about my friends like that. It puts pictures in my head and weirds me out."

"That's why I do it." He grinned. "Anyway, for some reason, Quinn thought I'd be able to talk some sense into you. As if *anyone* can talk ol' Stonewall Bristow into doing something he doesn't want to do."

If anyone could, it would be Raffi. Gabe respected his youngest brother more than any other man on the planet, and Quinn knew it. That sly bastard.

"For the record," Raffi added and rested his chin on his laced fingers, "I think it's a great idea. Way better than Dad's plans for you."

True. The job the Admiral had lined up for him at the Pentagon was—God, he didn't even know what to call it. "Boring" came to mind. So did "mindless."

"Gabe, can I ask you something?" Raffi said after a moment of silence.

"No, but that's never stopped you before." Resigned to the lecture he knew he was about to get, Gabe limped over to where his jacket lay on the bed, light glinting off his rows of medals. It always surprised him how many he had. He just did his job and never much cared about the number before—but, man, now he'd never get another one. And how fucking depressing was that?

"Well, I'm curious," Raffi said. "Did you turn Quinn down because you really don't want to go private, or because it would put you on level with Darth Vader in Dad's eyes?"

Inwardly, Gabe faltered, his heart doing a little two-step even though his hands stayed calm, his face schooled into an expressionless mask. "I don't see why it matters. I'm not going into the private sector. End of story."

"It does matter. Big time." Raffi watched him with a rare serious look in his eyes. "That's it, isn't it? Look, Gabe, if you're holding yourself back because of the Admiral's narrow-minded views—well, we both know how I feel about that. Tell him to go fuck himself sideways with a spoon, then do what makes you happy. And you, brother dear, are only happy if you're out in some godforsaken wasteland of a country, risking life and limb, saving the world. Go work with Quinn."

"No."

"At least think about it? For me?"

"Fine." He was so going to find Quinn and throttle him for dragging Raffi into this. "I'll think about it, okay?"

• • •

It took several hours of elbow rubbing with political so-and-sos before Gabe finally tracked Quinn down in the crowd. He stood in the most shadowed corner of the room, naturally, stiff in his dress whites, eyeing the horde of D.C.'s most powerful as if he expected an attack at any moment.

Not a surprise.

Quinn had earned the nickname "Achilles" during BUD/S training. A warrior to his marrow, all but indestructible since nobody had found his heel yet. His only concession that this was a party and not an op was the slender flute of champagne he held.

Gabe stalked toward him.

"This place is a terrorist attack waiting to happen," Quinn muttered and lifted his glass in a salute to the room.

Yeah, it was, and securing the damn mansion had been a nightmare, but that was beside the point. "Seriously, Q, you're a rank bastard for siccing Raffi on me."

His lips twitched. "Did it work?"

Gabe thought about the glittering crowd he'd been forced to schmooze with all afternoon and held back a wince. Did he really want the rest of his life to consist of politics and state dinners? Because if he lived in D.C. fulltime, the Admiral would guilt-trip him into attending. More importantly, did he really want to live under his father's thumb again? Oh no. Make that, oh *hell* no.

"Yeah," he admitted. "It worked."

"Good."

"But answer me something first. Why don't you want to command this private team by yourself?"

"You know me." He took a long swallow of champagne. "Would rather take orders than issue them."

"Since when?"

"Since always. You have command in your blood. Me, I'm just one of the rank and file."

"Quinn—"

"Incoming." Quinn eyed the Admiral, who had spotted them and was making a beeline for their position. For some reason, the Admiral had never liked Quinn, pictured him as a bad influence even though he was the most squared-away guy Gabe knew.

"Better get back to the party before Admiral Stick-up-the-Ass blows a gasket," Quinn said. "Meet me outside in twenty. If you're serious, there's someone here I want you to meet. Oh, and you can remember to thank me for saving your sorry ass from a desk job anytime now."

He wasn't joking.

Gabe snorted in response. "You really are a bastard." He waited until Quinn lifted his glass to his lips before adding, "But Raffi thinks you're hot."

As he walked away, he had the great pleasure of watching the unflappable Achilles choke on his champagne.

• • •

Gabe slipped outside twenty minutes later, found Quinn and another tuxedo-clad man on the terrace overlooking the garden. Well, if it wasn't Tucker Quentin. A businessman with sights on a senate seat, Gabe recognized Tucker from other political shindigs around Washington, but had never spoken to him before.

"Ah, the man of the hour. Lieutenant Commander Bristow," Tucker said as Gabe hobbled toward them. His foot hurt like hell, but he'd left his damn cane inside somewhere.

"Gabe," he corrected. "I'm not in the Navy anymore."

"Don't give me that load." Tucker flashed a smile worthy of his Hollywood roots. "We get out, but we never leave. I've been gone from the Rangers for ten years, but my men still call me L.T." He held out a hand. "Tuc Quentin."

Gabe ignored it. "I know. So you're the guy that put the idea of a private hostage rescue team in Quinn's head."

"No," Quinn said. "I heard Tuc was thinking of putting one together and approached him about funding us."

Tuc nodded. "On paper, you'll be employees of Quentin Enterprises, specifically HumInt Consulting, Inc., but save for a quarterly expense report and the occasional contract I'll throw your way, I plan to have nothing more to do with your team. If you come to me for advice, of course I'll be glad to give it, but otherwise it's yours to run as you see fit."

"Why?" Gabe asked.

"I already have several teams working for HumInt, plus a multi-billion dollar empire to run." His lips twisted. "I think I'm quite busy enough."

"No, I mean why are you doing this? People don't hand out free money and expect nothing in return." Especially not savvy businessmen, but Gabe couldn't figure out Tucker Quentin's angle.

Tuc leaned his forearms on the balustrade and studied the garden in the courtyard. "That garden's amazing."

"What are you getting out of this?" Gabe repeated.

"Quinn's right. You're tenacious as hell. Perfect for this job."

Yeah, right. Gabe bit back the automatic response. If that were true, if he was perfect for any command position, the Navy wouldn't have tossed him and his bum foot to the curb. He shifted his weight, suddenly very aware of the pain.

"Why?" Gabe asked again. Meaning, *why me?* But he'd be damned before putting a voice to that insecurity.

Tuc twirled the stem of his champagne glass between his fingers. "The brother of one of my men was taken hostage recently and we were unprepared to handle it. I don't want that happening again. I'm a big believer in being prepared, and you have an admirable reputation in the spec ops community. I only ask that if I contract you for a job, it's given top priority. You of all people must understand how important my men are to me. They're family."

Gabe briefly met Quinn's stare and then nodded once. He understood, all right, and his respect for Tuc ratcheted up a notch. "Should the occasion call for it, you and your men will have top priority."

"Thank you. So." Tuc finished his champagne in one swallow and pushed away from the balustrade. "Quinn tells me you have a team lined up from the dossiers I gave him."

Gabe honestly didn't know and looked at Quinn, who nodded and said, "We had six men submit resumes."

"Their qualifications?" Gabe asked.

"Couple ex-CIA spooks, an FBI negotiator, a Delta Force

medic, an explosives tech…" His eyes slid away for the barest instant before he continued. "And a Marine sniper. They're all experts in their fields—"

"Whoa, wait." Gabe held up a hand. "What sniper?" He got nothing but a whole lot of stubborn silence in response and shook his head in disbelief. "Goddamn. You're talking about Seth Harlan, aren't you? The same Seth Harlan that—"

"I recommended him for a position. He's an excellent sniper," Quinn said with an expression on his face that dared Gabe to argue. Well, he'd take that dare.

"Q, are you out of your fucking mind? Harlan's unstable."

"He's better now."

"Good for him." When Quinn just gave him a long stare, the kind that always made him feel like a complete ass, he added, "Listen, I give the kid credit for surviving what he did, I do. And I know you have a soft spot for him, but he's traumatized. Who wouldn't be? I don't want that kind of baggage weighing down my team. Think about it. What if he has a psychotic break in the middle of an op?"

Quinn held his gaze a moment longer, then swore softly. "Yeah, you're right. I know you're right, but—shit. All right. Harlan's out." He turned back to Tuc. "The only man I haven't been able to reach yet is the linguist, Jean-Luc Cavalier. Apparently he lives in the middle of the bayou and has spotty cell service."

"If you want him, you'd better find a way to get in touch," Tuc said. "Because I already have a job for you. I was recently contacted by Zoeller and Zoeller Insurance Company, on behalf of Bryson Van Amee. Have you heard of him?"

Gabe had. "He's in imports and exports and does a lot of

subcontracting for the military."

"That's right. Bryson was taken hostage this morning in Bogotá during a business trip. The FBI fears one of the guerilla groups may be responsible."

Gabe nodded. Wealthy American businessman plus Colombian paramilitary—yeah, the math added up, and the sum didn't look good for Bryson Van Amee.

"The FBI is working with his wife, Chloe," Tuc continued, "but Zoeller and Zoeller wants to free him before a ransom is paid, or else they'll be liable for a hefty kidnap and ransom insurance payout."

"Does the FBI know what Zoeller's doing?" Gabe asked.

Tuc gave a thin smile. "What do you think?"

That'd be a big negative. Okay, he wasn't all that crazy about working against the FBI—well, maybe "against" was too harsh a word, since they all wanted the same results. Still. It somehow seemed a betrayal of his former career.

"I understand your hesitation," Tuc said after the silence stretched too long on his end. "Believe me, I do. I had some bad moments when I went private. But I'd also like to point out that the FBI hasn't sent a team in after him and isn't planning to. They're hoping to simply talk his abductors down or, if all else fails, pay the ransom. He's not important enough to them. Even with his government contracts, he's a small fish in the grand scheme of things, and Uncle Sam could care less about what happens to him. But that man's damn important to his wife and kids, his sister, his company—and you're his best chance at survival."

Gabe considered it. He had two choices. Go wheels up, sneak in under the FBI's nose, and bring Bryson Van Amee home to his family, or gimp back to his boring new job at the Pentagon, where he would forever be under the Admiral's thumb. Yeah. When put that way, there was really only one choice.

"Q, we have to get mobilization orders to the men," Gabe said, his mind already working through the logistics. He checked his watch. "Tell them to be ready at—wait, do you have a plane for us?" he asked Tuc.

"Fueled and ready to go. You'll also have helos and a HumInt pilot at your disposal here and in-country."

"Perfect. We'll need one to dig Cavalier out of his hole in the bayou."

Tuc snorted. "Good luck with that."

"Tell the men to be at their local airport for a 0400 pickup," Gabe said to Quinn. "I'll swing by Louisiana and grab Cavalier, then meet you at…" He trailed off.

"I have a private airstrip about forty miles outside New Orleans," Tuc suggested. "My pilots all know where it is."

"That works. Thanks. We'll come up with a plan of attack once everyone is together and we have more intel, but we need to get moving."

"On it," Quinn said, already dialing. He tucked the cell phone between his shoulder and ear as he strode toward the relative privacy at the other side of the balcony. "Hey, Marcus, it's Quinn…"

Tuc turned toward Gabe and held out a hand. "I'll have all the information you need before you leave. Welcome to HumInt Consulting, Bristow."

Gabe shook the offered hand. And tried to tell himself he hadn't made a pact with the devil.

NEW ORLEANS, LA

Jean-Luc Cavalier was drunk.

And naked, buried underneath a pile of equally drunk and naked women. Three women to be exact.

None of them moved when Gabe knocked on the wood doorframe of Cavalier's shack, so he let himself in through the screen door.

"Cavalier." Gabe nudged the guy's head with his boot.

Jean-Luc mumbled something in French and palmed one woman's ass, gave it a squeeze, then drifted back to sleep with a smile.

Jesus Christ. This is what his life had come to? Scraping a drunk linguist off the floor so that he had enough men for an op? He never would have found one of his SEAL teammates like this if they were waiting for a call to go wheels up.

Gabe sighed, picked a half-empty bottle of wine off the end table, and dumped the contents over Jean-Luc's face.

"Huh? Wha—?" Jean-Luc sputtered and blinked up at Gabe. "*Merde!*" He scrambled to his feet and cussed in a lively string of Cajun French. His shoulder-length blond hair looked as if someone had styled it with a handheld mixer. "I didn't know she was married. I swear. She didn't have a ring."

"Which one?" Gabe asked, eyeing the women as they stirred to life. *Girls Gone Wild*, the morning after. Not pretty.

"Any of them!"

Gabe had to clear his throat to hide a laugh. "I'm nobody's

husband. I'm your new boss, Gabe Bristow."

"Oh." He looked confused at that and ran a hand over his face. Then, "Ohh. HORNET."

"HORNET?"

"I thought all you military types like acronyms." He rooted around through a heap of discarded clothing, tossed some to the women, and pulled on a pair of khaki shorts. "HumInt Inc.'s Hostage Rescue and Negotiation Team is a mouthful, so I shortened it. HORNET."

Leave it to the linguist to come up with something like that. "We have a job in Colombia. That is, if you're still interested."

"Fuck, yeah. I've been bored mindless."

"Looks it," Gabe said.

• • •

The plane arrived at the private airfield fifteen minutes past 0800. Thank God. If Gabe had to listen to another of Jean-Luc's tone-deaf renditions of whatever song came over the radio, he might just draw his firearm and shoot the man.

It was a big plane. Bigger than Gabe had expected, and each of the five men already aboard had claimed a row of the plush seats for himself. The former FBI agent, Marcus Deangelo, dozed in the second row, a plaid fedora pulled down over his face, his legs crossed at the ankle, blocking the aisle. Jean-Luc reached over the seat and flipped the fedora off his head.

"Hey!" Marcus snatched his fedora back, blinking against the light. "Asshole. I should—whoa, it's the Ragin' Cajun." He laughed as he sat up and slapped Jean-Luc a high five. "Dude, you smell like a wine cellar."

"Better than a Calvin Klein cologne ad." Jean-Luc grinned and plopped into an empty seat in the fourth row beside Eric Physick. "Harvard! Where y'at? How's post-Company life treatin' ya?"

Former CIA analyst Eric "Harvard" Physick chuckled and set aside the crossword puzzle he'd been working on. "I should have figured you'd sign on for this. I'm fine. How about you? Learn any new languages lately?"

Jean-Luc answered in a musical string of words. Harvard tilted his head to one side, listening. "Is that… Yucatec Maya?"

"That it is. I said 'you bet your ass, I have.'"

"Fluent?" Harvard asked.

"Pretty damn close."

"That's what, thirteen now? You've been busy."

"You have no idea. Let me tell y'all about the night I had."

Within minutes, Jean-Luc had everyone on the plane laughing at his night of adventure with the three women. The jet coasted toward the runway and the seatbelt light came on with a ding.

Gabe sat next to Quinn in the front row. "So, what do you think?"

Laughter exploded behind them. Quinn shook his head, but didn't look up from reading the file on his lap. "It's going to be interesting. To say the least."

"That the intel Tuc sent?"

"Yes." He handed it over as the plane picked up speed and pushed them back in their seats. "Bryson Van Amee is worth around a quarter of a billion dollars."

"Has a ransom demand been issued yet?" Gabe asked.

"About an hour ago, according to Tuc's sources. Sixty-two point five million."

"That's pretty damn high for one guy."

"No. What it is, is damn specific. In fact…" Quinn slid a calculator from the bag at his feet and punched in some numbers. "It's exactly a quarter of Van Amee's worth."

And, Gabe noted, the maximum amount Van Amee's kidnap and ransom insurance would cover. "That can't be a coincidence."

"So what are we dealing with?" Quinn asked. "Tangos who do their homework?"

"Too soon to tell." The plane leveled out and a moment later, the seatbelt light went off. "Suppose it's time to brief the troops."

Quinn grunted. "If you can call them that."

Gabe stood and braced his hands on the backs of the seats on either side of the aisle. Pain spiked through his foot, but he'd be damned if he relied on his cane. Last thing he needed was to show any sign of weakness in front of this ragtag group.

He waited a moment. When nobody quieted down, he put his fingers to his mouth and gave a sharp whistle that echoed around the plane's interior in the silent aftermath.

"Gentlemen, listen up. I'd like to introduce myself before we get started. My name's Gabe Bristow. You've all been dealing with Quinn, my XO, but from now on, you'll answer to me."

"Do you expect us to salute?" Ian Reinhardt asked. His motorcycle jacket creaked as he raised an arm and gave a cheeky two-finger salute. "Sir."

So this was the explosive ordnance expert. After reading everyone's dossiers on the way to New Orleans, he'd known Ian might be a problem. The guy was bad attitude personified. "No, I don't expect that. However, showing some respect for a fellow teammate wouldn't hurt."

"Bite me," Ian said.

Oh, yeah. This was going to be fun. "Do I look like a fucking vampire, Reinhardt? And if you have a problem with my leadership…" He turned, walked to a closet at the front of the plane, grabbed one of the parachutes he'd asked Quinn to pack, and tossed it to Ian. "Strap in. The door's right there. Go find yourself a new job."

Ian caught the chute and his dark eyes locked on Gabe's in a game of chicken for a long moment. Then he flashed a smile that held just an edge of malice and tossed the chute back. "Nah, I don't have a problem with you, Bristow. I like your style. We'll get along fine."

"Let's hope, because I have no use for disrespectful assholes on my team. Those guys get their teammates killed, and I want everyone here to go home to their families when this is over. You clear on that?"

Ian grunted something that may have been an agreement. Or, more likely, a fuck you.

Gabe decided he'd have to chat with Reinhardt about his attitude at some point in the next few hours.

He took a moment to replace the parachute in the closet, then returned to his spot in front of his men.

"Our objective is to find and rescue this man, Bryson Van Amee, before any ransom money is paid." He opened the folder Quinn handed him and held up the businessman's photo. "He's forty-three years old, five-eleven, one-eighty, with thinning brown hair, brown eyes. He co-founded The Bryda Corporation twelve years ago with his college roommate, has been married to his wife, Chloe, for five years, and is the father of two young boys, Ashton, five, and Grayson, three. His parents are deceased, so he also provides for his younger sister, Audrey, twenty-seven, a struggling artist."

"In an ideal situation," Quinn said and passed around copies of the file, "we'd have trained together for a couple months before taking on our first mission, but we don't have that luxury. Most of you have been on this type of op before, so we're confident we can pull together and bring Bryson home to his wife and kids."

"This is truly a trial-by-fire, gentlemen," Gabe agreed. "We fail and this man will at best live the next few years of his life in some Colombian jungle shithole. At worst, he dies. Neither of those outcomes is acceptable." He gave them a moment, letting the grim reality of this mission settle into their minds. The lighthearted mood dissipated as everyone got their game faces on. "I expect you to know the information in this file inside and out by the time we land."

"Has there been a ransom demand yet?" Marcus Deangelo asked.

"Sixty million and some change," Quinn said. "It's all there in the file."

"Who's taking responsibility?" Harvard asked.

"A new terrorist faction calling themselves *Ejército del Pueblo de Colombia,* the People's Army of Colombia, or EPC," Gabe said. "All we know about them is that they broke off from the Revolutionary Armed Forces of Colombia about six months ago and have been on a terror campaign ever since.

"That's where Harvard comes in." He turned toward Eric Physick, who had a rep as one of the best analysts ever to work for the CIA. A genius with more brain than brawn—something

Gabe would have to fix if the kid wanted a chance of staying on this team. "We need you to gather as much intel as possible on the EPC. Who, what, where, how—get me everything available. We're working against the clock. The FBI will only be able to stall the ransom drop for so long and I don't want to go up against these guys blind."

Harvard nodded, picked up his laptop case, and unzipped it. "You'll know the basics by the time we get to Colombia. The rest will take me a little longer."

"Thanks." Gabe refocused on the rest of the men. "Okay, so here's how the team's going to work. Harvard will control base camp and all the comms, including all contact with the hostage takers, should it come to that. Harvard, make a list of everything you might need and you'll have it when we land."

The kid nodded, but didn't look up from his computer.

"Jesse Warrick will function as our medic. Anyone gets hurt, we defer to him. If you need anything, Jesse, let either Quinn or me know and we'll get it for you."

Jesse tipped the brim of his Stetson back with one knuckle and patted the bulging bag on the seat next to him. "I travel with my own supplies, thanks," he drawled. "But I do want access to medical records and everyone needs to have a physical exam in the next twenty-four hours so I have a baseline reading should one of ya get hurt."

"Done." Gabe studied the group. "We'll rely on Jean-Luc as our translator. Anyone else fluent in Spanish?"

"Mine's passable," Jesse answered.

"All I remember from Spanish class is *un burro sabe mas que tu*," Marcus said and Jean-Luc snorted a laugh.

"'A donkey knows more than you?' Nice, Marcus. If we need to insult the EPC into submission, we'll know who to call."

"All right, gentlemen," Gabe said. "Enough joking around. We have a little over four hours until we land. Read up and catch whatever sleep you can, because once we're on the ground, we're on the move."

CHAPTER THREE

BOGOTÁ, COLOMBIA

"Nice digs," Jean-Luc said from the passenger seat of the rented 4Runner. "Nice neighborhood. I didn't think Colombia had nice neighborhoods."

Gabe ignored him and leaned on the steering wheel to study Bryson Van Amee's apartment building and the surrounding neighborhood. It *was* nice. Affluent. Clean. Full of sprawling parks and red brick buildings with a subtle British flair to the architecture. A million steps up from the barrios he'd seen during his past two trips to Bogotá. Of course, he'd been assisting the Colombian Army in hunting for the brutal leader of a drug cartel, not searching for an unfortunate American businessman caught in the wrong place at the wrong time.

"I don't think the snatch happened inside his place," Gabe said, "but it won't hurt to check it out." He needed to get a feel for the kind of person Van Amee was. A survivor, he hoped, or else they'd be dragging a body back to the States.

"Security guard on the front door," Jean-Luc pointed out. "Cameras, too. IP-based, which means they probably archive their footage."

"How do you know?" Gabe had seen the cameras, but as far as he knew, there was no way to tell whether they were on an IP network or closed-circuit TV just by looking.

"My brother-in-law owns a security company in New Orleans," Jean-Luc said and raised a pair of binoculars, focusing on the closest camera. "I help out with installing systems when he's short staffed, and...*oui*, I know that brand. I can call him, but I'm pretty sure it's an IP camera. We should ask to see their footage."

Gabe shook his head. "I don't want to risk tipping anyone off that we're looking."

Jean-Luc lowered the binoculars and grinned. "I like the way your mind works, *mon capitaine*. Very James Bond."

"No," Gabe corrected, "very practical. Van Amee's limo driver, Armando Castillo, reported him missing when he didn't show for his scheduled pick-up. Building security had no clue anything was wrong until Armando raised the alarm." He scanned the building, looking for faults in its security. At first glance, he didn't find many. A guard here, a camera there, angled just right. Not necessarily unassailable for a trained operative, but a newly formed, ragtag terrorist faction would have a rough time of it.

"Leads me to believe the EPC has someone on the inside," he continued. "How else would they know who to hit and when? They had to have surveillance on him."

"I'll call Harvard, see if he can hack into their network." Jean-Luc flipped open his phone, spoke for a moment, gave the camera's brand name and apartment's address, and nodded. "Harvard says it's a go. He'll have the footage for us in an hour." He closed the phone and slid it into the front pocket of his button-up shirt, which he wore open over a Pink Floyd T-shirt. "So, *mon capitaine*, we have time to kill. You want us to sneak a peek inside?"

"Not yet. I'm going to recon the block first. You stay here and keep eyes on." Gabe climbed out of the 4Runner and grabbed one of the radios Harvard had given him before they left the safe house. "Anything suspicious, radio me. Don't go in by yourself."

"Aye-aye. But, uh…" Jean-Luc reached into the backseat. "Shouldn't you take your cane?"

"Goddammit." He snatched it from Jean-Luc's hand. The only reason he had the fucking thing was Jesse Warrick, after getting a load of his medical history and doing a physical, insisted he use it more. Since he told his men to defer to the medic, he couldn't very well go against his own order.

"God*dammit*," he said again and Jean-Luc laughed as the car door shut.

• • •

Nothing.

Not that Audrey had expected a glaring neon sign with an arrow that said, *Find Bryson Here*, but, well, at least one clue would be nice. The apartment was disgustingly tidy, so like Bryson. No ruffled pillows, no dust on the rosy hardwood floors, no leftover dishes in the sink or crumbs on the marble counters. The coffee pot appeared unused and the fridge sat mostly empty. Also not a surprise. Brys couldn't cook worth a damn, somehow managing to burn everything he toasted, nuked, or fried up in a skillet. Like the time he'd tried to make Mama's famous casserole shortly after their parents died to cheer her up and ended up with half of Savannah's fire department on the front lawn.

Audrey smiled a little and ran a finger along one of the unused frying pans hanging above the kitchen's center island. Yes, they had their issues, but she couldn't have asked for a better big brother.

Now he was gone.

Her smile faded, but she wouldn't let the surge of stomach-churning fear get to her again or else she'd spend the next several hours hung over a toilet like she had when she realized she'd witnessed his kidnapping.

God, that short call might be the last time she ever talked to him.

No. No, she refused to think that. Bryson deserved better than that from her. He'd go to the ends of the earth to find her if she was in trouble. She couldn't do any less than the same.

But where to start?

Audrey drifted over to the window that took up one whole wall of the living room and stepped out onto the balcony. So many buildings, people, and parks in this quiet neighborhood alone. She had no idea where or even how to start looking. Chloe, the Wicked Sister-in-Law of the West Coast, had been next-to-no help.

"Don't get involved," Chloe had said. They simply had to do what the kidnappers wanted. Pay a ransom, get Bryson back. No police involvement. "Everything will be all right," she had said. "Trust me."

Uh-huh. Audrey would trust her the day Chloe admitted her boobs, butt, and the age on her ID were all fake. The only thing that woman had ever done right in her miserable life was give Bryson two sweet, adorable sons.

Audrey had ignored Chloe and called the FBI, who hadn't seemed all that interested, but said they would "look into it." Wasn't the FBI supposed to be all about finding kidnappers? At least, they were on *Without a Trace*. So she tried every other alphabet soup bureaucracy she could think of, and even Bryson's insurance company, in hopes someone could do something. But everyone said it was someone else's jurisdiction, except the insurance company, which was more worried about their bottom line than her brother's wellbeing. As soon as she hung up with them, she called her manager, canceled her show, and started packing her bags. If nobody was willing to help, she'd just find Brys herself.

Somehow.

On the street below, a man with a cane caught her eye as he climbed out of a dented blue 4Runner parked at the curb. He didn't look Colombian. For one thing, he towered head and shoulders above everyone he passed. He had dark close-cropped hair and light skin and wore a simple white short-sleeved shirt over olive green cargo pants. His footwear looked an awful lot like combat boots. Even two stories up, she could feel the waves of command radiating from him.

He seemed to be looking for something.

No, not looking. Canvassing. That's what all those cop dramas Mama used to like called it. Canvassing the neighborhood. Er, casing? She always got those confused, but that was beside the point. He didn't belong here, and jangled all of her mental warning bells.

Did he know something about Bryson's abduction? If not, why else would a man like him be here?

With a hard lump of fear rising in her throat, she watched him turn the corner at the end of the street, then she looked at the 4Runner he'd abandoned. From what she could see, it appeared to have local plates and another man sat inside. Okay, maybe she was overreacting. Maybe they were tourists, and the man with the cane was searching for a restroom. Or they were lost and looking for their hotel. Or they—

The man inside the vehicle lifted a set of binoculars and focused them directly at her.

Audrey ducked back into the apartment. A car door slammed shut a heartbeat later.

Oh God, oh God, oh God.

Heart pounding, she scanned the room. The apartment was too open and airy, too minimalist to offer any decent hiding place. Maybe he wouldn't be able to get in. The security guard at the door hadn't believed that she was Bryson Van Amee's sister, and it had taken a lot of wheedling and charm to access his apartment.

Footsteps pounded hard and fast down the hallway and her hope plummeted. The man obviously knew tricks to get by security guards. Big surprise. Did he also know how to get inside a locked apartment?

When the knob rattled and she saw the point of a knife slip between the door and frame, she got her answer.

What had she been thinking coming here alone? Yes, she'd wanted to find her brother, but not like this. Not as a fellow captive.

The door clicked and opened, catching on the chain she'd at least had the foresight to slide home.

"*Policía*," the man called, but his Spanish carried an accent she couldn't place and she didn't believe him for a second. "*¡Abra la puerta!*"

Uh-huh. Hell would most definitely freeze over before she acknowledged his command to open the door. Way she saw it, all she had going for her was the element of surprise. He figured someone was inside, but he didn't know who or where or whether she was armed.

She grabbed the closest thing, a heavy glass lamp on the end table beside the couch—such a girly weapon and not as heavy as she'd hoped, but it'd still make the fake policeman see stars—and moved to the right side of the door.

"*¡Policía!*"

Ri-ight. And if she had a cup of tea and a biscuit, she'd be the Queen of England.

Holding her breath until her ears buzzed, Audrey waited for him to kick the door, her hands beginning to sweat on the lamp. Any second now. Any…second…

The door flew open, banging into the opposite wall, and she went into pure adrenaline-fueled fight or flight mode, slamming the lamp down as hard as she could on his blond head. Once, twice, a third time for good measure, her heart hammering so hard she thought for sure it was going to pop out of her chest and join in on the beating.

The fake policeman collapsed with an *umph* and she scrambled over his big body. And, boy, was he big. A solid lump of muscle lying dazed on the floor, blocking her only escape. He looked more like a frat boy than a kidnapper in his Pink Floyd T-shirt, jeans, and Nikes, one of which connected with the back of her left knee, buckling her leg.

She managed to keep from slamming face-first into the floor by catching herself on her hands and knees. Tried to crawl away from her attacker, but he snagged her pant leg. On instinct, she kicked out, crashed the heel of her sandal into his nose, and wished like hell that she were wearing a stiletto instead. As blood spurted, he lost his grip and she scrambled to her feet.

He cursed in a language that was definitely not Spanish and, ignoring his bleeding nose, he was back on his feet as if he hadn't ever been down.

Who was this guy, the freaking Terminator? If he was this resilient, she didn't want to stick around and meet his friend with the cane.

"Hey, stop! I just want to talk to you." His English was perfect, barely accented, and he repeated the command in Spanish.

American, some tiny, rational portion of her brain realized as she darted toward the stairs at the end of the hall. Still, that didn't mean he was a friend. He wouldn't have kicked down the door if all he wanted to do was have a simple chat. She hit the stairs at a sprint, half-expecting him to vault over the railing and cut her off at the bottom. He didn't, but a glance over her shoulder as she crashed through an emergency exit at the back of the building proved he was still right behind her.

He had a gun now, holding it alongside his leg.

Oh God.

She turned to flee down the alleyway toward the street and smacked into a rock wall of a chest covered with a white short-sleeved cotton shirt.

Audrey screamed. And screamed. And screamed.

• • •

Gabe wasn't entirely sure what just happened. One minute he'd been reconnoitering the alleyway, wondering if Bryson had been taken from here because it had easy access to two different streets at both ends, and the next, a wisp of a woman shot out of the apartment building's emergency exit like her ass was on fire. Then she took one look at his face and gave a bloodcurdling horror movie scream. As a SEAL, he was trained to handle most anything an enemy could throw at him, but a hysterical woman? What the fuck was he supposed to do with her?

"Shh," he said. "It's okay. I'm not going to hurt you."

She didn't seem to hear him over her screaming. Or maybe she spoke Spanish and didn't understand him. She had smooth, tanned skin and light brown hair, but he'd seen enough light-skinned Latinos in his travels to know that wasn't the best judge of ethnicity. He dug around his admittedly rusty Spanish repertoire for the right words: "*Tranquillo. Está okay. No voy…a hacerte daño.*"

She screamed.

Jesus.

At wit's end, he clamped one palm over her mouth and circled her slender neck with his other hand, felt her pulse pounding wildly against his thumb as he applied just the right amount of pressure. She slumped into blessed silence. He had to drop his cane to catch her before she hit the ground, and the extra weight ignited fireworks of pain in his foot.

Great. Now what?

Her head lolled against his shoulder, her hair tickling his nose. Balancing her in one arm, he used his free hand to smooth back the silky strands, which were not so much brown as the color of the finest gold rum. He got his first clear look at her face and felt a tug of familiarity. Freckles dappled the bridge of a nose that he could only describe as "cute," like something on a doll. High cheekbones, a wide mouth that she probably thought was too big for her face if she judged herself by society's standards of beauty, but that he found fascinating. He suddenly very much wanted to see her smile.

And then it clicked. He *had* seen her smile before. In a photo while briefing the men.

This was Audrey Van Amee. His hostage's sister.

Gabe had a moment of no-fucking-way, but then the door slammed open again and Jean-Luc, his nose bleeding down the front of his shirt, skidded to a halt.

"You got her."

"What are you doing?" Gabe demanded. "I ordered you to hold your position."

"She was in Van Amee's apartment." He holstered his gun, then tried to staunch the blood flow with the edge of his shirt, which gave his voice a nasally sound. "She spotted me and took off. What else was I supposed to do?"

Gabe shut his eyes, drew a calming breath. Patience, he reminded himself, was a virtue. "Follow orders."

"Fuck orders. We're not the military, and I didn't have time to get you on the horn."

Police sirens wailed in the distance. Shit, as if this couldn't get any worse.

"We'll talk about this later." Talk. Yeah, that's what they'd do. After he reamed Jean-Luc a new one. This sort of reckless, Dirty Hairy shit was not happening under his command. "Get the car."

"What about her?"

He looked at the unconscious woman in his arms. Her freckles stood out in stark relief against her pale face. Her eyes moved restlessly behind lids fringed with some of the longest lashes he'd ever seen.

The police sirens screamed closer.

"Well?" Jean-Luc asked.

Poor woman would wake up with a hellacious headache from the pressure-point KO, but not for at least a half hour. Leaving her unconscious in this alleyway was just not an option.

"She's coming with us." They needed to talk to her and find out what she was doing in Van Amee's apartment. She'd also benefit from a once-over by Jesse when she woke up.

Jean-Luc grinned. "If you really want a date, I know plenty of willing women. We don't have to kidnap one." He stopped grinning and studied Gabe's face. "Whoa, you're serious."

"Car. Now."

Jean-Luc shook his head and broke into a jog. "And here I thought we're the good guys."

· · ·

"What the…?" Quinn's jaw didn't drop open when Gabe limped into the safe house carrying the unconscious woman, but came pretty damn close. In typical Quinn-like fashion, he shook off the shock fast.

"Help him," he ordered Marcus, who stood beside the door with a cup of aromatic Colombian coffee in hand.

"I got her." Gabe waved everyone back. Marcus Deangelo, with his California surfer good looks and brimming with all of that Italian lover charm, was not laying even a pinky finger on her. He angled through the group, heading toward the nearest bedroom.

"What happened?" Jesse asked, trailing behind, medical bag

in hand.

"Long story."

"No, it's not," Jean-Luc said as he shut the front door and propped Gabe's cane against the wall. "I found her in Van Amee's apartment."

"So , what the hell, Jean-Luc? You knocked her unconscious?" Jesse said.

"Nah. Our esteemed *capitaine* did that." He pressed two fingers to his neck and mimed a faint to demonstrate.

"Like a Vulcan death grip? Cool." Marcus took a drink from his cup. "Can you teach me that shit?"

"She'll be fine," Gabe muttered and shouldered into a small bedroom off the living room. The narrow cot he laid her on squeaked under her slight weight. She moaned, but otherwise didn't stir. "She'll wake up with a headache, nothing more."

Jesse crouched beside her, checked her vitals, and then stood. "Seems okay, but I wouldn't advise makin' a habit of the Vulcan death grip, 'specially with such a little thing as her." He snagged his medical bag from the floor beside the bed and went to the door. Glancing back, he opened his mouth to say something, but then looked at Quinn, shook his head, and walked out. "Hey, Jean-Luc, lemme take a gander at your nose. Looks broken."

A whole minute passed in silence after the room emptied. Quinn stood beside the door, studying the woman with unreadable eyes, a slight frown pulling down the corners of his mouth.

"I couldn't leave her," Gabe said. Quinn was one of only two men on earth he'd ever felt the need to explain himself to. His brother Raffi was the other.

"I didn't say anything."

"You don't have to. Listen, Q, things got fubared. Jean-Luc, that stupid jackass, went against orders and chased her through the building with his fucking gun. Someone called the cops and I had to make a decision. Leave her and possibly lose any information she might have, or bring her with us."

He purposely left out the part about the tugging in his groin every time he looked at her.

"Well, shit." Quinn rubbed a hand back and forth over his high-and-tight. "We're here to rescue a hostage, not create an international incident by kidnapping a native."

"She's not a native. Look at her. Don't you recognize her?"

Quinn studied her face for several moments. Then his eyes rounded. "Audrey Van Amee. Shit."

"Yeah, and she's not our hostage."

"You just abducted her."

He set his jaw. "She's not a hostage."

"What if she knows something about her brother? We can't let her go."

"We'll have to convince her to hang around until we find Van Amee, but we're not going to keep her tied up or locked in a room."

Quinn's expression gave nothing away, but Gabe was good enough at reading his best friend to know he thought it was a shitty plan. And it was, but Gabe refused to hold anyone against their will.

Jean-Luc was right. They were supposed to be the good guys.

"So," Quinn said after another long beat and showed the barest hint of a smile. "Wanna go give Jean-Luc a taste of SEAL discipline?"

CHAPTER FOUR

Audrey woke to the thrum of a baritone voice issuing orders and turned her head toward the sound. Holy God, what was that racket? Her mind swam, temples throbbed in beat with her heart. Better yet, what on earth did she drink last night? She wasn't a drinker by nature, but every once in a while her friends would drag her out to a dance club on the beach and she'd go a little margarita crazy. Is that what she'd done last night? Must've been a doozie of a time since she wasn't in her own bed—

Bryson.

It all flooded back. Chased out of Bryson's apartment by the fake policeman. The man with the gold eyes and cane. Her brother's abduction.

Oh God.

She blinked against her headache and looked around the room. Small. Empty. A wood crucifix hung over the narrow bed she lay on, but there was no other furniture. No lamp to use as a weapon and no window to escape from, naturally. The door sat open about six inches. Through the opening, she could make out movement in the other room and hear that commanding voice barking out orders like a drill sergeant, but couldn't tell what was going on or who her captors were. Did they have anything to do with Bryson's abduction? If so, seems like they'd make sure to keep her under lock and key instead of leaving the door open.

Of course, maybe they were all armed to the teeth, which was why they had no worries she'd try to escape.

Well, only one way to find out.

She drew a breath and pushed herself upright, waiting a moment for her head to stop its tilt-a-whirl act before swinging her legs off the edge of the cot. Her first few steps were a little wobbly, but she felt steadier by the time she reached the door and gave it a push. It opened easily.

The fake policeman was doing push-ups in the center of the room, while the man with the cane walked around him like a predator zeroing in on its weakened prey.

"Arms straight!" He tapped the man's buckling arm with the tip of his cane. "You want to start over? We've got no place to be until Harvard finds that video footage."

Okay. Americans. She let out the breath she hadn't realized she was holding. Yes, being American didn't automatically preclude them from bad guy status, she knew that. Plenty of bad Americans out there in the world, but her instincts told her these men meant her no harm. Maybe they were even here to help. Maybe they were FBI or…

Not. She studied the group of men—soldiers, apparently, although most of them weren't dressed like it—standing around the perimeter of the room. One, wearing a blue plaid fedora and sipping a cup of coffee, took bets from the others. Definitely not FBI. Or anything else official. Mercenaries, then?

Audrey bit her lip and took two steps backward into the bedroom… But then what? She stopped moving, glanced back at the bed. She hadn't come to Colombia to lie in some tiny room and cower with the sheets pulled over her head.

She studied the group again and decided to go with her instincts. They hadn't locked her in the room. If they had wanted to harm her, they had plenty of opportunity to do so when she was unconscious. So who were they and what did they want from her? The only way to find out was to talk to them.

The fake policeman finally collapsed, sweating and gasping, and even though he'd chased her and scared the bejesus out of her, she couldn't help the twinge of pity as he rolled to his side and gripped his ribs, his face bright red, his teeth clenched. The other soldiers let out hoots until the man with the cane sent them all a look as lethal as a gunshot wound.

"Would you gentlemen like to join him?"

That shut them up and they all faked interest in something else real fast.

To Audrey's surprise, the man with the cane's whole demeanor changed from brutal drill sergeant to—well, she didn't know, but he was nearly gentle as he gripped the fake policeman's hand and hauled him upright. "You okay, Jean-Luc?"

"Hah, that's all y'all got? Piece of—" The man—Jean-Luc, apparently—winced. "Piece of cake." Blood leaked from his nose, over his lips, and he swiped at it with his arm. "But, uh, I'll listen to orders next time. Save you the…the humiliation of not breaking me."

"Good idea." The man with the cane smiled—and, whew, that was some smile, softening the hard lines of his cut-granite face. He patted Jean-Luc on the back. "Go see Jesse. You're bleeding again."

Jean-Luc tried to walk on his own, but stumbled a little and slammed a hand onto the nearest piece of furniture, a table filled with electronic equipment, to steady himself. The man with the cane caught him under one arm while another man, who looked more like a soldier than everyone else with his military haircut and urban camouflage pants, wedged a shoulder under his other arm.

"Dizzy," Jean-Luc muttered. He suddenly didn't look good at all, pale as bone despite his tanned complexion.

Audrey had a feeling he hadn't elaborated about their scuffle in Bryson's apartment. He probably had a concussion from her hitting him with the lamp.

"I hit him on the head." When seven sets of eyes turned her way, she realized she'd spoken aloud and her heart took up residence in her throat. Some of the gazes were mildly hostile, others assessing, and still others showing a spark of male interest, but one particular set of hazels focused on her like sunbeams. Not as gold in the artificial light of the overhead lamp as they had been in the gloomy natural light of the alleyway but more greenish-gold, they swept over her, lingering a second longer than was necessary considering the situation. Then he seemed to catch himself and ripped his gaze away, again focusing on Jean-Luc.

"Why didn't you tell us?" he asked in that smooth, calm baritone.

Jean-Luc blew a raspberry with his lips. "Aw, it was nothing. Glancing blow."

"No, it wasn't," Audrey told the man with the cane. "I hit him three times with a lamp. He really scared me." But since they hadn't tied her up and none of them had yet to attack her or threaten her in any way, she was beginning to think that had been a fluke. Maybe these guys were at least partly on her side.

"*Pardon*," Jean-Luc said and looked genuinely apologetic through the blood leaking down his face. He collapsed into a chair someone had pulled up and a man wearing a Stetson—a medic, she assumed, since he carried a bag of medical supplies—pressed a compress to his nose, then flashed a penlight in his eyes. He tried to wave the medic aside, but the medic wasn't having any of that.

"Either you let me do an exam, Jean-Luc, or I knock you out. Then I'll know for sure you have a concussion."

He grumbled but let the medic take his vitals without further fuss and refocused on Audrey. "Things got a little out of hand back there at the apartment, *cher*. For that, I am sorry."

"It's okay." She felt the man with the cane's eyes on her again but pretended not to notice. "I apologize for hitting you. And, uh, kicking you in the nose."

"Jesus, Jean-Luc," the man in the fedora laughed. "She beat the shit outta you."

"Hey, Marcus, got a gift for ya."

"Yeah?"

"Yeah," Jean-Luc said and flashed him the middle finger, which made Marcus hoot with laughter.

"That's enough, gentlemen." The man with the cane, again catching himself staring at her, snapped to attention. She watched it happen, saw him yank on the reins of tightly held control.

How often did he let go of those reins? Not nearly enough,

she guessed, and she had the inexplicable urge to force his hand.

As he directed his men, Audrey realized she was staring right back at him and gave herself a mental kick. Bryson was in danger. She didn't care how intriguing and, yes, sexy the man with the cane was. He wasn't important right now. Nobody was, except Bryson.

When he refocused on her, his eyes were like citrine, cool, calculating, but still sparking with inner fire that no amount of training or control could hide.

"What's your name?" he asked.

"I'm..." She considered giving an alias for all of a half-second, but that would only complicate matters. Given all the computer equipment in the room, her real name wouldn't stay secret long... if they didn't already know it. Her art show was getting a lot of press, not only in Central America, but also in the States. All they had to do was look for one of the many interviews scattered over the internet with accompanying photos of her. For the man in the corner pounding away at his laptop keyboard, she bet that would be the work of a minute.

"I'm Audrey Van Amee."

He nodded as if she'd confirmed what he already knew, but, damn him, he didn't introduce himself or any of the other men.

"And you are...?" she prompted.

"Looking for your brother."

Could he be more deliberately obtuse? She jammed her hands onto her hips. "I kind of figured that, given that you were staking out his apartment. What I want to know is if you're working *for* or *against* him."

Please, please, please say for.

"For," he said, without a blink of hesitation.

Audrey discovered she was holding her breath again and let it out in a soft exhale so as not to draw attention to the fact. She thought it better that she appeared confident and strong in front of these pseudo-soldiers, but what would she have done if her instincts had failed her and these were the bad guys? Her stomach jittered at the thought.

Bryson was right. She really should start thinking situations like this through before running her mouth. Then again, she'd never been in a situation like this before and was pretty much winging it.

"Who hired you?" she asked. Although the man with the cane had the bearing of a general and his friend in the camouflage pants was most definitely a soldier, they had to be mercenaries. The rest of the group was too ragtag to be official military.

When he didn't answer, she huffed out a breath. "Do you know who took Brys?"

He ignored the question. Big surprise. She got the feeling he never answered questions not to his liking. "With all due respect, ma'am—"

"Oh, tell me you didn't just ma'am me."

Again, he ignored her. "You need to go back to Costa Rica. You're just as much a target here as your brother was. Let us handle this. We'll bring him home."

How did he know she lived in Costa Rica? And what else did he know about her? The idea that he knew more about her than she did him doused her manufactured courage with ice and goose bumps raced over her skin. Even so, she had nothing to hide, and she sure wasn't falling for that whole let-the-professionals-handle-it, your-brother's-in-good-hands bit. She'd heard of too many incidences where the so-called professionals were not enough.

"Would you leave?" she asked. "If it was your brother, would you leave without him?"

His jaw tightened just a little bit, telling her she'd hit a tender spot. "Not the same. I'm trained for this."

"Oh yeah? And just how many hostage rescue situations have you been in, Mr. I'm-Trained-For-This?" She'd be surprised if even one. Soldiers of fortune, or at least the few she'd met in Costa Rica, talked and walked big, but as soon as the real action started they were nowhere to be found. She'd tried to hire one before trekking to Colombia but discovered his claims were just alcohol-fueled bravado and nothing more. And, yeah, she was still miffed at that. Stupid men and their stupid egos.

"Over fifty," he said placidly.

"Well, see, that's—a lot." O-kay, talk about having an argument blow up in her face. The man apparently knew his stuff. Maybe her brother was in good hands. She didn't dare to hope. "Who are you?"

He exchanged a look with Mr. Camo Pants, a thousand words passing between them without either of them making a sound. Then he shrugged.

"My name is Gabriel Bristow. Gabe."

Gabriel. It suited him. He even looked a little like the painting her uber-religious mother had of the avenging angel.

Gabe went on to introduce each of the other men in the room. Jean-Luc Cavalier was the fake policeman she'd already had the pleasure of meeting, but he swept into a bow as if this was their first introduction, murmured something delightful sounding in French, and kissed her hand. Her opinion of him did a complete one-eighty. In fact, she melted into a big, gushy puddle of girly giggles and didn't even hate herself for it.

Jesse Warrick, the medic, touched the brim of his Stetson with a polite, "ma'am"—somehow when he said it in that cowboy drawl, it didn't sound as condescending as it had when Gabe said it earlier.

Fedora guy was Marcus Deangelo. He nodded toward her wrist. "You do much surfing in Costa Rica?"

She glanced down, at first not sure how he'd drawn that conclusion. Then she remembered the surfboard charm on the bracelet her brother had given her for her twenty-fifth birthday. "Sometimes."

Marcus grinned and wagged a finger in the air between them. "You. Me. We're gonna talk." He held up his coffee cup. "Want some?"

"Oh, very much. Thank you."

Gabe made some displeased grumbling noises until Marcus returned with a mug, then continued with the introductions.

Eric Physick, whom everyone called Harvard, was the computer geek tapping away at his laptop keyboard. He looked up and offered a distracted smile when Gabe said his name. His glasses sat crooked on his nose. Audrey had to fight the urge to straighten them and comb down his spiky mop of brown hair.

Ian Reinhardt leaned against the wall in a motorcycle jacket with bad attitude rolling off him in waves. He said nothing to her, but his lip curled in a faint sneer of disdain.

O-kay. Mental note: she never wanted to be in a room alone with him.

Finally, camo pants, Travis Quinn, gave her a solemn nod, but kept his distance.

Such an odd assortment of men. She wasn't sure whether to cheer, laugh, or cry that they were apparently her brother's only hope since the FBI was doing jack to save him.

"Nice to meet everyone," she said when Gabe finished the introductions. She might be frightened out of her wits and confused as hell, but she was a Southern girl, born and bred. Mama would fly down from heaven and tan her hide good if she wasn't polite, of that she had no doubt.

"But," she added, "that still doesn't explain *who* you are."

"We're HORNET," Jean-Luc said.

"*Horny* is more like it," Gabe muttered and gave him a blistering stare. "Keep your eyes above her neck."

Jean-Luc grinned shamelessly. "Aw, *mon capitaine*. No worries. I wouldn't dream of stepping on your turf."

His *turf*? Audrey scowled at them both and yanked at the slipping neckline of her tank top. In the sticky heat of the jungle, she often went braless, and hadn't changed that habit since arriving in Bogotá, despite the cool, rainy climate. A half-inch more and she'd have had to ask Jean-Luc for Mardi Gras beads in exchange for the show. Not that she had a problem with nudity. If she could get away without wearing clothes, she would, but she needed to keep these guys focused. And one surefire way to get a man off task was to flash him.

"What's HORNET?" she asked.

"That's not what we're called," Gabe said. "We're a private hostage rescue and negotiation team. And you're right, we have been hired to bring your brother home."

"Who hired you?"

"That's confidential."

Audrey huffed out a breath. Pulling teeth was easier than getting information out of him. A pit viper's teeth, to be exact. "Maybe I can help."

"No, you can't. And every second we waste explaining ourselves to you is another second your brother spends in captivity. So you need to back off, Ms. Van Amee, and let us do our job."

"Gabe," Harvard called across the room. "I got it."

Without another glance in her direction, Gabe strode over to stand behind Harvard and studied the computer monitor. "Go back to his first appearance."

Since nobody had told her to stay put, Audrey drifted over to see what Harvard was doing. An image of her brother leaving his apartment building showed on the computer screen. The timestamp in the corner read 5:58 a.m. Forever prompt—that was so like Bryson. His pixelated image left the screen.

"Another angle?" Gabe asked.

Harvard pecked a few keys and Bryson's image returned to the far left corner. He waited there for something, impatient.

The limo, she thought as Bryson checked the screen of his phone and answered her call. A few minutes later, the limo arrived and a tall dark-haired man opened the door for Bryson. A moment after that, the vehicle pulled away from the curb with her brother inside.

"License plate?" Gabe asked.

"Partial. I'm already running it. And the phone call…" Harvard rewound the footage to check the timestamp. "…came in at 0620. With a little finessing, I can get into his records, see who he spoke to."

"Do it. Also see if—"

"It was me," Audrey said and Gabe turned narrowed eyes on her.

"What?"

"It was me," she repeated. "I called him. I have—was supposed to have an art show this weekend in San Jose and wanted to make sure he remembered. He didn't."

Gabe straightened away from the computer. "What else did he say?"

She shrugged. "Typical Bryson stuff. He had to work. He was off to another meeting."

"Where?"

"He didn't say. I started lecturing him on how he works too much, how he's missing out on his sons' lives, and how his doctor said he needed to take it easy." She noticed a faint scowl pass over Gabe's hard features at that, but he hid it in a blink.

"The medical records I have for your brother don't mention any serious conditions," Jesse Warrick said, concern in his voice.

"Uh, no, he doesn't have any," she answered. "I mean, nothing that he needs medicine for or anything. He just had some chest pains last summer. They ran tests and are keeping an eye on him, but so far, it seems to be an isolated incident. The doctors think it was caused by a panic attack."

Jesse looked at Gabe. "The records I have don't mention anything about chest pain."

Gabe appeared frustrated and said something back, but she didn't hear him because Quinn asked from across the room, "Did you hear anything else when you were on the phone with Bryson?"

She glanced over at him. Such solemn intensity. He made her

uncomfortable, so she returned her gaze to Gabe. "I heard a man's voice say in Spanish that Bryson needed to relax, that nobody was going to hurt him because he—" She had to stop and clear away the lump forming in her throat. "Because he was worth too much money. After that, the line went dead."

"So naturally you jumped on the first flight to Colombia and put yourself at risk." Gabe held up a hand when her mouth opened to fire back a defense. "Forget it. What else did Bryson say? Can you remember anything else about that conversation?"

Oh, what a condescending, overbearing...

No, she told herself and clenched her teeth to reign in her temper, *don't let him get to you.* There would be plenty of time to rip into him later. Now, she had to focus.

For Bryson.

She shut her eyes, replayed the conversation for the hundredth, maybe thousandth, time in the last twenty-four hours. "He didn't say anything else to me. When the limo arrived, he had a short conversation with the driver. I couldn't hear all of it, but I think the driver introduced himself as Jacinto."

Gabe snapped his fingers and turned to Harvard. "Any clear shots of the driver's face?"

"Not clear, boss. One profile. Pretty grainy, but I might be able to clean it up. If I can get a clear enough picture, I'll find you a name, birthday, and the name of his last one-night-stand."

"Do it. How's the EPC research coming?"

"Getting there. I have some possible EPC hangouts that need checking."

"That's what I like to hear." He clapped Harvard on the back before turning to the rest of the group. Watching him take command was like seeing a tank roll over everything in its path, and Audrey stood back in awed silence as he addressed his team.

"We're going to split up, check out those addresses. Jesse, you said your Spanish is passable, so you and Marcus will be alpha team. Quinn, Jean-Luc, and Ian, bravo team. Each will recon half of the addresses Harvard dug up. Stay in constant radio contact in case one of you needs reinforcements. Harvard will stay here on the computers."

Quinn frowned. "What about you?"

"I'm going to talk to the real limo driver, the one that reported Bryson missing, Armando Castillo."

"How do you plan to do that?" Quinn asked. "Your Spanish sucks. You should take Jean-Luc with you."

"*Sí,*" Jean-Luc agreed. "You shouldn't go alone."

"No," Gabe said, and his tone dared anyone to argue. "Quinn's Spanish is just as bad as mine, if not worse. Unless Ian…"

Ian shook his head.

"Point made. Jean-Luc goes with bravo."

"Gabe, man." Quinn sighed and dragged a hand over his short hair. If it was anyone else protesting, Audrey suspected from the way Gabe's shoulders tightened that he'd bite their head off and pick his teeth with their spinal cord. But the others wisely kept their mouths shut and let Quinn do the talking.

"When we were on the teams—"

"Teams?" Audrey knew of only one branch of the military that referred to itself as "the teams," and studied the men with renewed interest. "You're SEALs?"

At her interruption, they both turned. Having two big, hard men give her such flinty stares should have scared her. And, okay, it did a little.

"Were," Gabe said at the same time Quinn said, "Yeah."

"Okay." She bit her lower lip. "Uh, wow."

Now that she knew, she wondered why she didn't see it before. Gabe carried himself not like a general, but like a Navy SEAL. She'd met a few guys retired from the teams while living in Costa Rica, and Gabe walked like a SEAL, talked like one. He even blinked like one. How could she have not noticed that? Having them on her brother's side suddenly felt a whole lot more like a benediction than a curse.

"On the teams," Quinn repeated, returning to their conversation, "we always use the buddy system."

"Goddammit, I know that," Gabe snapped.

Quinn didn't back down, didn't even blink. "Good, 'cuz it's not changing now that we're out. You're taking someone who knows the language with you."

"Mind telling me who? We don't have enough men."

Quinn's jaw tightened. "Maybe HumInt has an asset in the city we can borrow. We're already borrowing a pilot, so—"

"I can go with him." Again, every eye in the room turned to her. Even Harvard stopped working to gape, and she bristled. "What? You need a Spanish speaker, and I'm fluent."

"Hell. No."

"Why not?" Anger flaring, she whirled on Gabe and jabbed a finger between his pecs. There was no give at all under his shirt. Like poking a concrete wall. She barely resisted the urge to flatten out her hand and rub it across all those hard muscles. Had to remind herself—twice—that she was annoyed with him.

"I've lived in Costa Rica for close to ten years now and I'm as fluent in Spanish as I am in English. And Armando—well, he doesn't know me personally, but he knows who I am, so he'll be more likely to talk. I'm an asset, numb nuts. Use me."

CHAPTER FIVE

Yeah, Gabe wanted to use her all right, but it had nothing to do with her Spanish fluency. Not unless she cried out in Spanish during an orgasm.

Whoa. He put the brakes on those thoughts as his cock twitched in expectation. It'd been way too long for him if Miss Mouth, here, was this big of a turn-on.

And why the hell did he find her name-calling such an aphrodisiac, anyway?

"No," he said between his teeth at the same time Quinn said, "That might not be a bad idea."

"*What?*"

Quinn shrugged. "Tactically, she's an advantage."

And the Machiavellian motherfucker never passed up an advantage. Gabe scrubbed his face hard with his palms. "She's. Not. Trained."

"Are you expecting opposition?"

Dammit. Quinn already knew the answer to that was a solid

no. It was the only reason he'd risk going by himself to talk to the limo driver. Really, Armando Castillo should own a freakin' phone. If he did, this all would be a moot point. "I'm not taking a civilian—"

"News flash, Gabe. We're all civilians now."

Civilian.

His mouth froze on a comeback as the realization struck with the same force as a sucker punch to the solar plexus. Fuck, that *hurt.* Way more than it should have, and he had a moment of pure panic as his diaphragm refused to expand and let air into his lungs.

He *was* a civilian now. Damn.

"So it's settled." Audrey turned to face Quinn. "I'll go with him and act as a translator."

Settled? Far from it. He couldn't take her anywhere with him unless it was to bed. Definitely not on an op, even one where he expected no resistance. She'd be a distraction of epic proportions, something that could get both of them killed in the wrong situation. Even now, he couldn't stay on task and found his gaze wandering to her pert little rear end, so close in front of him he wouldn't have to reach far to get a handful.

But how could he admit that in front of his men? Between Jean-Luc disobeying orders and Ian's bad attitude, the natives were already restless, and if he admitted to a weakness—a woman, for shit's sake—there would be anarchy.

He forced his mind back on task before the pulse in his cock became a full-on boner. Audrey wasn't trained, true, but she spoke the language and knew the mores of Hispanic culture better than any of his men. She was better equipped to tell whether the limo driver was evading, hiding something, or downright lying to them.

He turned to her. "Could you shoot a firearm and not hit me if the situation came down to that?"

"I was born and raised in the South, honey, but I'm no southern belle. I shoot what I aim at," she said in a tone so coated with sugar he was surprised her teeth didn't rot. Then she flashed a smile as bright as that sinful yellow tank top she wore. "But it's still up in the air whether I'll aim at you or not."

Marcus let go an appreciative whistle and Jesse muttered, "Dayam."

Gabe rubbed his jaw. Last thing he needed was for this Southern spitfire to go all Annie Oakley on his ass, but he pulled his SIG Sauer P226 from the holster at the small of his back and handed it over. When he saw the way she tested its weight and checked the chamber in smooth, efficient movements, some of his trepidation vanished. The woman really did know how to handle a firearm. Thank God.

"All right, you're with me. Marcus," he called across the room, "do you have contacts within the FBI that can keep their mouths shut?"

"Nah, boss," Marcus said, and something that looked a lot like guilt darkened his features. Then he moved his shoulders as if shrugging off a weight. "You know, with the way I left... nobody talks to me now."

Figures. Gabe didn't know the nitty-gritty of Marcus Deangelo's retirement from the FBI, except that he'd left with a less than sterling reputation. "Then find someone who will and get us a sitrep without causing a stir."

"Sitrep?" Audrey asked.

"Situation report," Gabe said through his teeth.

"Sure thing, boss," Marcus said with his usual smile back in place and a cheeky two-finger salute.

Patience is a virtue. Patience is a virtue. Patience. Is. A. Goddamn. Virtue.

Gabe repeated it to himself like a mantra. Didn't work. It may be a virtue, but he'd never been all that virtuous and still wanted to throttle Marcus.

He put a hand on Audrey's back and guided her toward the door. "The rest of you, gear up and move out, but stay in touch with each other. We'll be out of radio contact, but I have my phone. We'll be back in a couple hours, tops."

With time dwindling steadily away, he couldn't waste any more than that.

Jesse trailed them outside. "Gabe, can I talk to you for a sec?"

Now what? He stopped, waved Audrey on ahead. "Make it fast."

"It's about Quinn." Jesse took off his hat and swiped a hand through his long, dark brown hair before replacing the Stetson and adjusting the brim. "He hasn't had a physical yet. Every time I approach him about it, he makes up an excuse. He hasn't given me access to his medical records, either." His dark eyes went to the front door as it opened and the man in question stepped out into the breezeway. "Granted, I don't know him all that well, but it seems like odd behavior, so I thought I should mention it."

Odd? And the grand prize for understatement of the year goes to Jesse Warrick. No, that was beyond odd. That was so completely unlike Quinn that at first, Gabe's mind couldn't assimilate what Jesse was telling him with the man he knew. He turned toward his best friend, who was leaning against the front door with his arms crossed over his chest.

"That true?"

Quinn's jaw cracked from the force of his back teeth grinding together. "I don't appreciate you going over my head, Warrick. You have a problem with me, you talk to me."

"I tried," Jesse shot back. "You brushed me off. Several times."

"I've been busy. In case you haven't noticed, we have a very limited window to find Bryson Van Amee."

"What I've noticed is you're defying a direct order from our boss."

"This coming from the guy kicked out of Delta for punching a ranking officer. Since when are you so hell-bent on rules?"

"All right, gentlemen. Enough." Gabe stepped between them before the heated argument escalated out of hand and, for one brief moment, wished for his former SEAL teammates. With them, there had never been scuffles like this during an op. Before and after, sure. But during, it just didn't happen. You followed orders to a T or someone got killed.

In fact, Quinn used to be by-the-book, strict as they come. Did a shoulder injury and discharge papers really make that big of a difference in him?

"Q, man, why are you fighting this? It's nothing. Let Jesse do the damn physical and give him access to your medical records so we can move on to more important things." He motioned toward the Jeep in the driveway where Audrey sat, watching them through the window. "That woman is counting on us to bring her brother home and you're wasting time we don't have."

"Exactly," Quinn said. "*Time we don't have.* I've been busy and haven't—"

Jesse grunted. "I've shoveled some mighty big piles of bullshit in my day, but yours is the biggest."

Quinn stepped forward. So did Jesse.

All right, this was getting ridiculous and Gabe was sick of listening to these two snipe at each other like ten-year-olds.

"Knock it off or you'll both have a meet-and-greet with the ground." He shoved Jesse back with one hand and jabbed the business end of his cane at Quinn's stomach. "You. Inside. You're getting that fucking physical now."

"Gabe—"

"Goddammit, I mean it. You wanted me to lead this team, so I'm leading it. And right now, you're being an epic jackass. If you were anyone else, you'd be done. Don't make me pull you off this op, Q. I'll hate it, but I'll do it."

The two men stared at each other over Gabe's shoulder for a long, heated moment. Quinn finally relented. He turned and walked, stiff-backed, inside. A second later, Jesse sighed and followed, but Gabe caught his arm.

"Call me if you have any more trouble with him."

"Sure thing, boss."

In the car, Audrey gave him a sympathetic look as he leaned his head against the seat and shut his eyes. After witnessing that spectacle, her faith in them as saviors had to be next-to-nil, and yet she laid a comforting hand on his arm.

"This is new to you, isn't it?" When he cracked an eyelid and shot her a sideways glance, she added, "Not the hostage rescue stuff. Seeing you work, I have no doubt that you know what you're doing there. But this set-up is new."

That was one way to describe a six-hours-old, never-trained-together team. New. He called it a goatfuck. Man, he should've passed on this mission. He'd been so eager to get back into the field. *Too* eager—and his team was suffering for it.

With a sigh, he sat up and started the Jeep. "That obvious?"

She nodded. "Everyone's testing boundaries. Not exactly jockeying for power, since they all seem to get you're in charge, but they're trying to figure out what they can get away with, what they can't. It's a natural progression for any newly formed group."

Yeah, but *Quinn*? He always liked to know where the boundaries lay and never, ever crossed a toe over them. What the hell was the matter with him?

"The same thing happened when Phil joined my dolphins," Audrey said, drawing his attention back to her. She sat buckled into the passenger seat, staring out the window at the passing Bogotá streets as he wound the Jeep through gathering traffic toward the edge of the city. He wondered if she was looking for her brother in the faces of everyone they passed. Probably.

"You have dolphins?" he asked, partly out of genuine curiosity but mostly to take her mind off Bryson for a little while.

She flashed him a brilliant smile before returning her gaze to the window. "Guess they're not really mine, but I think of them that way. They hang out around my dock and visit me throughout the day. Rata, Matahina, Hika, and Phil."

"Phil?"

"He's the newcomer. Just showed up one day. Rata didn't like having another male around his pod, but they're buddies now. Took some time and quite a few fights, though." She patted his arm. "Your pod has a lot more alpha males in it than Rata's. You'll get the kinks worked out."

But will it be in time to save her brother? He knew that was what she was thinking, and gave her props for not saying it aloud.

"Why'd you name him Phil?" he asked after a moment of bumping along in comfortable silence. "Why not something more exotic?"

"He's not an exotic guy. He's happy and sweet and laid-back. Phil suited him." She shrugged, and the strap of that slinky yellow tank slipped off her shoulder, showing a whole lot of golden brown skin and freckles.

No tan lines. Jesus.

The image of her stretched out naked on a dock with dolphins dancing in the ocean around her took up residence in his brain right next door to his libido. He tried to shake it by recalling the directions to the limo driver's house that he'd committed to memory. A forty-five minute drive southeast to a small town in the Amazon region where jungle tangled around the base of the mountains.

And he was still picturing her naked.

It was going to be a long ride.

• • •

"There. That wasn't so bad, was it?" Jesse pulled his stethoscope from around his neck, tossed it inside his medical bag, and snapped the clasps closed. "Want a lolly now?"

"Fuck you." Quinn grabbed his shirt and stuffed an arm in the sleeve, muttering something that sounded like, "I hate doctors," with expletives thrown between each word for good measure.

Jesse shook his head. Different dance partner, same ol' tune. He had almost come to miss it since leaving the military. He'd tended to lots of guys like Travis Quinn back then—burned out and perpetually as mean as a caged bull because of it, but in for the long haul because they had nothing else. The type that knew he wasn't invincible and just didn't give a rat's hairy ass. The type that didn't exactly have a death wish, but neither did he have anything to live for.

It was a sad, lonely place for a man to be, and could have so very easily been Jesse if it weren't for his little boy. He'd already been on the edge of it when Connor was born, which was why Lacy divorced him and threatened to take away his son two months later when he got kicked out of Delta Force. Shit, he couldn't even blame her for it. He'd been a piece of work back then. Pissed off, depressed. That threat was the boot in the ass he'd needed to pull himself together, and he'd done it right quick. His boy meant everything to him.

Quinn needed something like that, something to mean everything, but he'd never open himself up enough for it. And he'd probably kick Jesse's ass to Jackson Hole and back for giving that particular medical opinion seeing's how he hated doctors and all.

"I'm not a doctor yet," Jesse said good-naturedly instead. He would be, though, then his son wouldn't need to worry about whether or not he'd come home alive from his next mission. HORNET was just a means to an end, a way to keep his skills sharp and bring in extra cash to cover the expenses of med school.

"Close enough. Are we—" As Quinn turned to grab his boots from the floor, something happened—Jesse saw it, like a flipped light switch blew a fuse inside his head. His face blanked. His eyes, though open, went vacant as the Wyoming plains in the middle of winter.

"Shit!" Jesse shot to Quinn's side, hat flying off his head from the speed of the movement, and wrapped an arm around his waist in case he toppled.

And, just like that, he snapped back. "What the…? Get the hell off me."

"Nah, pal, you should have a seat." And a freakin' CAT scan. Unfortunately, the latter wasn't readily available in Bumfuck, Colombia. The former was, and Jesse maneuvered Quinn into a nearby chair, then reopened his medical bag. "How long have you been blacking out?"

"I haven't."

Jesse snorted, looped a blood pressure cuff around Quinn's upper arm, and clipped a pulse oximeter to his finger. "I already made a point about your bullshit earlier, so I'll refrain from beating a dead horse by repeatin' myself. How long?"

"It's nothing," he muttered. "I haven't eaten. I'll get some food and be fine in a few minutes."

"Are you diabetic?" No answer. "Goddangit, you might as well tell me. I'll find out."

Quinn said nothing, just stared mulishly at the opposite wall, his jaw clenched so hard his right eye ticked. His blood pressure and pulse were a little high, his O2 low. Not good, but expected after an episode like that. Whatever *that* was.

As soon as Jesse ripped the BP cuff from his arm, Quinn was out of the chair, headed toward the door.

"Quinn."

He stopped, still said nothing, but his shoulders tensed.

"I need you to release your records to me."

"You'll get them. Right now, we have work to do."

Yup, Jesse thought as he packed away his supplies and picked his Stetson off the floor. But the sixty-four thousand dollar question was, when? He had no doubt Quinn would take his good ol' time about releasing them.

Well, he'd just see about that. By hook or crook—probably crook, which was just fine by him—he'd get his hands on those medical records ASAP. Then, depending on if he found what he suspected he'd find, he'd have to take the issue to Gabe.

CHAPTER SIX

Bryson rolled over in bed and something hard snagged his wrists. He jolted awake, opening his eyes into the darkness of his bedroom.

No, not his bedroom. Enough ambient light from somewhere illuminated the concrete block walls and a metal staircase descending into the middle of the room from the floor above.

"Wha…?" Blinking, he looked at his caught wrists and at first didn't understand the steel bracelets. Except for his wedding ring, he wasn't the jewelry wearing type. Why would he be wearing…

Handcuffs.

Bryson screamed, jackknifing on the mattress. Oh God, Oh God, Oh God, this wasn't happening. Dreaming, he had to be. A horrible nightmare he'd soon wake up from and—

His stomach revolted and he rolled off the pallet only to discover his feet and waist chained to the concrete wall. Vomit surged up his throat, stained the front of the thousand-dollar suit he still wore. Distantly he heard a door open and footsteps rattle the stairs. Voices.

"What the fuck's wrong with the gringo?" someone asked in Spanish, his voice the squeaky, immature sound of a teenager not yet through puberty.

"It's the ether," a deeper voice replied. He remembered that voice. Jacinto. "Made him sick."

Ether?

Oh God, the limo. He remembered now, in such vivid detail, the memory seared. The dizziness, the panic, the sleepiness. Jacinto wearing a bug-eyed mask and telling him to let it happen, that nobody would hurt him, that he was worth too much money. He'd been gassed. Kidnapped.

Bryson puked until there was nothing left in his stomach. Dry heaved until tears streamed down his face and his ribs screamed in pain from the violent, useless spasms. Then he collapsed, wishing he'd slide back into the comfortable oblivion of unconsciousness.

"Señor Van Amee," Jacinto said.

Bryson felt a boot nudge his side. Something pressed to his ear.

"Talk."

He tried. Couldn't do anything but moan.

"Get him up."

A pair of hands hauled him upright and his head spun, kicking off another round of dry heaves. Again, Jacinto pressed something to his ear and ordered, "Talk!"

"Bryson?" Chloe's tear-choked voice was like a balm, soothing over the worst of his pain. "Bryson, baby, are you there? Are you okay? Talk to me, baby. Please."

He opened his mouth, found his tongue was like sandpaper as he tried to wet his lips. "Chloe."

"Oh God." She broke down crying. "We're going to bring you home, baby. We're going to pay anything they want, okay?"

Pay them anything they want. It was the logical thing to do, but God, it pissed him off. These cretins took him from in front of his own apartment building, scared his wife and kids and probably his sister, and now they were demanding money from his family? And after they got his money, they'd just kill him—he wasn't a stupid man and knew they'd never let him go. He'd seen their faces, could identify them. And after they dumped his body somewhere, they would do it all over again to someone else.

No. No, they wouldn't. It ended here.

"Don't pay…them a…dime."

"Brys?"

"I mean it. Not one—"

Jacinto swore in Spanish, yanked the phone from his ear, and backhanded him so hard his vision flared white and stayed white for a long five seconds. Pain exploded through his face and blood spurted from his nose, over his lips, the coppery taste of it filling his dry mouth.

"Chloe, listen to me!" He didn't know if she was still on the phone or if Jacinto had hung up on her. "Don't let them get away with this. Don't pay them, whatever threats they make, whatever—"

"*¡Cállate!*" A boot landed hard in his side and something cracked. Suddenly, he couldn't draw a full breath without pain splintering his every thought and he collapsed onto the concrete floor with bone-jolting force.

Jacinto grabbed his tie and hauled him upright. Breath that reeked of cigarettes and coffee and something spicy invaded his nose as a broad, dark face pressed so close, an irrational fear that

Jacinto was going to kiss him flitted through his brain.

"I speak *Ingles,* asshole," Jacinto said in thickly accented English and jerked on the tie, cutting off his oxygen. "Try something like that again, I will kill you. I don't need to keep you alive now that they have proof of life. Remember that."

LOS ANGELES, CA

As far as second communications went, that wasn't the worst. Wasn't the best, either, and a hard knot of dread settled in FBI negotiator Danny Giancarelli's stomach. He set down the phone and exchanged a knowing glance with his partner, then they both turned to Special Agent in Charge Frank Perry.

"What—what was that?" Chloe Van Amee's voice was high, verging on a screech. She looked from one of them to the next, eyes frantic, complexion white despite her tan. "We're going to pay them, right? Yes, of course we're going to pay them. Brys doesn't know what he's saying. We have to pay them. We—"

"Mrs. Van Amee," Danny said since Frank Perry didn't seem to care to step up and do his job to calm the woman. "This isn't unusual. Your husband is frightened, feeling out of control, and trying to take back whatever control he can."

"Oh God." She doubled over in her chair and covered her face with her hands.

Standing over Chloe's shuddering form, Rick O'Keane arched a brow. Danny gave his partner an almost imperceptible shrug. It might be true. Bryson was no doubt frightened, but usually hostages were willing to pony up anything for their release. Wasn't often he heard a hostage say not to pay.

God, he wished Marcus Deangelo was here. His former partner knew how to handle family members better than any other agent in the office.

"We're obviously dealing with professionals," Frank Perry said, and Danny turned in his seat to stare at him. "Don't worry, Mrs. Van Amee. They don't want your husband's life. All they want is the money."

Hell. He can't know that after two very short freakin' phone conversations with the HTs—hostage takers. They didn't know anything yet, other than Bryson was still alive, his ransom was around sixty million and some change, and the HTs wanted the exchange to happen as soon as possible.

O'Keane looked just as thunderstruck, and nothing much surprised the Irishman. He cleared his throat and jerked his head toward the corner of the room in a we-need-to-talk gesture.

"Perry." Danny stood and motioned him toward the corner as well. "Let's talk."

Perry ignored them both. "Mrs. Van Amee—Chloe. Is it okay if I call you Chloe?" When she gave a watery nod, he took the chair across from her that Danny had vacated. "Do you have access to funds for the ransom payment?"

Another nod.

"My suggestion is that you start making calls, whatever you need to get the ransom money ready. Your husband's best chance, *our* best chance, is to pay what they ask."

"Now I think we're getting ahead of ourselves," the suit from the insurance company said. Always protecting that bottom line. Danny couldn't remember his name and frankly didn't care to know it, but in this instance, he had to agree with the man.

They had the resources to send someone to Colombia and get Bryson out. A team of SEALs stationed in Coronado trained with Danny's office, as well as several other Special Forces units—any of them could go in after Bryson.

Problem was money. And politics. Always came down to those two gems. Even as wealthy as the Van Amees were, a rescue operation cost serious bucks, and Bryson wasn't important enough to waste that kind of time or manpower. It was easier to pay the ransom.

Not important enough.

Danny thought of Van Amee's two little boys, Grayson and Ashton, who reminded him so much of his twin sons. So young and frightened, with a mother who didn't seem to give two figs about them.

Okay, he knew he had to cut Chloe some slack for the dismissive way she treated them. Stressed way beyond what most normal people experience in their lifetime, she was cracking, and everyone handled that differently. For all he knew, she was Mother of the Year under normal circumstances.

Not important enough.

Goddammit, but Bryson Van Amee was important. Those two little boys deserved to grow up with a father. Who was he to take that away by not doing everything in his power to bring Bryson home?

But that was the problem. It wasn't in his power to make the call. It was Perry the Prick's.

Frustrated, feeling the constraint of bureaucratic red tape, Danny ground his teeth but kept his mouth shut.

CHAPTER SEVEN

COLOMBIA

Gabe stepped out of Armando Castillo's shabby but well-kept house and slid his sunglasses on against the glare of morning sunshine. Chickens clucked and strutted around the house and a worn shed he assumed was a barn. A scruffy mule grazed behind a fence that had seen better days and wouldn't hold back a more ambitious animal. Skinny stray dogs sniffed the pitted dirt streets of a barely there jungle village for scraps.

The air already sweltered, promising a day as thick as pudding with humidity, and Gabe's shirt clung to his spine. Compared to the persistent coolness of Bogotá, it was as if they'd entered a different country.

He checked his cell phone to call Harvard and found no signal. Not a surprise, but being out of contact with his team in the middle of guerilla country with an untrained civilian woman in tow made him twitchy. Since leaving the city, the hair on the back of his neck prickled in a near preternatural sixth sense—if you believed in that sort of thing—that usually warned him someone was watching.

Laughter erupted from the house behind him and Gabe shook his head in complete awe. How Audrey went from giving Armando Castillo the third degree to becoming the limo driver's new best friend was beyond him. He'd watched it happen and still couldn't understand *how* it had happened. One minute, grief and guilt devastated Armando's lived-in features as he explained someone had called in and changed Bryson's pick-up time the morning of the abduction. The next, Audrey had him grinning and joking with her like they'd known each other forever. Maybe if Gabe knew Spanish, he'd understand how she managed that. Then again, maybe she just possessed a certain…magnetism or something.

God knew she drew him like the proverbial doomed moth to a flame.

Which ticked him off in a big way. Never before had a woman fascinated him to distraction like this. He liked to keep his love life—if he could even call it that; sex had been completely off his radar since the car accident last year—as orderly and precise as everything else he did. But she had the potential to destroy his meticulous life like a wrecking ball through concrete.

So he shouldn't even consider Audrey Van Amee in that way. Idiot.

Warning prickled along the back of his neck again and he straightened, scanning the area. He couldn't see anything out of the ordinary, but that didn't mean much. He excelled at spotting tails, but he wasn't dumb enough to think that nobody in the world was better at tailing than he was at spotting them. He checked his watch then rubbed a hand over his jaw, which was in desperate need of a date with a razor.

What the hell was that woman doing in there, anyhow? They had just about overstayed their welcome and needed to get gone.

Ten minutes later, just as he was about to go drag her out of the house in a fireman's carry if need be, Audrey emerged carrying a basket. Armando and his tiny wife, who had a voice that rivaled a foghorn, trailed behind. Gabe pushed away from the car, only to have to wait another five minutes as they chatted.

C'mon, woman.

He caught Audrey's gaze and hitched his chin toward the Jeep. She crinkled her nose—and, dammit, he shouldn't have found that expression as endearing as he did—then pointedly turned her back on him. He got the feeling she would have stuck out her tongue if they weren't in mixed company.

Frustrated, he yanked open the Jeep's door with enough force to rock the vehicle. He was tapping his fingers in succession on the steering wheel when she finally decided to bless him with her presence, and slammed the Jeep into gear almost before she had the door shut.

"Oh, for God's sake." She caught herself on the dashboard with one hand while protecting her basket with the other. "Impatient much?"

"In case you've forgotten, we're working on a limited watch." He shot her a narrow-eyed glare. "We don't have time to sit around and chitchat with the friendly locals, especially when there are a lot of unfriendly locals in the vicinity."

"I haven't forgotten." Audrey straightened and buckled herself into the seat. "And I wasn't wasting time." She reached into her basket and brought out a printed sheet of paper that she fluttered in front of his nose.

"Holy shit. You actually got something out of him?" He grabbed it from her. Spanish. Of course. He really needed to learn the language. "What's it say?"

"Yes, I did." She scowled and snatched the paper back. "But we're lucky Armando even let us inside, not to mention told us anything. It's extremely rude to come calling without bringing a gift, you know."

"What's it say?" Gabe repeated though his teeth.

Audrey sighed. "It's the itinerary Bryson filed with the limo company so they'd know when he needed their services. And…" Again, she dipped a hand into the basket, brought out a smaller handwritten piece of notebook paper. "Even though they didn't have a name for the man that called in and changed Bryson's pick-up time, they have the phone number he used."

Okay, that was slightly impressive. When he left the house to try and contact his team, he'd figured that well of information was tapped out. "We'll give that to Harvard to trace as soon as we're back in contact."

"You didn't get a hold of them?"

"No signal."

"Y'all really should have satellite phones," she said, as if it was common sense.

"Why didn't we think of that?" He infused the words with as much fake incredulity as he could muster. "I'll get right on that as soon as I get us out of guerilla country, rescue your brother, and keep this haphazard team of mine from killing each other. Top of my list. Promise."

"You're such a grumpy butt."

Gabe sputtered. He'd been called a lot of things in his life, mostly names incorporating creative variations of four-letter words in many different languages. But this took the cake. "A what?"

She flashed that smile, the one that lit up her eyes and crinkled her nose, and his irritation instantly faded. That probably should have annoyed him, but it didn't.

"It's something my brother…" Just as quickly as it appeared, her smile vanished and she turned away to stare out the window.

Gabe let a whole five seconds of silence pass before he couldn't stand the sadness he felt weighing down on her. "Something your brother…what?"

"Just something he used to say when I had a mood on as a child," Audrey said, still staring out the window. "I always thought it was so ridiculous I forgot whatever I was mad about." She finally looked at him again and a hint of her previous smile ghosted over her lips. "Did it work for you?"

"Yeah. And, wow, I never pegged you for the manipulative type."

Now her smile returned full-force, and for a moment, Gabe found himself so dazzled he almost forgot to watch the winding road in front of them.

"I'm a woman, duh," she said. "And a Southern woman, to boot. Manipulation is what we do best."

Gabe forced his attention back to the road. "What else is in there?" He hitched his chin toward the basket on her lap.

"Food for the guys from Armando's wife."

At the mention of food, his stomach growled mightily,

reminding him he hadn't eaten since his retirement party, and then only a couple hors d'oeuvres. "What kind of food?"

"Empanadas, buñuelos, some fruit, coffee."

He held out a hand, wiggled his fingers. "Hand over one of those empanadas."

"We need to teach you manners." She rolled her eyes but slapped one of the wrapped packages into his palm. "You're lucky they included enough for you. They thought you were very rude. Which, you are."

"I'm hurt," he muttered around a bite of flavorful beef and fried dough. "Crying on the inside. Got coffee?"

She sighed, but produced a thermos and poured some coffee into the lid without spilling a drop as they bumped over a road that hadn't seen construction in a good decade or more. The hot, dark aroma that only came with real Colombian java filled the car. She waited until he inhaled the empanada before handing over the cup, but they hit another bump and his head banged on the roof. The coffee sloshed everywhere. He swore as the car that had been riding his ass for the past mile blared its horn.

"You should buckle up. If Colombians are anything like Costa Rican drivers, it can get vicious." Calmly, she poured another cup. Then, despite her lecture, unbuckled herself and turned in her seat to hold the coffee to his lips. "Careful, it's hot."

Something twisted his gut, a sharp clench of emotion he didn't dare put a name to, not to mention analyze.

"Uh, thanks, I got it now." He took the cup, their fingers brushing in an innocent, fleeting touch. That clench in his gut slid below the belt. She had soft hands, small and elegant, flecked with colorful bits of paint, and a visceral image of those pretty fingers tracing over his body, her palm closing around his cock and stroking hard and fast the way he liked, took root in his brain.

The Jeep hit another bump and sent a pinch of pain through his groin. He winced and she drew away, retreating to her side of the car. Her eyes looked a little dazed, her lower lip swelling up under the constant worrying of her teeth. Silence stretched between them, growing more uncomfortable with each passing second.

At last, she looked at him. "You feel it too, don't you? From that first moment, there's been something between us. Chemistry."

Should've known she'd not shy away from it. Audrey Van Amee may be quirky, rash, and as capricious as his intel claimed—though he was starting to doubt that last one—but nobody could accuse her of not having spine. Which shamed him for considering, even for a second, denying the…chemistry, or whatever it was. Lying was probably the right thing, the professional thing, to do. But, hell, if she couldn't see the erection still throbbing against the fly of his cargo pants, she should visit a doctor about that vision problem, because the damn thing was as noticeable as the Washington Monument.

"Yeah," he admitted. "I feel it. Obviously."

Her gaze dropped to his lap, and lingered just long enough that he had to shift in the seat to relieve some of the growing pressure between his legs. She licked her lips and he wanted to groan.

"Must you do that?"

Big caramel brown eyes snapped to his. "Do what?"

"That thing with your tongue. It's not helping my situation over here."

She sent him a wicked grin. "Why? Does it distract you?"

"You know damn well it does."

"Hmm." Slowly, ever so slowly, she traced her tongue over her lower lip. "Good."

"No. Not good. Not if you want to see your brother again."

Her smile faded and hurt flared in her eyes before she turned away from him. Direct hit. Dammit, he was an asshole, but he refused to take it back.

She rode in silence for several miles, and Gabe got the feeling she'd retreated to somewhere inside herself. Maybe he'd been *too* abrupt in shutting her down. He wasn't always the most tactful of men, but he had to make his intentions clear from the go so there were no crossed signals and hurt feelings later on. Yes, she was sexy. Under different circumstances, maybe he'd have even acted on his attraction. But not here. Not now. Probably not ever, if he wanted to remain professional—and he did. If word got out that he'd had a fling with a family member during an op, the team would be ruined before they even had a chance to make a name for themselves.

Out of the corner of his eye, he caught the glimmer of wetness on her cheek and glanced over. Tears streamed from her eyes in steady rivulets. Okay, now he really felt like an ass.

"Audrey, I'm sorry. That was—"

"No." She sniffled and wiped her eyes with the backs of her hands. "I went too far. I just… I guess I need the distraction, even if you don't." She squared her shoulders and turned in the seat to face him. "We're not going to get to Bryson in time, are we?"

"We'll find him."

"Don't sugarcoat it."

"I wouldn't know how." He took his eyes off the road long

enough to meet her gaze. "My team will rescue him, Audrey. There is no other alternative."

A smile fluttered over her lips. "Thank you."

"You're welcome."

Silence again, but this time she didn't turn away. Her eyes stayed on him, studying him, and he started to feel like an abstract painting that she couldn't figure out.

Up ahead, traffic had halted on the narrow road. He pulled up behind the last car in line, popped open his door, and stood on the runner. Some sort of accident, maybe, but with the way the road curved to the left, it was too hard to tell. He considered walking up and checking it out, but the idea of leaving Audrey alone in the car sent an icy shiver through him. And no way was he taking her. What if it was a guerilla roadblock?

Fuck.

He ran through a mental list of their options. Couldn't turn around. Another car—the one with the horn-happy driver—had already rolled to a stop behind them, blocking that escape. He couldn't run, but Audrey could. Maybe he could distract them long enough for her to disappear into the—

Audrey alone in the jungle. Cold. Wet. Vulnerable to all manner of predators.

No. His mind instantly and violently rejected the image. He was probably getting ahead of himself, anyway. For now, the best course was to wait on high alert. Could be nothing just as easily as something serious, and he didn't need to draw any undue attention to them either way. He sat back down, shut the door, grabbed his SIG, checked it, and realized her gaze was still on him. She hadn't even spared the stopped traffic a glance.

"What?" he snapped, his legendary nerves of steel fraying. He felt more exposed with her eyes on him in the close confines of the Jeep than he ever did HALO jumping into the most brutal enemy territory.

She turned her head to one side, golden honey-brown hair cascading over one slim shoulder. Sunlight glinted off her ear. He hadn't noticed she was wearing earrings before, little turquoise sunbursts that were fanciful and charming and suited her to a T.

"You're really not my type, Gabe."

"Ditto, sweetheart," he said, keeping one eye on the stopped traffic. Why were those stupid turquoise earrings so freaking sexy, anyway?

"I can't figure out why I'm so attracted." Fine lines etched into her brow as she narrowed her eyes at him. "Okay, you're hot stuff, but you're also impolite, domineering, abrupt, sarcastic—"

"Stop. My ego can't take much more flattery."

She grinned at his deadpan tone. "See? And still, I *like* you." She sounded shocked. "Once this is over and my brother's safe, maybe I'll walk on the wild side and go against type, just this once. See if I'm missing anything. I'll have to think about it."

His cock jerked, offering itself for her experimental walk on the wild side, and he clenched his teeth against the hot and raw surge of lust. *No can do, buddy.* "Think about it all you want, Audrey, but nothing's going to happen."

"Why not? You want it. If I decide I want it, too, there shouldn't be a problem. We're both consenting adults."

"It's unprofessional."

She made a very unladylike sound. "I'm starting to think it's not me that needs a walk on the wild side. Do you ever just...I don't know…cut loose?"

When he only gave her a bland stare, she added, "You know. Raise hell, let your hair down, kick up your heels, sow your wild oats… Oh, c'mon, Gabe, work with me. I'm running out of euphemisms here. I bet you were a wild child in your day."

"Yeah, 'cuz I've had so much time to run wild." He laughed, but it wasn't a pleasant sound, even to his own ears. "Forget that I'm a little busy trying to save your brother. Never mind that I spent the past year trying to save my foot, then my job. And every year before that, I was too busy trying to be the best damn SEAL I could be. So, no, I don't ever *cut loose.*"

"What about when you were a child?"

She asked it so casually, he didn't think twice about answering. "Same goes. I went to a military academy."

Audrey gave him a look so full of—Jesus Christ, was that pity? He ground his back teeth and reached into the glove box for an extra ammo clip, then jammed it into the side pocket of his cargos. She had no reason to pity him. He'd had a good life and liked it just fine the way it was. Or at least he did. He still wasn't sure how he felt about the new course he'd taken in the past twelve hours, but that didn't rate her pity.

Up ahead, a shout of alarm drew his attention, and what he saw made his heart drop into his gut. Eight guerillas with AK-47s were going from car to car, yanking people out, lining them alongside the road with their hands on their heads, while another two rifled through each empty vehicle.

A raid.

Great. Just great. Should've known this would happen. Murphy's fucking Law.

"What's going on?"

He ignored Audrey's question and bent over to unlace his left boot with one hand while he dug for his cell phone with the other.

"What are you doing?" she asked.

"You might wanna grab your gun now."

She blinked and, if he wasn't mistaken, some of the color drained out of her face. "W-what?"

"The gun I gave you back at base. You might need it."

"You mean to… shoot? No." She shook her head. "I'm not shooting anyone. I don't shoot people."

Gabe lifted his attention from his boot to stare at her. "You don't *shoot people*? So what was all that shit about not being a southern belle and shooting what you aim at?"

"I aim at paper targets! Shooting is a hobby. A sport. Something I did for fun with my dad." She waved a trembling hand at the guerillas. "I'm not like them. I don't kill."

"If you don't kill them first, they are sure as hell going to slaughter you without a second thought."

"I don't kill," she repeated. "Maybe we can talk to them."

"And afterwards we can all hold hands and sing *Lean On Me*. Christ, what world do you live in?"

"One where violence breeds violence."

"Yeah, that's exactly right." He jerked a thumb at the guerilla soldiers methodically making their way down the line of cars. "But when violence is the only language your enemies know, you gotta learn to speak it, too."

Jaw set at a stubborn angle, Audrey vehemently shook her head. "I won't kill anyone."

Figures he'd end up in the middle of a raid with a peace-loving, flower-sniffing hippie.

"Then make yourself useful and keep watch," he gritted out between his teeth and made sure his phone was on silent mode before sliding it down into his boot. Thank the technological gods for razor-thin phones. With his boot laced, it was all but invisible, and if the guerillas patted him down, it would go unnoticed. If they made him strip, then he might have some issues.

One of the cars up ahead contained a family, and the guerillas were no gentler with the two little boys than they were with the adults. The kids' mother cried out as one guerilla shoved the older boy hard enough that he hit his head on a tree stump and went limp.

"Oh my God," Audrey whispered. Her hand covered her mouth in shock even as she reached for the door. "We have to—"

"Stay here." He caught her arm. "It'll be bad enough for us once they realize we're American."

And when they saw that he was armed. But he couldn't hide his firearm in his boot. The SIG was a veritable death sentence for him, and all but useless against all those AKs. It wasn't so unusual for him to be outnumbered and outgunned—for a SEAL, it was just another day in the life, what he was trained for. In theory, he should be able to take three or four out before they got him, but that wasn't a theory he particularly wanted to test when Audrey's life was at risk, too. What would happen to her after they killed him? He shuddered to think.

She struggled against his hold. "But the boy—"

"His parents have him. Don't draw any unnecessary attention to us, Audrey. They'll notice us soon enough."

CHAPTER EIGHT

The moment the warning left Gabe's lips, wheels screeched as the car behind them shot into reverse, kicking up gravel that pelted the Jeep like hail. Shouting, the guerillas left their captives to run after the escaping car, those wicked-looking guns locked to their shoulders, firing without sense or aim. Bullets peppered the windshield and Gabe grabbed Audrey by the back of the neck, shoving her down. Her breath whooshed out when the heavy weight of his body covered her and jabbed the gearshift into her ribs. Every second felt like forever, every heartbeat her last. She closed her eyes and prayed like the good Catholic girl her mama had raised her to be. Someone was making a hiccupping sound, and for a long, confused moment, she couldn't figure out who it was.

Gabe's arms circled her, crossing over her chest so that his hands covered hers where she held them clasped between her breasts. She felt his heartbeat against her back, heard his soft, even breaths in her ear. Calm. Cool. And so insanely collected, he was almost a robot.

Just another jungle jaunt for the man who didn't know how to cut loose.

Hysterical laughter bubbled up, but caught on the growing knot of fear in her throat. Realizing she was the one making those hiccup sounds, she clamped her mouth shut and ground her teeth to keep more noise from slipping out.

Gabe gave her a tight, reassuring squeeze. It shouldn't have helped. She shouldn't have felt safer with him wrapped around her, because he wasn't any more bulletproof than she was. But, oh God, did it help.

Minutes, hours, *days* later, the gunfire slowed. Then stopped altogether.

"Stay quiet." Gabe squeezed her again, lightly this time, and she felt him shift his weight, his face lifting from where he had it buried in her hair. "Oh, fu—"

Suddenly he was gone, hauled off her by rough hands. The passenger side door flew open and more hands reached in to grab her and yank her out of the air-conditioned Jeep, into the stifling heat of the jungle afternoon. A cacophony of sights and sounds bombarded her senses as the guerillas shoved her over to stand with the other captives. Monkeys screeched in the treetops, several people were sobbing, others shouting in jungle-accented Spanish. The car that had tried to get away hissed steam from under its hood as its bullet-riddled radiator leaked. Three bodies lay sprawled on the pitted road, seeping bright red blood even as the guerillas went through their pockets. The air reeked of jungle-rot, gunpowder, blood and bowels.

Two of the men—God, they were more like boys—held Gabe

by the arms while a third got in his face and interrogated him in Spanish. "Who are you? Are you police? American military? Answer me!"

Gabe looked as if he was talking about the weather as he shook his head and said repeatedly, "No Spanish. *No hablo Español.* No Spanish."

The guerilla asking the questions hooked the strap of his AK-47 around his back and reached to pat Gabe down.

The gun. What had he done with his gun?

Or... oh, God. The gun he'd given her! She'd stuffed it underneath her seat before they left Bogotá, sure it would be of no use.

Audrey looked toward the Jeep, where two other men— boys—were ripping through the contents of the basket Armando's wife had given her. They stuffed the buñuelos and empanadas in their mouths like they were starving and filled their pockets to bulging with the fruit. When they found the sheet with Bryson's itinerary, the smaller of the two called out to Mr. Interrogator, who stopped frisking Gabe to read it. They'd called him Cocodrilo. She could see how he came by the nickname. He had dark, beady eyes, a long nose, and a prominent brow that resembled the ridges over a crocodile's eyes.

Cocodrilo scowled at the printout, then at Gabe. "Who are you?"

"*No hablo Español,*" Gabe repeated, even though she was certain he knew enough Spanish to understand the question.

"*No hablo Español, no hablo Español, no hablo Español,*" Cocodrilo mocked and jabbed the butt of his rifle into Gabe's stomach with enough force that he dropped to his knees, grunting in pain. But he didn't stay down. Almost as soon as he touched the ground, he was back on his feet. Or foot. He hadn't used his cane once since leaving Bogotá and was favoring his right side a little, but not enough that the guerillas noticed or else Audrey was sure they'd attack that weakness.

"What if I kill your woman?" Cocodrilo motioned with one hand and a guerilla grabbed Audrey by the wrist and dragged her over. He drew a long blade, dirty with mud and God knew what else, from his belt and made a show of pointing it at her pounding heart. "Will you speak Spanish then?"

Gabe's jaw tightened. Apparently, he didn't need to speak the language to understand the intent. "No, wait. Stop. Don't hurt her. *Hablo…un poco, pero…no hablo…lo suficiente…*ah, goddammit." He rubbed a hand over his head. "*…mantener una conversación.*"

Listening to him struggle through the sentence to save her tugged at her heartstrings and tapped into a store of courage Audrey didn't know she had. Anger replaced fear. She refused to be the stereotypical damsel in distress, not when knowing the language gave her a distinct advantage over her wannabe knight in shining armor. She turned to face off with Cocodrilo, startled to realize she was taller by a good four inches and older by nearly ten years.

"He doesn't know enough to have a conversation," she said in Spanish. "I do."

"Audrey," Gabe said softly in warning.

"Shut up."

His eyes widened in surprise. She imagined not many people talked back to him like that and he'd be licking the wounds to his male ego for the next week. Well, too bad. This situation didn't call for his particular dictatorial brand of management.

"Talk to me," she urged Cocodrilo. "I'll translate for him."

Cocodrilo eyed her up and down. "Who are you?"

"My name is Audrey. That's Gabe."

"Why are you in my jungle?" Cocodrilo demanded.

"We were just visiting some friends up the road."

"What friends?"

"I'm sorry," she said as gently as she could, thinking of Armando and his sweet wife and their five kids. "I won't tell you that."

She expected to be shot on the spot, or at very least hit with the butt of the rifle like Gabe had been. Instead, Cocodrilo gave a toothy smile that did his namesake proud.

"Are you American?" he asked instead.

"Yes." She thought it better not to lie.

He nodded, looked at the printout again. "What is this?"

"My brother's itinerary. He's been taken captive." She hesitated and looked at Gabe, searched his unreadable expression for help. He wouldn't approve of what she was going to say next, but what if this was their shot at finding Bryson?

She drew a fortifying breath and turned back to Cocodrilo. "I want to make a deal for his release."

• • •

Gabe didn't like that he had no idea what they were saying. The few key words he caught, though, made him curse.

Hermano. Brother.

Cocodrilo looked interested. Then got that glint in his eye, the one that says *cha-ching* in any language, and Gabe knew Audrey had made a possibly fatal mistake. He glanced toward the brush alongside the road where he had tossed his gun as the guerillas yanked him out of the Jeep. Luckily, Cocodrilo was distracted by the itinerary before he found the extra clip in Gabe's leg pocket. The clip wouldn't do him much good without his gun, and he didn't think he'd be able to get to the weapon without one of the guerillas noticing. But the cell phone in his boot had GPS. His team would be able to track him as long as the phone's battery held out.

A little guerilla with spiky black hair ran to Cocodrilo's side, shouting in a panicked tumble of Spanish that Gabe couldn't begin to sort out, not to mention comprehend, but the name Mena came up repeatedly in their exchange.

Mena.

Really, could this goatfuck get any worse?

He kept a close eye on Audrey's face and when she frowned, he guessed it could. Cocodrilo snapped out orders and the men scrambled to pocket their loot from the cars before letting everyone, including the family with the injured boy, leave.

No such luck for him and Audrey. The muzzle of a gun jabbed his lower back, nudging him off the road.

"*¡Vamos!*" Cocodrilo said and forged a path into the jungle.

• • •

Well, that had been a colossal waste of their precious time.

Quinn breathed a deep sigh of relief to be out of the 4Runner as he strode toward the front door of the safe house. Stuck in a car with Ian and Jean-Luc for several hours was not his idea of a good time, akin to sitting beside a grenade sans pin and in front of an off-key jukebox that somehow knew every friggin' song that came over the radio.

In Spanish.

Quinn knew at least seven ways to kill a man with his bare hands, and Jean-Luc was damn lucky he hadn't utilized them. He'd been tempted, but Gabe would frown upon a dead linguist, so he'd restrained himself—and Ian, who more than once lunged over the seat, intent on strangling the tone deafness right out of Jean-Luc.

After canvassing the suspected EPC hangouts Harvard had dug up, they were no closer to finding Bryson Van Amee. The first two addresses had seemed abandoned. At the next two, they had seen a lot of suspicious activity, including several drug deals, gang activity, and prostitutes soliciting their wares, but no signs of anyone held against their will at either place. Hopefully alpha team had better luck. If not, they were SOL in the intel department, which did not bode well for their mission or their hostage's continued state of breathing. That is, if he still was.

Harvard sat planted behind the computer, doing his geek thing, when Quinn pushed through the door. "Anything?"

Harvard took off his glasses and rubbed his eyes. "Tons of information, but we're still wading through it all."

"Give me what you got."

"I matched the picture I pulled off the security cameras to Jacinto Rivera. He isn't a known member of EPC, but he's associated through his brother, Angel." He hit a few keys on his laptop and the printer next to his work station spit out a sheet. Standing, he stretched his arms over his head, then retrieved the printout and handed it to Quinn.

"From what I can gather, the nominal head of the EPC organization has little to do with the everyday decision-making.

Instead, he nominated five generals to control each region of the country. Angel Rivera operates in the Andean Region, which includes Bogotá. I haven't dug up the names of the other generals yet, but I do know the Amazon Region is controlled by a man known as Cocodrilo, who has a nasty reputation as a sadist."

"What about Angel and his brother?" Quinn asked. "What are their reps like?"

"Despite his name, Angel Rivera's no angel. He has as many as fifty kills under his belt—nobody knows the exact number. Could be more. If he likes your shoes, he'd have no problem stabbing you in the gut in the middle of the street and taking them. If he doesn't like your shoes, he might still stab you for the insult to his well-developed fashion sense.

"His brother, Jacinto," Harvard continued, "is just as cruel, but also stupid as a bag of shit. Angel's never been pinched by the law, but Jacinto's spent most of his life behind bars. His last stint was for attempted armed robbery of a bank here in Bogotá. He served twenty-two months of a seven year sentence and was released with a full pardon, which leads me to believe his brother has at least one high-up politician tucked safely in his pocket."

"So the EPC is definitely involved in Van Amee's abduction," Quinn concluded.

"Could be," Harvard said. "But also could be Jacinto acting on his own or with one of the many gangs he has ties to."

"So you're saying we still don't know."

"We still don't know," Harvard agreed. "But we will. I just need more time."

"That's a commodity we're running very low on, Eric." Quinn let out a long breath. "Have you told Gabe about this yet?"

"He isn't back," Harvard said. "Hasn't checked in, either."

Quinn's heart gave one hard thump of panic. It was all he ever allowed it. "That's not like Gabe. He always checks in."

"I was wondering about that. Think he ran into trouble?"

He hoped not, but it was possible. Hell, likely. Gabe, the single-minded, meticulous guy Quinn knew and loved like family, wouldn't skip a check-in unless he was unable to make the call.

The door opened and every eye in the room turned toward it in expectation. Jesse and Marcus stopped short.

"What?" Marcus said.

Shit, Quinn thought. "Did you two find anything?"

Jesse nodded. "No sign of Van Amee, but we took a gander inside one of the warehouses on our list. Just happened the lock on the side door was busted." He grinned at Marcus.

"Imagine our luck," Marcus added with an expression of complete innocence as he drew a lock pick kit from his coat pocket and set it on a side table.

"Damn near pissed ourselves when we stumbled into a bomb-making factory," Jesse said. "C4, semtex, all the good stuff, and this…" He reached into the side pocket of his medical kit and brought out a bag filled with a yellow crystalline substance that he held out to Ian. "Found it stored in these bags like this. Figured you'd know what it is."

"Explosive D," Ian said, taking the bag. "Also known as ammonium picrate. Very stable. Used in armor-piercing shells."

"Well, shit," Marcus said. "They had enough of that stuff to blow a hole in an armored car."

"And then some," Jesse agreed. "Looks like they're gearing up for a war."

Probably are, Quinn thought and rubbed a hand over his chin, hearing the rasp of a two-day beard against his palm. Fuck, he didn't want to deal with this. He wanted to take orders, not issue them.

Where was Gabe?

He snagged his cell phone from his pocket and dialed Gabe's number as he spoke: "We have to take that warehouse out of commission. Ian?"

"Oh yeah," Ian said, showing the first hint of emotion besides the hostility on a constant low burn beneath his skin—excitement. The EOD expert needed a major attitude adjustment, but that was a problem for Gabe, as commanding officer, to handle. Quinn was just another of the rank-and-file, which was how he liked it. He had enough to shoulder without adding the weight of command.

"What will you need?" he asked Ian, listening as Gabe's phone rang and rang and rang and—voicemail. He hung up on the automated voice telling him to leave a message.

"A backpack, pliers, a good length of fuse." Ian paused, considering. "If we can't find safety fuse, I could rig it up with visco, but it's not my first choice. Visco will be easier to find, but it burns with an external flame and can ignite any chemicals in the immediate area, which could cause problems in the warehouse. And someone needs to watch my back so I don't have to worry about the baddies putting a bullet in my brain while handling the explosives."

"I'll go," Harvard volunteered and stood. "I need to get away from the computer before my eyes cross."

Quinn considered him—Jesus, did the guy ever see the sun? But he was in good shape, if a little on the wiry side of fit, built like a runner. He had so much potential, like a tadpole just before BUD/S training. Too bad they hadn't had the time to tap into it before this op.

"No, we need you here, working on intelligence gathering." He ignored Harvard's deflated expression and considered his options. Since Harvard had to stay and work the radios and computers, Marcus had no military training, and Jean-Luc's was rusty, that left Jesse and him for trained operatives.

He turned to Jesse. "What do you think?"

"I agree we need to get rid of that warehouse, but we don't have enough men," Jesse said. "Up to you, though."

Perfect. So it was a judgment call, all on his shoulders. Quinn kept hoping his phone would ring, Gabe calling him back, so that he could pass the ball to him and let him make these decisions.

"All right. Ian, how long will the warehouse job take?"

Ian lifted a shoulder. "Half hour to an hour tops."

One hour to cripple the baddies' operation. Christ, he couldn't turn that kind of opportunity down. Maybe they could even use the explosion as a distraction, giving them the extra time they would need to search the EPC's other hangouts.

"Jesse, you'll go with Ian to the warehouse," Quinn decided. "But before you blow it from the map, make damn sure Van Amee isn't being held inside somewhere. I want as few casualties as possible."

He studied his remaining team. Three men. Dammit, he needed another, and wished Gabe hadn't talked him out of inviting the sniper, Seth Harlan, to join the team.

No choice. Harvard had to go out into the field, after all.

"Jean-Luc, Harvard, take the 4Runner and follow Gabe's trail to the limo driver's house, see if he ran into car trouble or worse. Keep in constant contact with me, and if you sense trouble, don't take any unnecessary risks. We can't afford to lose more men. In the meantime, Marcus and I will pay a friendly visit to Jacinto Rivera's current address, see if we can't find any clues as to Bryson's whereabouts." He considered the group for a long moment, then shook his head. "Let's do Gabe proud and not fuck this up, guys."

CHAPTER NINE

They marched for miles, deep into the heart of the jungle, through thick undergrowth to the base of the mountains where the trail started a winding climb. There, the guerillas finally decide to stop for a water break.

Biting back a groan, Gabe settled onto a boulder the size of a coffee table and wiped sweat from his eyes with one arm. His bum foot and leg burned like stepping into a fire pit every time he put weight on it. Never thought he'd see the day he wanted that damn cane—but, Christ, he needed it. And admitting that, even to himself, chaffed.

He wasn't stupid enough to turn down the water his guards offered him, even though he wanted to reject it on principle. He glugged down half the bottle and kept his eyes fastened on the trailhead, hoping to catch a glimpse of fawn-colored hair or the glint of a turquoise earring.

Where was she?

He had tried to keep Audrey in his sights, knowing the

guerillas favored a divide and conquer strategy when it came to taking captives, but she quickly fell behind. The twist of trees and vines swallowed her and her guards and he hadn't seen them since. Had they taken her somewhere else?

His phone vibrated against his ankle. Damn. Hadn't he set it on silent mode? He willed it to stop when the spiky-haired guerilla from earlier settled on another boulder nearby. The scrawny kid laid an AK-47 across his lap, then took a buñuelo from his bag and started breaking off pieces to eat. The phone vibrated again. Gabe coughed to hide the sound, pretending his water went down the wrong pipe.

Spiky Hair looked unconvinced. "Do you have a microchip?"

At first, Gabe thought his rusty Spanish skills had led him to misunderstand, but then Spiky Hair repeated the question slowly. Yes, he'd definitely asked if Gabe had a microchip, like one came standard in all Americans. God. A bunch of sci-fi nerds were holding him hostage. Somehow, that made it all worse.

He shook his head.

"Because if you do," Spiky Hair added, "and I find out your government is tracking you with satellites, I will kill you and take your woman."

Gabe caught the general idea of the threat and had no doubt the little shit meant what he said. And really, given that the phone in his boot was equipped with GPS, Spiky Hair had cause to be concerned. Gabe hoped whoever just called him—Quinn, probably—remembered the feature.

"My woman, where is she?" he asked. Claiming Audrey as his didn't scare him as much as it should have, but that might be due to the fact he had ten trigger-happy teenagers threatening them both with death and God knew what else. In the face of that, freaking out about his attraction to Audrey seemed a tad ridiculous. "Where is she?"

Spiky Hair shrugged. "Who knows?"

That succinct answer was easy enough to translate. Well, at least Spiky Hair didn't say she was dead.

Hah, look at him. Suddenly Mr. Optimistic. Gabe rested his elbows on his knees and dragged both hands through his hair, surprised to find them shaking. Adrenaline afterburn, mixed with the long hike and his mostly empty stomach. It had nothing to do with the terror that clamped hold of his chest every time he thought of Audrey. In the jungle. Alone.

He heard her before he saw her. She emerged from the jungle, her face flushed, her tank top sticking to every dip and curve of her body. Instead of the sandals she'd had on, someone had given her a pair of too-big rubber boots like farmers wear to muck out stalls. She moved awkwardly in them, crashing through the underbrush with a gun to her back and tears streaking her cheeks.

When she spotted him, her chest heaved and relief filled her bloodshot eyes. "Gabe!"

He had the oddest urge to sprint to her, scoop her up in his arms and kiss her until both of them were gasping for air, but as pleasant a thought that was, his foot wouldn't appreciate the running part. It now throbbed in beat with his heart and he had little doubt it was so swollen he would need to cut his boot off. So instead, he held out a hand to her. She took it in a tight grip as if she was afraid to let go and sat beside him on the boulder.

The guerillas gathered on the other side of the small clearing and watched them with a mix of fear and awe. They were so freakin' young, all of them dirty and skinny and scarred. Gabe didn't have to wonder how bad their childhoods must have been to force them into life with the *Ejército del Pueblo de Colombia*. He'd seen it all too often in his SEAL career.

"Something's wrong," Audrey whispered.

He had to bite his tongue to suppress the urge to say, "Ya think?" He nodded toward Cocodrilo, who was already chopping at the undergrowth on the switchback leading up the mountainside. "You shouldn't have told him about your brother."

Surprise flitted over her features. "You caught that?"

"I do know some Spanish, Aud. I know what *hermano* means."

She nodded wearily. "Maybe if I hadn't said anything about Bryson, they'd have let us go with everyone else."

He doubted that, but said nothing. He offered the rest of his water.

"Oh, God," she said. "Thank you."

Gabe watched her drink it down in the same greedy gulps he'd taken. Her neck and chest were pink like her cheeks. A fine sheen of sweat made her skin shine in the waning evening sunlight, captivating him. She started to choke on the water and he drew the bottle away from her lips.

"Easy. Don't make yourself sick."

"Sorry." She coughed once more and dragged the back of her hand over her mouth. "I kept asking them for water, but they just pushed me on and on and on until my throat felt like sand and I couldn't walk anymore because I kept tripping over my sandals. Then they gave me these instead."

She curled her legs up to her chest and took off the rubber boots. Blisters covered most of the flesh on both her feet and

Gabe's blood went volcanic with rage. He wanted to kill her guards for that mistreatment, and gave serious consideration to ripping through the group right now with his bare hands. He could snap at least three necks before they realized what was happening, another three or so before they took him down—but that would leave Audrey in a very bad place. No companionship, no protector, just her and the guerillas, who would probably take Gabe's death as an invitation to do whatever they wanted to her. He couldn't let that happen and drew a deep breath, forcing his fury down to a simmer.

Audrey grimaced, touched the largest bubble on her left big toe, and lifted her gaze to his, looking like a child not understanding why she had been punished. He wished he could explain it to her, but he didn't understand it, either.

"Are you okay?" he asked.

"Y-yes." The word came out shaky, but then she firmed her lips and nodded. "Yes, I *am* okay. We *will be* okay."

With a determination that rivaled any he'd seen in BUD/S, she slid the boots back on then turned her full attention on him. Her fingers feathered over his cheek, light as a breeze.

"You're in pain. Is it your bad foot?"

"I'm fine." Except that he really, really wanted to lean into her touch.

"Uh-huh. That's why you're white as a ghost." She held up a hand to cut off his protest and took another sip of water. "Yeah, yeah, save it. I know you're a regular Terminator."

Gabe smiled. Couldn't help it. The woman was amazing.

After a moment filled with the sounds of the jungle and the steady swing-chop-swing of Cocodrilo's machete through the foliage, she sighed. "Those dead men back on the road…"

"What about them?" Gabe prompted when she trailed off.

"Cocodrilo's afraid of them."

"They're not going to do him much harm. You know, considering they're dead."

"Gabe." She pushed out an exasperated breath. "Not them, specifically, but who they worked for. Luis Mena."

"Shit." The name brought to mind a round, almost grandfatherly face. A face that had been on the Department of Defense's watch list for years for suspected drug trafficking activities, kidnapping, extortion, terrorism, and so many murders nobody knew the exact count. The DOD intelligence gatherers claimed Mena's operation was based out of Cartagena. And hadn't he seen that city listed on Bryson's itinerary? Bryson, who was in imports and exports….

Yeah, he'd known this was going to get nasty from the moment he heard the guerillas whispering Mena's name. He just hadn't realized that Bryson may also have a hand in that nastiness.

"There's something else," Audrey said, then folded her lips together when Cocodrilo snapped, *"¡Silencio!"* over his shoulder.

She moved closer to Gabe's side, lowered her voice. "I didn't catch all of it. Spiky Hair was talking too fast and his accent's… but I got the gist. They found a GPS unit in the car they shot up. It was tracking our Jeep." She paused, waited until his gaze met hers. "Mena's men were following *us.*"

• • •

"I don't get why Quinn doesn't want me out in the field."

Jean-Luc glanced over at Harvard, seated in the passenger

seat of the SUV with a mulish expression on his pretty-boy face, before returning his attention to the crappy jungle road.

"You're a computer guy."

"I've trained…" Harvard winced. "A little."

"Well, you're out now, true?" Jean-Luc said.

"On a bullshit assignment."

Jean-Luc didn't think it was bullshit. From what little he knew about Gabe Bristow, something was seriously wrong if the man didn't check in. "Gotta start somewhere."

Harvard's shoulders slumped and Jean-Luc couldn't stand seeing the guy so down in the dumps. "C'mon, give me a smile, *mon ami*. You're out from behind a computer, the sky's blue, the air's hot, and who knows? Maybe we'll even meet some Colombian cuties and finally rid you of your virginity."

Harvard sent him an I-am-not-amused glance over the rims of his glasses.

"Uh, how about some music?" Jean-Luc asked after a turbulent moment of silence. He flicked on the radio. "Ah. Do you like cumbia rock?"

The radio station cut in and out, but it was clear enough that he could pick out the song and sing along, tapping his fingers to the beat on the steering wheel. Good song with a good rhythm. It made him want to find a sexy Colombian woman and dance until their feet fell off. Then he'd take her to bed for a little horizontal dancing….

Mid-daydream, Harvard answered, "No," and switched the music off. The curvy Colombian fantasy disappeared.

Jean-Luc sighed. "It's an acquired taste."

"So's your singing."

"I'll have you know, my mama says I'm an excellent singer."

Harvard rolled his eyes and opened his mouth to say something, but stopped short. "Hey, hey, stop." He hit Jean-Luc's arm with the back of his hand and pointed through the windshield as the 4Runner cleared a sharp curve in the road. "Look."

Up ahead, a Jeep and a sedan sat abandoned in the middle of the road, facing them. Both of the Jeep's doors hung wide open and bullet holes had turned the sedan into an expensive hunk of Swiss cheese. He counted four bodies, their blood mixing with the dirt road into red mud, and swore softly in Cajun.

Harvard was out the door before Jean-Luc could stop him. He moved smoothly, kept his rifle at the ready, and cleared both vehicles, all quick, efficient, and quiet-like.

Maybe, Jean-Luc thought as he followed, they had all underestimated genius boy's abilities. "Where did you learn to do that?"

"*Call of Duty.*"

Or maybe not.

"They're not here," Harvard said and shouldered his rifle. "But the weapon Gabe gave Audrey before they left is still under the seat. His sunglasses are on the dash and his cane's in the back. There's a basket upturned in the passenger seat. Looks like it had food in it."

"Keys still in the ignition," Jean-Luc observed and leaned in to try the engine. It fired without so much as a hiccup. "No car problems."

"Bullet holes in the windshield, but I don't see any blood on either seat." Harvard scanned the jungle, then started a sweep of the area, walking in ever-widening circles around the vehicle. "No blood on the ground, either. Don't think they were hit."

"Huh." Jean-Luc fisted his hands on his hips, looked at the Jeep, the sedan, the dead bodies, then the spot he'd parked their 4Runner. "Looks like someone was shooting at the men in the sedan, and Gabe and Audrey got caught in the crossfire."

"Guerillas?" Harvard asked.

"Most likely."

"Think they were captured or made a run for it?"

Jean-Luc studied the gnarled twist of jungle choking both sides of the road. Not much place for them to run, but he supposed it was possible. Gabe knew his stuff, so if anyone could get them out of a sticky situation, it would be him.

"Hey, got something."

Jean-Luc turned to see Harvard kneeling next to a ditch carved out alongside the road by water flowing off the mountains during the rainy season. Now it was dry and overgrown. With the barrel of his rifle, he held aside a huge leaf to reveal a SIG Sauer P226. No way to be sure, but it looked like Gabe's.

Harvard frowned. "Wherever he is, he's without a weapon."

"That kinda puts a kink in the idea that they ran for it." A man like Gabe wouldn't run without his gun, no way. And if they had run, and for some reason he had to abandon the gun, seems his first course of action would be to get in contact with the team and order an exfiltration.

"Is his cell phone there?" Jean-Luc asked. He hadn't seen it in the Jeep, but moved over to take a closer look as Harvard explored the ditch.

"Nope," Harvard said.

"*Merde.*" Jean-Luc straightened as he heard another car

rumbling down the mountainside. He motioned to Harvard. "Grab the gun, take the Jeep, and try to get a hold of Quinn as soon as you have a signal. I'll meet you at that little gas station we saw ten klicks back."

He waited until Harvard was on the road before searching for a pen in the 4Runner's glove box and scribbling the sedan's license plate number on his hand. He didn't have time to search the dead men's pockets for ID—didn't want to risk being caught at the scene of a crime by whoever was headed this way—so he snapped a picture of each of them with his phone, hoping Harvard could dig up their names from the photos.

After one last look around, he got into the 4Runner and started up the mountain, passing another SUV headed down. He adjusted the rearview mirror and watched the vehicle stop beside the sedan. Four men got out. One surged over to a dead body, scooped it up and cradled it, crying into its hair. A lost loved one, brother or cousin, and Jean-Luc felt for the man. That shit sucked.

The other three tangos drew guns and looked around, much the same as he and Harvard just had.

So it was the bad guys, after all.

He saw the exact moment that they remembered passing him, because they all ran for the SUV and it skidded into a U-turn, kicking up dirt.

And let the games begin.

Jean-Luc grinned to himself, switched on the cumbia rock station, and stood on the gas.

CHAPTER TEN

Night closed in fast on the jungle floor, throwing dank shadows across the path, slowing their progress to a crawl. Just when Audrey thought she couldn't possibly take another step for fear of breaking an ankle out of exhaustion and lack of visibility, they emerged into a clearing soaked in the orange-red glow of evening sunlight. Pretty pink and red flowers bloomed in neat rows across the field. As a backdrop, blue mountain peaks stretched toward the saturated sky, with wild green jungle climbing as far up the slopes as the mountain allowed. For a moment, she forgot her aching feet, her exhaustion, her bone-deep fear, and yearned for her paints. She would never be able to do the stunning scenery justice on canvas, but boy, did she want to try. She'd paint it in soft, warm watercolors and call it, *End of the Road.*

Beyond the colorful field sat a cluster of thatched-roof huts that she prayed was their final destination. The guerillas all but dragged her through one of the rows between the flowers, seemingly as excited to get there as she was. Gabe would be waiting—she couldn't think otherwise—and the notion of seeing him again spurred her onward even with overwhelming exhaustion plaguing her every step.

As soon as they renewed their forced march up the switchback, they'd been separated again despite his efforts to stay with her this time. Hours had passed since he and his guards disappeared up the trail ahead of her. The first hour after she'd lost sight of him, she kept thinking they'd turn a corner in the path and find him waiting. During the second hour, with still no sign of him or his guards, she wondered if they'd taken him somewhere else. The third, as fatigue started dragging her down, she spiraled toward depression, fearing he'd been led to his death like a lamb to slaughter, and that she was next.

Then she spotted him, seated on a crate by a sputtering fire, eating a plate of rice with his fingers. The flood of relief made her knees go weak. Gabe was no lamb. More like a mountain, as tall and sturdy and rugged as the one they'd spent the day climbing, the only solid thing she could anchor to in all this craziness.

Spotting her, he stopped eating, a handful of white rice halfway to his mouth, and his ears reddened with embarrassment. That was…kind of cute. She had noticed the careful way he ate back in the Jeep with the empanada, but now, given the situation, it was even funnier. Who'd have thought the big, bad former SEAL had the table manners of her grandma.

Without a word, she sat beside him and scooped up a handful of rice. He gave a faint smile lined with fatigue and pain and continued eating, leaving the last half for her. When they finished, the guerillas prodded them toward one of the huts. Gabe was limping now, and each time he put weight on his bad foot, his mouth tightened with pain.

Audrey wedged herself up underneath his arm. He made a move to push her away and she tightened her hold.

"Don't you even think about it, bub."

"I'm fine."

"Liar. You need help."

"It's okay, Aud. I'm fine. I can do it—"

"Gabe. Shut up."

He grumbled under his breath, but then, surprisingly, his arm circled her waist. That he didn't put up more of a fight just went to show how much pain he was actually in. They must have made quite a sight hobbling across the camp together, because the guerillas all stopped eating to watch. Some pointed and laughed. Others returned to their meals like it was SOP to have two injured and exhausted Americans in their midst. Well, it probably was.

Bastards.

Audrey mentally spit the vilest curses she could think of in both English and Spanish at them until they locked her and Gabe inside the hut. She helped him sit on a pile of feedbags, then stamped her foot and fumed at the closed door.

Gabe chuckled softly. "Are you done cursing them out yet?"

She stamped her foot one more time for good measure before facing him. He lay stretched out on the feedbags, one arm thrown over his eyes, breathing in slow, deep breaths. His complexion had drained of color and held the faintest tint of green.

God, he must really be in pain, and here she was feeling sorry for herself. She settled onto the dirt floor at his feet and began working the laces off his boots. His jaw clenched so hard she saw a tick start below his eye.

"Audrey, stop. It's fine."

"Right. This foot is so far from fine, it's in another zip code."

"Okay," he said through his teeth. "It will be fine. Just leave it alone."

"Not happening." His grumbles, so like she imaged a displeased bear might sound, made her smile. "How'd you know I was cursing at them?"

"That you were stomping around like a five-year-old wasn't a clue?" His mouth flattened, but she thought she saw a small lift at one corner. A smile? "And my youngest brother does the exact same thing. Mostly to The Admiral's back."

"The Admiral?"

"My father. He doesn't like us to call him Dad. We've always called him by rank."

Audrey took an instant and intense dislike to the man. "Oh, yeah? Did he make you salute at the breakfast table, too?" Incensed on his behalf, she pulled a little too hard on the lace and Gabe sucked in a sharp breath.

"Oh! Oh, I'm sorry." She gentled her touch. "Better?"

"Yeah." He drew another breath. Let it out, and closed his eyes. He was silent for a long time. "And he did make us salute sometimes."

Audrey stared up at him in horror. "I was being sarcastic."

"I'm not."

Good Lord. Military school, a tyrant for a father. What an unpleasant childhood Gabe had endured. If it could even be called a childhood. It amazed her that he escaped with any semblance of sanity.

She sent up a quick prayer to her parents, suddenly a million times more grateful she'd had them, even if it was for too short a time.

Audrey got the boot unlaced. His foot was twice its normal size, and sported more shades of purple than she'd ever seen outside a canvas. She bit her lower lip. Should she cut the boot off? Then he'd be barefoot tomorrow if they continued marching. But if she didn't, the boot might cut off his circulation, putting him in danger of losing the foot altogether, and the loss of a limb would be hard on a control freak like him.

Okay, the boot had to come off.

She scanned the walls of the dim, dusty hut. No windows and only one door, most likely locked or guarded or both. It seemed to be a storage shed, packed with feedbags for the mules she'd heard braying somewhere in camp, but nothing to cut through leather.

Well, duh. Unless their captors were complete idiots, they'd check for anything that could be used as a weapon before putting her and Gabe inside.

"Left boot," Gabe said, startling her. He'd been quiet for so long she thought he'd passed out from the pain.

"What?"

"Look in my left boot. There should be a Swiss army knife that Cocodrilo didn't find."

How did he do that? He always seemed to know what she was thinking. Unless she was muttering to herself? She did have a tendency to do that when stressed.

Audrey moved around him, unlaced his other boot, and dipped a hand inside the leg. Her fingers brushed the hard muscle of his calf—did the man have even an ounce of fat on his body?— then closed around a plastic square. His phone. She gasped and flipped it open, only to see it searching for service. Disappointment crashed down on her, bringing tears to her eyes. For a moment there, she thought they would be able to call for help. They'd get out of here, then Gabe and his team could focus on finding Bryson and this nightmare would finally be over.

But, no. They were still stuck in the middle of the jungle with a useless phone, wasting time Bryson didn't have. "How's the battery?" Gabe asked.

She swiped the back of her hand over her eyes to clear her watery vision and checked the indicator. "Little under half."

"Damn. Let's hope we're outta here before it runs down."

"What good is it? It doesn't have a signal." She set the phone aside and dipped into his boot again, this time avoiding his calf and finding the small knife. She opened it and stared at the blade. As far as weapons went, it was pitiable, but she was still glad they had something. She moved back to his bad foot and started cutting.

Gabe winced. "It has GPS," he said of the phone. "As long as the battery holds out, Quinn will be able to track us."

One good thing, she supposed. Still, she'd rather it have a signal.

Was the team even still searching for her brother? Or had they abandoned the search to launch a rescue mission for her and Gabe? God, she hoped not. Her brother *needed* their help. At least she had Gabe. Bryson had nobody, and the thought of him locked away somewhere, alone and frightened, brought on a fresh round of tears.

"Hey." Gabe reached out and brushed his thumb over her cheek. "We'll be okay."

"I'm more worried about Bryson. Do you think the guys are

still looking for him?"

"I know they are."

"Okay." She sucked in a fortifying breath through her nose. "Then let me take care of that foot."

She worked at the boot in silence, using the tension in his body as an indicator of when to take a break. Because God knew the macho man SEAL wouldn't cry uncle if his life depended on it.

After what seemed like forever of her going all Jack the Ripper on the boot, it finally lay on the floor in shreds, and his foot ballooned now that the pressure was off it. Scars covered the top of his foot and ran in surgical lines up his calf to his knee. He was missing his middle toe, and another appeared mangled. No wonder he needed the cane.

"I, uh, know it's not very pretty," Gabe muttered. He kept his eyes off both her and his damaged foot.

"Feet rarely are." Aching for him, she closed the Swiss army knife then gently picked up his foot and placed it on her lap. "How did this happen?"

As soon as the question left her lips, she wished she could call it back. She wasn't sure she wanted to hear about the time he was captured and tortured by terrorists. Or the time he stepped on an IED. Or—

"Car accident," he said. "About a year ago now. We were on our way back to base after a weekend leave and some asshole kept playing leap frog with us on I-95—you know, speeding up to get ahead of us then slowing way down. So Quinn tried to pass him on the right and the guy got pissed, cut us off. Quinn swerved to miss hitting him and this semi came up behind us out of nowhere."

A semi truck? Audrey's heart performed a quick swan dive

into her stomach. He was lucky to be alive. "Oh my God."

"Yeah, I said that a couple times when it blindsided us." His lips inched up into a hint of a smile. "Sent us over the median. Quinn got thrown through the windshield after the first flip and, lucky him, he missed the face-to-face meet and greet with a concrete support. I was pinned upside down by my leg for four hours. The docs didn't think I'd keep it. It's—"

His voice caught, and she watched emotions battle over his face before he locked them down and cleared his throat. "It's the reason I'm no longer on the teams. Little tough to be covert when there's so much metal in there, I can't even get through airport security without a big hassle."

If it looked this bad now, his foot and leg must have been a mess a year ago. It was truly amazing that he was even walking. Then again, maybe not. She'd never met any man as stubborn and indomitable as him, and if he'd made up his mind to walk again after the accident, by God, nothing short of an apocalypse would have stopped him from walking.

But if he wanted to stay that way, they needed to get him professional medical attention. All she knew about medicine was what she'd seen on *House* and *Grey's Anatomy*.

She soothed a hand over his calf and felt his muscles jump. "Can you wiggle your toes at all?"

His big toe moved about a centimeter, but that was it. Probably not a good sign. Okay, now what?

"I... I think we need to wrap it."

"Cut up one of these." He thumped his palm on a feedbag. "The burlap should work."

"Won't be comfortable."

"Neither was the boot."

"Good point." Audrey hurried to drag one of the burlap sacks off the pile and cut it open. The sweet, earthy scent of oats filled the hut as she dumped it out. Using the knife, she cut five strips and went back to his side, again lifting his foot onto her lap. "This will probably hurt. I wish I had something to give you for the pain."

"Don't worry about it." Releasing a long breath, he laid back and shut his eyes. "I've dealt with worse."

Yes, she bet he had. Pain was a hazard of his former job, but she absolutely hated the thought of hurting him in any way.

"Just get it wrapped up for me, okay?" he said. "After I stay off it and keep it elevated for the night, it'll be good as new tomorrow."

Somehow, she doubted that. As gently as she could, she set to work wrapping the burlap strips around his foot, starting at his swollen ankle.

"So," she said after a moment, hoping to distract him. "You have a brother, huh?"

"Two."

"Older, younger?"

"Both younger."

She smiled a little, thinking of Bryson, and couldn't help but draw comparisons between her older brother and Gabe. If the situation demanded it, she had no doubt Gabe would and had killed. Bryson wouldn't take your life if you crossed him, just everything that made your life worth living. Both men were also cocky know-it-alls in their own ways. Both were fiercely protective. Inflexible. Domineering. The biggest difference was in their attitudes. Bryson tried to play nice, he truly did, and he was careful to never be rude even as he cut you down. Gabe didn't bother.

Knowing how difficult growing up with Brys had been, she almost pitied Gabe's little brothers. "Bet you bossed them around all the time."

He made a noncommittal sound. "I don't get along with Michael, my middle brother. He's too much like our father. He even married an ice queen of a woman who is so much like our mother, it's frightening. And my youngest brother, Raffi? Nobody bosses him around. He's ... uh, free-spirited. You'd like him. He acts on Broadway."

Something changed in Gabe's demeanor when he spoke of his youngest brother. Audrey couldn't quite put a finger on it, but he...softened. "Tell me about him."

"Where to start?" Gabe stayed silent for a moment, then gave a quiet laugh. "I'll never forget the look on The Admiral's face the day Raffi announced he was not going into the military. I believe he said something like he wanted to dance and sing and act and he was going to drama school in New York, fuck you very much." Pride filled his voice. "Priceless. Our old man looked like he was going to shit monkeys."

Audrey picked up another strip of burlap, held it in place with her thumb where the last one ended, and lifted his foot to continue wrapping. "Raffi sounds like my kind of guy."

Gabe's smile dropped into a dark scowl. "Yeah, well, don't get any ideas. He's gay."

"Even better." When his frown deepened, she smothered a laugh and finished bandaging his foot, tying the burlap in a tight knot to keep it from slipping. She bent over and placed a gentle kiss on the knot. "There. All done."

She looked up to find him staring at her with an odd expression on his face. "What, Gabriel? Nobody ever kissed away your pains as a child?"

"No. My mother wasn't exactly…" He trailed off and seemed to struggle with an inner demon for a moment, then shook his head. "Uh, yeah, you know what? I won't even make excuses for her. She sucked as a mother. She never should have spawned once, not to mention three times."

Emotion rose into Audrey's throat and it took two swallows to choke back the automatic denial that popped to mind. If his mother never had children, he wouldn't be here now. With her.

Good lord, was that really how he felt about himself? That he never should have been born? What a way to go through life.

"That's a shame," she finally managed. "Every child should have someone to kiss their injuries better."

That odd expression of his turned shuttered, unreadable. "Thank you, Audrey."

Her heart swelled, which was just plain stupid. A thank you, especially a grudging one, was nothing more than an expression of appreciation, even when coming from a man who rarely said the words. "Any time."

Kicking off her boots, she crawled up on the feedbags and stretched out beside him. They lay together in silence, listening to the chatter of the guerillas by the fire. She could make out bits and pieces of the conversation—bawdy observations about her body, crude challenges issued toward Gabe, speculation over how much money they would get from the United States government for two captives, and how they planned to spend said money. As if they would see any of it. She wanted to shout to them that their leaders were playing them for fools, the rich using them to line their own pockets, while they spent their days marching through the jungle, living off blocks of sugar and white rice.

Did they hold her brother in a camp like this? Maybe he was even somewhere in this camp. Had they forced him to march for miles through the jungle? He wouldn't last long if they had. Bryson never had been a good outdoorsman, hated camping or anything even remotely rustic. Her lovely little hut on the beach in Quepos, Costa Rica had appalled him so much last year that he'd immediately gone out and bought her that awful condo in the tourist trap section of town. Unable to see past the hut's lack of comfortable amenities, he just didn't get it. Didn't get her. But he tried to help her the only way he knew how, and God love him for that.

Tears welled. As much as they didn't see eye to eye, she still loved her big brother. He had to make it through this. She'd try harder to see things his way, she would. Just as long as they both made it out of this hellhole of a country alive.

"Audrey," Gabe said very softly next to her ear, drawing her out of her thoughts. She hadn't felt his body shift toward her, but there he was crowding her personal space, big as the mountain she'd compared him to earlier. His hand traced lightly down her arm, dipped to follow the curve of her waist, and finally settled on her hip.

His breath tickled her ear. "I have another injury that needs kissing."

She smiled into the gathering dark. "Do you?"

"Mm." He rolled her over and propped himself up on one elbow, bending down until his mouth hovered millimeters above hers. "Right..." He bussed his lips over hers, caught her lower lip in a gentle tug that she felt all the way to her womb. "…here."

Gabe claimed her mouth in the same take-charge way he did everything else, obliterating all but the need to feel more of him. No fear. No worry. Even the pain in her blistered feet faded. For a moment, it was just her and him, a man and a woman enjoying each other.

His tongue met and danced with hers, lighting up nerve endings in places she'd forgotten existed. His hand tightened on her hip, drawing her against all that hard muscle of his chest, and her fingers snaked into his hair, hugging him closer still.

Yes. This. It was exactly what she needed. A distraction. A tender, loving reminder that she was still alive. How had Gabe known she needed this when she herself hadn't realized it until now?

He kept his lower body off her, but his erection still prodded her side, especially when she sucked on his tongue and his hips surged involuntarily. Reaching down with her free hand, she cupped him through his pants and went utterly wet at the size of him.

Cripes, he was a *big* man. She figured he'd be fairly well-endowed since he towered well over six feet of solid muscle. But she never expected… She pressed her palm into him and let him thrust against her hand. Whew. She didn't know if he'd even fit comfortably, but sure couldn't wait to try.

With a groan, Gabe drew her hand away as she fumbled to free the buttons of his fly.

"Easy, honey. We can't do this now." After rearranging himself, he pulled her close. "Get some sleep."

She snorted out a laugh. "You want me to sleep after *that*?"

"To be continued," he said. "When we're both in better shape and have more privacy. Believe me." He cupped her breast and gave it a light squeeze. "We're nowhere near close to finished."

"Sadist." Even as the word left her lips, she yawned. She was so very tired all of a sudden, the sexual buzz having tapped out her last energy reserve. He was right; she needed sleep.

Seemed he was always right. That might get annoying.

"Can you...hold me for a while?" She felt silly asking, like a child afraid of the dark. But the dark had never been so frightening before, and she needed the human contact.

Gabe pushed her hair back from her face and pressed a soft kiss to her forehead. "I planned on it."

"Let me know if I hurt your leg."

"You won't."

Audrey sighed and curled into his side, taking strength from the heat of him, the solidity of his body and character. He was a good, honorable man. Funny to find one now in this place, under these horrific circumstances, after all her years of looking. She just hoped they both lived long enough to explore their budding intimacy.

God, it was all so surreal. She couldn't help feeling as if she'd wake up any minute in her hammock outside her cabin with a killer margarita headache and the vague notion she'd had a crazy dream. But she wouldn't. This was no dream, Gabe was no dream man, and they were both in a lot of danger.

As the day started to sink in fully, tears spilled over. "Gabe?"

"Mm?"

"Do you have a plan to get us out of here?"

"Yes."

The confidence in his succinct answer eased her fears, but only a little. "You're not just saying that, are you?"

"No, Aud, I'm not." He shifted and pulled her more firmly against his side. "Do you smell that? Almost like burning plastic?"

She sniffed the air, nodded. The scent did have a plastic smell, but also carried the chemical undercurrent unique to all hard drugs. "They're smoking something."

"*Basuco*, the dregs left over from the cocaine-making process. They're out there celebrating. They think they've hit the jackpot with us, but they're too cocky for their own good. Come morning, they'll all be drunk and stoned, and I'm going to cause some problems for them with the farmers that live in this village."

"How?"

"I'm going to kill one of their cows."

Audrey sat up, an automatic objection jumping to her lips. But when she saw the hard, determined line of his jaw and the flatness in his golden eyes, she knew protesting would be a useless endeavor. Still, she had to try. "Do you have to kill it?"

"It's the cow's life or ours, Audrey," he said without remorse. Those flat eyes met hers, and she wondered at the sudden stranger lying beside her. How could this be the same man who had been so tender with her only moments ago? "Livestock are like currency around here, and the last thing Cocodrilo wants is to piss off the local farmers. It'll cause chaos, and that's what we need to escape."

He was right. She knew it, but God, she hated the thought of some poor animal dying to save her. "Will you be kind to it, at least?"

His features softened a fraction and he caught a strand of her hair between his fingers. He wound it around his hand, studied it like the color and texture fascinated him.

"Gabe?"

"Yeah." He abruptly dropped the strand. "The animal won't feel a thing. I'll make sure of it."

"Thank you." After a moment, she settled beside him again, but her heart stayed lodged in her throat. "I'm really scared."

Gabe's arm tightened around her shoulders. "Yeah, I know. But I promise I won't let anything happen to you. Trust me."

Trust. Funny thing, that. Since her parents' deaths, she'd never trusted anyone to take care of her but herself. Not even her brother. But, as she tumbled into the oblivion of sleep tucked safely in Gabe's embrace, she realized she completely trusted him to do as he promised.

CHAPTER ELEVEN

It had been a long, long time since Gabe woke up with the warm sweetness of a woman curled beside him. In fact, had he ever? Most of his past lovers, those that he'd stayed with longer than a weekend fling, had always elected not to spend the night, either because of their own busy schedules or his.

But this…

This felt good. This felt right. He could learn to love this.

Still half asleep, marveling at the sensation of Audrey's small breasts flattened against his arm, he slid his free hand over her curves. She wasn't voluptuous, not like the women Quinn liked and therefore usually found for the both of them. Actually, now that he thought of it, he liked the full-figured ladies okay, but slim women with just a handful of breasts were what really cranked his engine. Almost every woman he'd ever had over the last twelve years was one Quinn hooked him up with. Well past time for him to start thinking with his own dick — and his dick wanted willowy Audrey Van Amee so badly it ached.

He wanted to slip his fingers under the waistband of her jeans and feel her. So hot and slick and ready for him. He'd start with one finger, curling it inside just enough that her hips would surge against his hand, begging for more. He'd give her another finger, and then a third, stretching her until…

She gasped his name.

Gabe came fully awake and, holy shit, he wasn't just fantasizing. He had two fingers buried deep inside her slick heat as she clung to his shoulder and writhed against him, on the verge of climax.

"Jesus." He started to withdraw his hand, but she caught his wrist and squeezed so hard he actually felt his bones shift. The look she gave him was so fierce, feral, and utterly feminine that his cock leapt with excitement.

"Don't you dare stop, Gabriel." She guided his hand between her legs and pressed her hips upward, taking his fingers in. "I need this. Please."

Fascinated, Gabe propped himself on one elbow and watched her face. She'd been so flippant about everything the day before that he should've recognized her attitude as a defense mechanism. Wound as tight as she was, she was bound for trouble if she didn't release some of that tension. And he wanted to do that for her, just this once. It wasn't exactly unprofessional. She had to be clear-headed, because when the opportunity presented itself, he'd need her help to get them out of here. An orgasm was just the quickest way to get her to relax.

Yup. This would be strictly a tactical move. Nothing more.

Gabe found her clit with his thumb and smiled when she hummed with pleasure. Head back, eyes squeezed shut, mouth opening into a little O, she was so open and unpretentious, so sensual without even trying to be.

He took her mouth in a deep, hard kiss, swallowing her moan as she came. Goddamn, but he wanted her, wanted to be inside her when she did that again. It took every ounce of willpower he possessed not to roll over, free his straining erection, and drill into her until they were both too weak to move.

Tactical move, indeed.

Shuddering, Audrey went boneless beside him. With his fingers still buried inside her, he felt her inner muscles ripple with the aftershocks of her orgasm. Slowly, oh so slowly, so that her plumped, sensitized sex felt every movement, he removed his hand.

A sleepy smile curved her lips as she lifted a hand to his cheek. He turned his face into it, nuzzled her palm once before planting a soft, open-mouth kiss right in the center.

"Gabe," she said.

"Hmm?" He continued kissing up her arm to her neck, enjoying the goose bumps his lips brought out on her freckled skin despite the humidity in their little hut.

Her fingers tunneled into his hair and rubbed his scalp in a massage almost as sensual as a handjob. "Will you let me take care of you now?"

He swallowed hard at the idea, but caught her other hand before it reached his fly. "I'd love for you to, but it won't be nearly enough. I'll want you even more than I already do and I won't be able to have you."

"Yes, you—"

"Not here." Gabe pressed her back as she started to sit up. "Not like this." He bent to kiss her nose. "Soon, though. When we're safe, and your brother's safe, I plan to take you to bed and not let you leave for, ah, let's say three days. Maybe four. We'll have to see how we're feeling by the end of day three. If we can still walk, it's on, so clear your schedule."

Audrey flashed a smile bright as a sunrise, just as he'd hoped. "I'd like that."

"Then it's a date." After another quick kiss, he pushed himself upright and took stock of his condition. Besides the raging boner and a mean case of blue balls, he felt pretty good. Had a bit of a crick in his side from sleeping on feedbags, and God Almighty, he needed a shower before he gagged himself.

Amazed that Audrey let him anywhere near her when he smelled like a three-week-old gym bag, he climbed off the feedbags and tested his foot. Still hurt, but not like it had last night, and the swelling had gone down. Nothing he couldn't handle.

Audrey sat up and watched closely as he strode toward the door. "How's your foot?"

"Not too bad." He tried the knob, surprised to find it unlocked. No doubt there was a guard stationed—

A body tumbled inside as the door opened.

"Aw, fuck." He gazed down at a young face staring with sightless, glazed eyes at the pre-dawn sky. The guard's neck gaped open in a morbid grin, sliced from ear-to-ear.

"Gabe, what's wrong? What—"

"Shh." He waved Audrey back and dropped into a defensive crouch, scanning the campsite.

Another body lay crumpled by the still smoldering fire pit, and a third at the edge of the poppy field. No sign of Cocodrilo, but he thought he saw movement near one of the buildings at his nine.

Had his team found him already?

Gabe cupped his hands around his mouth and whistled, mimicking a birdcall, then listened for five long seconds. No answer. Not Quinn. Shit.

Staying low, he edged far enough out into the open to snag the dead guard's AK-47 and an extra clip of ammo, then ducked back inside the hut. As far as shelters went, it was pretty pathetic, and they had to get out in case a firefight erupted. The thin wood walls wouldn't stop even a low caliber round from a pistol. Something more heavy duty from an assault rifle would tear the hut—and anyone inside—to shreds.

They'd have to make a run for it. Only problem with that was he was down to one boot. And wouldn't you know, the dead guard had tiny feet. He bent over and began unlacing his other boot.

"Gabe?" Audrey climbed to her feet, staring at him with fear-widened eyes. "Oh my God, is that blood?"

"Not mine." Absently, he wiped his bloody hands on his pants and then kicked off his boot. He'd move faster barefoot. He checked the AK over and ejected the magazine, disappointed to see it half empty. "Goddammit."

What the hell had the kid been shooting at? Certainly hadn't been his attacker, or else Gabe would have heard. Fuck, the idiot deserved to die if he didn't know any better than to walk around on guard duty with a half loaded weapon. Gabe pocketed that clip, hoping he wouldn't need it, and loaded the fresh one, jacked the charging handle.

"Where's my knife?" he whispered.

"Uh…" Audrey scrambled to their makeshift bed, running her hands over the bags that still held imprints of their bodies.

She pulled the folded knife from a crack between the wall and the feedbags and handed it to him. "Here. What's happening?"

"Someone's killing off our guards."

She gasped and looked at the closed door. "Your men?"

"Don't think so."

"Oh God." Her knees wobbled and she sank to the feedbags, shaky hands covering her face. "When will this nightmare end?"

"Hey." Gabe slung the AK-47 over his shoulder and gathered her in his arms, securing her against his chest with his chin on the top of her head. "I promised nothing's going to happen to you and I keep my promises. Stay steady and do what I tell you and we'll be fine. Okay?

"Audrey?" he said when she didn't answer, and lifted her chin with the crook of his finger. "Can you stay steady for me?"

Her eyes shimmered with tears, but she nodded. So strong. A lesser woman would be an unstable mess right now. Hell, most Average Joe civilians would be, too. That she kept it together with no training to rely on was amazing to him.

"I won't fall apart now." With a watery smile she added, "Can't make any guarantees for later, though."

"Now's all I need." He pressed a quick kiss to her forehead before releasing her. "When I open the door, be as quiet as you can and run straight to the poppy field. Don't wait for me. Run until you reach the other side, then hide. I'll whistle twice when it's safe." He whistled softly in one short burst followed by a longer one. "If you don't hear that, stay put."

Biting down hard on her lower lip, she nodded again. Gabe turned toward the door, rifle aimed, heart thundering behind his ribs. It should have been steady—this was a cakewalk compared to other situations he'd been in as a SEAL—but Audrey changed the stakes. All that mattered was that she got out alive.

A quick glance at her showed him she was ready. Or as ready as she was going to be. He sucked in a breath, held it until his heart slowed, let it go in a slow exhale, and pushed open the door.

"Go."

• • •

Jacinto Rivera's current flop was three blocks down from the warehouse Ian and Jesse planned to make a crater, which really wasn't a big surprise. The fact that it was less than a half step up from a shithole, however, was. Knowing what Quinn knew about Angel Rivera's love of luxury, he'd assumed Jacinto rode on his brother's coattails, living the good life for nothing. This was not the good life.

After clearing the apartment's second floor—not that anyone cared who they were or what they were doing; in this kind of neighborhood, people kept out of their neighbor's business— Quinn had stood lookout while Marcus made short work of the flimsy lock on Jacinto Rivera's door. The nearly empty apartment smelled like spoiled milk, food gone over, and rotting flesh.

"Ugh." Marcus raised his brows at the stench and lifted the edge of his shirt to cover his nose as they slipped inside. "Something's dead."

Well, wasn't Deangelo a regular Sherlock Holmes. Quinn scanned the tiny apartment. "Let's hope it's not Jacinto Rivera."

If so, they were back to square one in their search for Bryson Van Amee, and time, that persistent fucker, kept ticking away. Everything that could go wrong so far already had. Harvard was having trouble digging up enough intel on the EPC, which was slowing down their search. The warehouse job was eating up time and manpower, but no way in hell was Quinn leaving all those explosives in the hands of the enemy. Oh, and let's not forget Gabe was MIA.

Best case, Bryson would resurface unscathed after the ransom, his insurance company sixty-some million dollars poorer. Or, more likely, his captors would kill him and dump his body somewhere it'd never be found and the insurance company would still lose a couple million to his estate. Either way, it'd count as a loss for HumInt Consulting Inc.'s newly minted Hostage Rescue and Negotiation Team, and that was just not acceptable.

"It's not Rivera," Marcus called and Quinn turned toward him. He stood in the small kitchenette off the main room, gazing into the open refrigerator. "Not unless he's small and furry. Stray cat, and it's been here a while. Looks like it starved to death."

"In the fridge?"

"Talk about your ironic death." With his shirt still tucked up over his nose, he lifted his head to study the rest of the apartment. His dark eyes crinkled in disgust. "Nobody lives here. How could they?"

Quinn made a noncommittal sound, not about to admit he'd grown up in an apartment in Baltimore not much better than this, with an alcoholic father that beat him senseless on a daily basis and a mother too stoned to care. It was something he'd never admitted to anyone. Not even Gabe.

His name had been Benjamin Paul Jewett, Jr., or Paulie, back then, and life had been Hell on Earth. The day Big Ben went on a drunken rampage and shot him and his mother was the best of Quinn's ten-year-old life, and how sad was that? Lying on his narrow bed, pumping blood from a hole in his chest, his stolen Gameboy still clenched in his hands, he'd thought, *I'm finally free.*

The police had busted down the door, carted Big Ben away, zipped his mother into a body bag, and shipped Paulie to a hospital, where he met Dr. Samuel Quinn and his ICU nurse wife, Bianca. They'd saved his life with so much more than excellent medical care.

Then he'd lost them, too.

"Yo, Q. You here with me?" Marcus's hand passed in front of his face and he blinked back to the present, silently cursing himself. He didn't stroll down memory lane often, and when he did, he never went that far back. He shook his head. He had to stop zoning out. Jesse was already suspicious about his medical condition and he didn't need to add more fuel to that fire by blanking on Marcus.

He also had to get out of this fucking apartment—it made his skin crawl with the memories of Big Ben. He cleared his throat. "Find anything?"

Marcus gave him a narrow-eyed once-over but then shrugged. "Nah. Place is cleared out. If Jacinto ever lived here, it wasn't recently."

Quinn nodded and started toward the door. "Let's go over and see how Ian and Jesse are doing at the warehouse. Maybe we'll get lucky and—" His phone vibrated in his pocket and he held up a finger. "Hang on." He checked the screen.

Harvard.

Even as his stomach dropped into his pelvic cradle with sickening speed, he tried to keep his voice level. "What did you find?"

The kid's voice was almost all static. "Nothing good."

And it wasn't. Gabe's Jeep abandoned on the road, windshield shot up, with no sign of him or Audrey.

Quinn rubbed a hand down his face, appalled that tears blurred his vision. There were so few people left in the world he considered friends, and even less he counted as family. Gabe was family. If that fucker went and got killed… Christ, he might just lose his grip on the thin shred of sanity he still had.

"…dead bodies," Harvard said, and Quinn snapped back, realizing he'd lost the thread of conversation.

Concentrate, asshole, he told himself. He'd never had a problem keeping on task before, but…well, a lot had changed. "What bodies?"

Harvard made an exasperated sound. "Four of them on the road. Looks like a shootout—"

"That Quinn?" Jean-Luc asked in the background. "Let me talk to him." Then, "Quinn, those bodies are trouble. I can't begin to explain what happened between them and Gabe, but some of their friends showed up as I was leaving the scene and came after me. I lost 'em. Wasn't easy."

And the hits kept coming. "Did you get any intel out of them?"

"Not from the guys chasing me. They had guns and they were pissed. I wasn't about to stop and have a hi-how-are-ya chat with 'em. But," he added before Quinn could protest, "I got the plate numbers of both vehicles and photos of the dead men. Already sent to Harvard's email, and he says he'll start on the IDs as soon as we get back."

"All right. You're sure there was no sign of Gabe or Audrey near the Jeep?"

"Positive." He mentioned how Gabe's cane and sunglasses

were still in the vehicle, and that they found his gun in the foliage beside the road. "Harvard thinks he ditched it."

"I agree. If guerillas ambushed them, he'd have wanted to pose less of a threat." Luckily, Gabe was a threat with or without a firearm. "What about his phone?"

"Couldn't find it."

So he ditched the gun, kept the phone…which had GPS. Thank you, Gabe, you smart son of a bitch.

Relief surged through Quinn, making his hands shake. He hoped like hell Marcus didn't notice.

"Get back to base ASAP," he told Jean-Luc, then disconnected the call and speed-dialed Jesse. "Change of plans. Hold off on the warehouse. We're going after Gabe."

• • •

"Go," Gabe whispered when the door opened. Audrey hesitated only a second.

It was a second too long.

The black silhouette of a man slunk around the corner of the hut, spotted them, and raised his gun without even a shouted warning. He never got a shot off; Gabe dispatched him with a burst of three quick, clean headshots. The man-in-black's eyes widened and, gun dropping from his limp hand, he crumpled where he stood. The AK-47's retort echoed off the mountainside and set off other gunshots around the camp in a daisy chain reaction of panic. The guerillas poured from their huts, confused, sleepy, and half dressed, right into the oncoming bullets of the attackers. Those that didn't drop dead went for their own weapons, and soon the clearing sounded like a firework show.

Bang, bang, bangbangbang. Boom!

Audrey shrank back. This was it. They were both dead. She'd never see her nephews again, never know if her brother made it home safe or if her paintings sold at the art show. She'd never find out if sex with Gabe was as good as she imagined it might be. Never know if their chemistry was purely an adrenaline-fueled consequence of the circumstances or something more.

God, she didn't want to die.

To her complete horror, Gabe grabbed her arm in a hard grip and flung her out the door. "Go!"

Go? Go where? Bullets flew, people fell to the ground moaning in pain or ominously silent, and she couldn't get her bearings. A young guerilla charged at her, caught her in the left side, and knocked her off balance.

Without hesitation, Gabe stepped up behind the kid and sliced through his jugular with the Swiss army knife. Blood spurted, splattering across her face and chest. She wanted to scream. Opened her mouth and nothing came out.

"Audrey!" Gabe's voice was all drill sergeant again. He easily spun and deflected a blow aimed at his kidneys from a knife-wielding man-in-black. "Move! Go, go, go!"

Audrey scuttled backward on her butt, watching Gabe in full hand-to-hand combat. He moved like an assassin. Quick. Silent. Mesmerizing.

And deadly. Can't forget deadly.

"Audrey, goddammit, go!" In the millisecond he took his eyes off his attacker to glance worriedly her way, the knife slashed deep across his bicep. He staggered back, stumbling as his bad foot went out from under him.

"No!" Audrey surged forward—but caught herself. What was she going to do to help, paint an unflattering portrait of his attacker? Right. He knew what he was doing. She didn't, so she had to gather her wits and follow his orders. She was doing nothing but distracting him, dividing his attention and putting him in further danger.

He'd told her to run through the poppy field, hide in the jungle, and wait. Scrambling to her feet in the slick dew-covered grass, she sent one last look over her shoulder. Gabe had straightened himself and sprung back into the battle with a dark, determined expression on his face.

She hated to leave him.

Sending up a prayer for his protection, she ran toward the poppy field.

CHAPTER TWELVE

Gabe saw her go out of the corner of his eye. About damn time—
except now that she was out of sight, his heart decided to imitate a
heart attack, causing him to hesitate and nearly end up with a knife
in his gut. Unacceptable. He had to screw his head on straight.
Getting himself killed would do Audrey no good.

He deflected another blow. His opponent liked going for the
kidneys and the stomach, never varied attacks. Gabe waited until
the knife came toward his bellybutton again, spun out of the way,
grabbed the guy's knife hand and twisted, all in one quick, fluid
motion. Felt the satisfying snap of bone in his opponent's wrist, but
kept twisting until the whole arm was chicken-winged behind his
opponent's back, shoulder straining not to pop free of its socket.
The man dropped hard to his knees.

The gunfire had slowed, so instead of finishing him off and
moving on to the next tango, Gabe decided they'd have a nice
heart-to-heart instead.

"Who are you?" Gabe leaned on his arm. He cried out, tears

spilling from his eyes as fast as the Spanish prayer from his lips. "Who are you? *¿Quién eres?*"

Tough man with the knife wasn't so tough without it. He babbled incoherently, or at least Gabe thought he was babbling. For all he knew of Spanish, the guy could be spilling classified information pertaining to every terrorist organization in the country of Colombia. He doubted it, though, considering the asshole just wet himself.

Movement in the poppy field caught his attention. He turned, saw Cocodrilo sneak away from the camp, not exactly following Audrey, but there was no way he'd miss her—she was only minutes ahead.

Time to put an end to this knife fight.

With the blade of his hand, Gabe knocked the still-babbling asshole out cold. Killing such a pathetic excuse for a threat wasn't worth the effort.

He grabbed his AK-47, which he'd dropped during the fight, then snagged the unconscious man's knife. A Bowie about fifteen inches long with a scuffed steel blade and rubber handle, it made a much better weapon than his little Swiss army knife. He sheathed it in his belt.

Now to get to Cocodrilo before he got to Audrey.

• • •

"I'll drop you two klicks to the west," HumInt, Inc.'s local pilot called over the beat of the helo's blades. Luckily, it only took a call to Tucker Quentin to find one ready and willing to fly without asking too many questions.

Christ, they needed a pilot of their own. Quinn sighed and

pinched the bridge of his nose. One more thing to add to the to-do list.

A quick look at Google Maps had shown the area mountainous, dense with overgrowth and lacking any decent roads in or out. A damn good place to hide, inaccessible except by air or foot, and they didn't have the time to hike in. Gabe's phone hadn't moved yet, but that could change at any moment. Flying was their best—and only, in Quinn's opinion—option.

Quinn looked over his shoulder at the men in the cargo hold. Jean-Luc, Ian, and Jesse sat grim-faced and geared up, ready for action. The decision to leave Marcus behind had been unanimous since he had no military training. He was a little peeved, but hopped right on the phone trying to get a hold of a man named Giancarelli, one of his former FBI friends, to get a sitrep on the case.

Harvard had also wanted in on the op, and it had been a hell of a time talking the kid out of it. He'd only relented after Quinn pointed out that he was the only person who could work the tracking program on the computer needed to find Gabe's phone. His voice had been a constant presence in Quinn's ear since leaving Bogotá, keeping him updated on the GPS and any new info Marcus found out.

And Quinn had a brain-splitting headache. Jesus, he hoped they found Gabe. He was so ready to hand back command.

"Let's be ready to move," he told the guys, unfastened his harness, and climbed into the back with them. He unlatched the sliding door and wind rushed inside, stealing his breath as he watched the helo drop closer to the ground. The moment the skids touched down, he motioned the men out with one arm, sent an

OK signal over his shoulder to the pilot, and followed them out into the waist-high grass of the field. The pilot took the bird up again, blocking out the morning sun long enough that Quinn's eyes adjusted to the brightness and he scoped their surroundings.

They stood in a deforested field high on the slope of a mountain, with its white-tipped peak rising over their heads to the north and a treacherous climb down to the south. The guerilla camp was two miles to the east, over some rugged terrain, and he hoped like hell the guys were up to the task of hiking it.

The plan was for the pilot to circle the camp and offer air support while they infiltrated from the ground. Not knowing how many tangos they were dealing with, and the fact that both Jesse and Jean-Luc hadn't seen battle in years, put them at a distinct disadvantage, so the helo's support was a major plus.

Once on the ground, Quinn pointed to Ian and Jesse and motioned for them to go south. Both experienced mountaineers— and, whoa, who'd have thought Ian had hobbies besides blowing shit up?—they carried climbing gear with their packs. Should they run into any steep drop-offs, they wouldn't have to waste time finding an alternate route. Quinn and Jean-Luc would approach from the north. They also carried climbing gear, but he prayed they wouldn't need it. He'd rather go back to doing log PT in BUD/S than climb any damn cliffs.

The team would rally at the coordinates of Gabe's phone. And if there was a benevolent higher power out there somewhere, they'd find Gabe and Audrey alive and in one piece.

• • •

The gunfire had settled down a while ago, but even as she strained her ears, Audrey still hadn't heard Gabe's all-clear whistle. She sat under a giant, leafy bush, shivering, swatting at the ants crawling up her legs, struggling to hold it together.

Blood. Violence. Death.

Death. Oh God, what if he was dead? What if that wicked knife hit an artery and he was bleeding out onto the ground while she cowered?

Another blast of gunfire ricocheted off the mountainside and she jumped.

Okay, this sucked. She wasn't a natural-born coward, but being tossed light years out of her comfort zone apparently turned her into one.

No. That wasn't true. She wasn't a coward. Now that her initial shock had worn off, she wanted to help. But didn't violence breed violence? At least that's what her mother had drilled into her childhood psyche. Violence solved nothing, but Audrey couldn't see how cowering peacefully under a bush during a firefight solved anything, either, and for the first time in her life, she wished she had a gun for a violent purpose. So she'd never killed anything more than a paper cutout. She *was* a good shot, but faced with taking an actual life, she had no idea if she'd be able to do it. She'd definitely not do it as easily as Gabe had.

Gabe.

Cripes, she didn't know what to think of him now. Part of her had always known he was dangerous. Deadly, even. A Navy SEAL trained to kill quickly and quietly. Even so, she never really assimilated that Gabe with the sarcastic, overbearing, and oh so tender one who needed a good lesson in manners, who spit fire at the idea of being nursed, who held her so gently and fended off her nightmares.

The way he'd slit that kid's throat…

Sure, the kid was one of the bad guys, intent on doing who-knows-what to her. But he was still a kid, probably not even old enough to legally drink in the States. Did Gabe have to kill him? And did it matter so much to her that he had?

She'd have to think about that. Just not now.

Where was he?

She peeked out from underneath the bush. Gabe told her to hide and stay put, and as much as she wanted to rush to his aid, the best way to help him was to do what he said, minimizing his distractions. He knew what he was doing— she had to keep reminding herself of that. He was the elite of the elite, trained to handle whatever an enemy threw at him.

Except that little niggling voice in the back of her mind— the one that had convinced her it was a good idea to come to Colombia and look for Bryson, bad idea that it was—kept saying Gabe may be elite, but he was no Superman. Bullets went through him as easily as anybody else. Maybe even more easily, since he was exactly the type of noble jerk to throw himself in the line of fire.

If he got himself killed on the misguided pretense of protecting the damsel in distress, she might just have to resurrect him and slaughter him again. She was no damsel. She was following orders. As career military, he should appreciate that.

Twigs crunched under someone's foot nearby and she saw a brown boot step into and then out of her line of sight. Audrey didn't dare move and caught her breath, holding it in until her lungs burned. The footsteps circled her, slowly, and headed back toward the guerilla camp. She let out her breath on a soft exhale and wiggled forward to peek out again.

Bright morning sunlight slanted through the trees, dappling the forest floor with streaks of yellow and shadows. Now that the gunfire had subsided, the jungle creatures made their displeasure with the early morning racket known, squawking and howling up a storm. Surely all that noise would cover any sound she made.

She just couldn't stay hidden anymore. Not only because of the damn ants still swarming over her legs, but because someone, like the owner of those brown boots, would eventually find her. She had to locate Gabe and somehow get him medical help if he needed it. Lord knows, stupid alpha male that he was, he could be half-dead and wouldn't ask for help.

Audrey scooted from underneath the bush and straightened slowly, half expecting a guerilla or one of the unknown attackers to jump out at her. That's the sort of thing that happened in movies. The inexperienced, unsuspecting leading lady who's too stupid to live gets taken hostage while her man's off fighting the good fight.

Uh-huh. She was so not going to become that cliché. She looked around for something to use as a weapon and found a small branch, the end sharpened to a point where it had broken off its tree. It was no Smith & Wesson Sigma, her personal favorite, but that sharp end wouldn't feel too good when jabbed into an attacker's stomach. And it was just the right size after she stripped off a couple twigs.

Now, where to start? The camp was the obvious choice, but every now and again, a pop of gunfire still sounded from that direction. Obvious, but probably not the smartest. The smartest choice was to run in the opposite direction, or continue hiding until Gabe finally showed up and gave the all clear. Neither appealed to her much. She had the sick feeling that Gabe hadn't arrived yet because he couldn't, so it was her turn to play knight in shining armor. Yes, she was terrified half to death, but she was *not* a coward, dammit. If Gabe needed her help, she'd give it.

Shaking, but determined, she held the branch out like a sword and retraced her steps through the jungle to the edge of the poppy field—and came face-to-chest with a man dressed in raid gear. Her gaze dropped instantly to his feet. Brown boots.

So maybe she was that too-stupid-to-live leading lady after all.

He caught her by the arms and clamped a hand over her mouth before a squeak of sound left her lips. Eight more men in raid gear made their way across the field—definitely not guerillas; they were too well dressed and equipped. Two of the men dragged an unconscious body from the poppy field behind them.

Gabe.

Blood poured down the side of his face. Bruises darkened his jaw and cheekbone, his lip split open. Whoever they were, they'd beaten the holy hell out of him. He lay motionless where they dropped him, so very still that she couldn't tell if he was breathing or not. Pain exploded in her chest. It hurt so bad she thought for sure she had to be bleeding internally.

No, he couldn't be dead. He was too…*stubborn*.

She flailed against the arms holding her, biting down hard on the palm clamped over her mouth and simultaneously thrusting the tree branch into his stomach. Somehow, her weapon got turned around and it wasn't the sharp end that hit his abs, but it was enough to knock him back a step. He released her with a loud curse and she ducked through the line of stunned men to get to

Gabe's side.

Breathing. Oh, thank God. And his heart beat strongly behind his ribs when she laid her head on his chest. Still, he looked like hell and his bad foot had swelled up, again turning an ugly shade of purple. Was that weakness how they'd managed to take him down?

A shadow fell over her as she hugged Gabe. She glared up at Brown Boots. "Who are you?"

Surprise flicked over his dark features that she spoke Spanish, but he recovered fast and answered a question with a question. "Are you with the EPC?"

"No. They took us hostage." She looked at Gabe. Anger heated her blood and she felt the flush of it creep up her neck into her cheeks. "Why did you beat him?"

"He killed one of my men," the leader said without remorse.

"Only because your man tried to kill us. We're just trying to stay alive and find my brother and get out of this damn country!"

"Your brother?" He sounded extremely interested and Audrey squeezed her eyes shut.

Dammit. Gabe said she shouldn't have told Cocodrilo about Bryson in the first place, and now she'd gone and made the same mistake with this new group. Someday she'd learn to keep her mouth shut. If it didn't get her killed first.

"Are you American, then?" he asked with a pronounced English accent. When she said nothing, he added, "Related to the American businessman, Bryson Van Amee?"

Figuring that for a rhetorical question, she stayed silent. So he already knew about Bryson. Wasn't that just lovely. Maybe the EPC hadn't taken Bryson at all, and these guys were responsible.

Better trained and equipped for it, she had no doubt they had taken hostages before. Had no doubt they'd killed hostages before.

Oh God.

The leader moved away and spoke in low tones to his men. She didn't hear much of the conversation, except for "the boss will want to see her," and that sounded ominous so she tuned them out. Turning her attention to Gabe, she found all the blood came from a small cut at his hairline above his right eyebrow. Thank goodness it wasn't bad. Might not even need stitches, but hopefully he had a hard head, because she really needed him to wake up concussion-free.

The group came to a consensus, and the two men that had been carrying Gabe returned to his side, picked him up by the arms and legs, and carted him away.

"Hey!" she said.

The leader held out a hand to her. "You are coming with us."

"No." She shook her head and held her ground. "I'm not going anywhere without…" What should she call Gabe? "Bodyguard" would probably get him shot, and "friend" wasn't a strong enough relationship to warrant her refusal. She hitched her chin and met the leader's eyes with a challenge in her own. "Without my husband."

His brows lifted, disappearing under the fringe of his dark hair. "Indeed. I hate to inform you, I don't need your consent."

"It'd make your life easier. If you leave him, I'll fight you every step."

"I could coldcock you."

"Yes, but I won't stay unconscious forever, and I'll wake up swinging. Unless"—she put a lot of stress on the word—"Gabe stays with me."

"Gabe?" he echoed and his entire posture changed, jaw hardened, eyes flashed with hatred so hot she'd have been unsurprised to find Gabe's unconscious body singed from it.

"Bloody fucking hell." He whistled to his men, who were about to dump Gabe unceremoniously into the jungle and probably kill him.

"Forget it. He's coming, too," he told them in Spanish. "But cuff his hands behind his back in case he wakes and do *not* take your weapons off him for even an instant." Then, he held out his hand to Audrey again. "Now, Mrs. Bristow, will you come with us?"

Like she had any other choice. Even though he'd framed it as a question, it was a command at heart.

Audrey ignored his offered hand and stood by herself, fearing she'd jumped out of the pot and into the fire. "You know my… husband?"

Brown Boots gave a clipped nod and looked toward the sky as a helicopter flew overhead.

Help? Audrey wondered and followed his gaze. She couldn't tell, but friend or foe, there was no way for the people in that chopper to see them through the dense treetops.

Brown Boots motioned his men to get moving then turned back to her. "I'd say it's a pleasure to make your acquaintance, but that'll just bugger things up when I make you a widow." He gave her a shove forward. "So shut up and walk."

. . .

"Looks like we're too late," Jean-Luc muttered and used the toe of his boot to nudge the still-warm body of a kid who'd had his throat slit ear-to-ear. He gazed up at Quinn, looking a little green, much like he had after Gabe fetched him, hungover, from the bayou. "Looks like someone not so nice got here first."

Quinn's chest tightened as he ducked inside the hut Gabe's phone had led them to, half expecting to see his best friend in a similar state as the kid out front. God, he didn't know how he'd react if—

The hut was empty.

Quinn covered his eyes with one shaking hand and felt the warm weight of Jean-Luc's palm come down on his shoulder. "It's okay, *mon ami*. This is a good thing."

Right. A good thing that Gabe wasn't dead on the dirt floor of this hut. Right.

Feeling ridiculous, Quinn shook off Jean-Luc's hand and cleared his throat. "Contact Harvard and see if the phone's moved."

Jean-Luc stepped out of the hut for better reception, which gave Quinn some much-needed privacy. He bent over and placed his hands on his knees, sucking in three long breaths.

Gabe was okay. Gabe. Was. Okay. He wasn't dead. Quinn hadn't lost another loved one. Not yet. Not yet.

Jean-Luc came back inside and cleared his throat softly.

Quinn straightened so fast all the blood rushed from his head, making him dizzy as fuck. "Well?"

"Harvard says the phone hasn't moved. He says, from your phone's signal, it looks like you're standing right on top of it."

They both looked around. A feedbag lay in the middle of the floor, cut apart, its oats scattered. There were also the remnants of a boot nearby.

Quinn squatted down and, using his knife, picked up the boot. Someone had unlaced it then sliced each side open.

"Gabe's?" Jean-Luc asked.

"Yeah. Man, his foot's probably all kinds of fucked up right now."

Dropping the boot, Quinn balanced his elbows on his knees and stared at the pile of feedbags. If the boot hadn't been moved from the spot it landed, that meant Gabe must have been lying back on those bags when Audrey—he assumed it was Audrey—had cut it off. So it was entirely possible the phone slipped out of his pocket, especially if this is where he'd slept last night. Quinn stood and ran his hand through every crack and crevasse between the bags.

Bingo. Gabe's phone. He flipped it open, saw the battery icon blinking red in warning, and powered it down. A second later, Harvard came over the radio.

"Achilles, Harvard. Over."

Quinn held out a hand for the radio. "Harvard, Achilles. Send your traffic." They'd decided en route that they'd use their nicknames for all radio contact in case someone was listening.

"Be advised, I lost Stonewall's signal," Harvard said. "Repeat, I lost Stonewall's signal. How copy?"

Quinn looked at the dead phone in his hand and sighed. "That's a good copy. Out." He started to hand the radio back to Jean-Luc, but instead hit the talk button again to find out Ian and Jesse's location. "Boomer, Achilles. What's your twenty? Over."

"Headed your way," Ian's voice said a second later. "With a present. Out."

Quinn and Jean-Luc shared a worried look.

"Is it just me," Jean-Luc said, "or did Ian sound waaay too happy?"

Yeah, he'd had a peculiar ring of…glee in his voice. Christ, what had that psycho done now? Quinn had thought that by pairing Jesse with Ian, the mostly sensible medic would dilute the EOD expert's particular brand of sociopathy.

Apparently not.

Shaking his head, Quinn strode to the door, more than a little afraid of what he might find waiting outside. Ian was dragging a bound, naked, and mutilated Colombian man across the camp like a recalcitrant puppy while Jesse walked behind, tight-lipped.

Disapproval and concern for the injured man rolled off the medic in pulses. "Okay, Dr. Lector, you can stop torturing him anytime now."

Quinn felt the same way. He was not so noble that he wouldn't use whatever means necessary to get what he wanted, but there was a line he wouldn't cross. From the looks of things, Ian had crossed it and then some.

"Ian," he said very softly, putting an edge of steel in his voice. "Let him go."

Ian didn't listen. Big surprise. He knocked the man to his knees, gripped his dark hair, and yanked his head back. Only then did the battered face covered in blood and snot ring a familiar bell.

"Recognize him?" Ian asked. When nobody answered, he scowled. "Did none of you read Harvard's reports?" He jerked on the guy's hair hard enough to make him cry out. "Meet Cocodrilo, the EPC's general of the Amazon region. And he's been quite talkative. In English, even. Told me some very interesting things you guys just might want to hear."

Ian let Cocodrilo drop to a sobbing heap on the ground and brushed his hands together. He arched a brow at Jesse. "You can apologize for that Hannibal Lector crack anytime now."

"No way." Jesse shook his head. "I don't care who he is. He's a human being and you still went way too far, *Lector.*" He stressed the nickname with venom.

Ian snorted. "Why don't you go spout that righteous shit to the families of all the people this asshole's tortured and murdered, huh? Let me know how well that works out for you."

"Shut up!" Quinn stepped between them and wondered how the hell Gabe dealt with shit like this without losing his mind. He could tell Jesse was itching to tend to the injured man and motioned him forward. "Jesse, go ahead and take care of him. And you—"

Ian's shoulders stiffened and Quinn had a sudden flashback to his youth. When Big Ben finished beating his mother and turned on him with a belt in hand, that look in his liquor-glazed eyes, and slurred, *And you, you little bastard...*

Well, shit. When that happened, he used to tighten up exactly like Ian did just now. Had someone once also used the contemptuous Ian Reinhardt as a punching bag? It seemed unbelievable—and yet the proof was there in his dark, wary eyes and defensive stance.

Imagine that. Quinn had something in common with the psycho.

"Good job, Ian." He said the words he'd so wanted to hear from his own father before he was old enough to realize they'd never come, and nodded in a show of approval. Abused kid to abused kid.

Ian looked so taken aback the expression on his face was almost comical. Blinking, he dropped the bad boy act and sounded apologetic when he muttered, "Uh, thanks."

Quinn waited a beat, letting Ian have a moment to compose himself. When his ever-present sneer returned, Quinn nodded and got back to business. "So, what did you find out?"

CHAPTER THIRTEEN

Coming back to consciousness was almost always as painful as getting KO'd in the first place, because it happened with a killer headache, churning nausea, and, in Gabe's case, a foot that ached like a son of a bitch. Even so, his first thought before he opened his eyes was of Audrey. Was she safe? Was she still hiding somewhere in the jungle, or had she been abducted by the men who jumped him?

Goddamn, they shouldn't have gotten the drop on him like that. He'd been too focused on the threat of Cocodrilo, too afraid for Audrey's safety, that he didn't see them until it was too late. And they weren't stupid like the guerillas—the moment they noticed his bad foot, they attacked the weakness, taking his legs out from under him. Once he hit the ground, he'd known it was game over. Oh, he still fought with every skill he possessed—it wasn't in him to do anything else—but it'd been with the certain knowledge that it was a hopeless fight. He was actually surprised he still drew breath, albeit painfully.

No matter. He had to get up, move out, and find Audrey.

Gabe pried open his eyes—and there she was, his lovely Audrey, kneeling beside him, haloed in sunshine. Freshly washed, her wet hair hung in a loose braid over one shoulder, and a filmy white dress hugged her slim body. Almost afraid she was a hallucination, he reached out a dirty hand and touched her cheek.

Warm. Soft. Real.

The crisp scent of citrus and clean woman drifted over to him as her hand covered his, and damn if his eyes didn't burn.

"You're okay." His voice sounded like a bullfrog's croak.

"So are you," she said softly, lacing together their fingers. "A little beat up, but the doctor said you'll be fine."

Doctor?

With his fear for her safety assuaged, their surroundings started to sink in. A hotel? Had to be. He lay on a plush, very large bed with translucent bronze drapes billowing from the canopy. A mural covered one whole wall of the wide-open room, giving the illusion you were staring out over a city in Greece. Directly across the room was a wall of windows that opened to a balcony and gave a breathtaking view of the sea, but it sure wasn't the Mediterranean. More like the Caribbean, since he was fairly certain they were still in Colombia, despite the room's decor. But how did they end up on the coast when they'd been in the heart of the jungle? And how long had he been out? And...

"What doctor?" He sat up, ignoring Audrey when she started making noises about him lying still. "Where are we? What happened?"

"Gabe, please, take it easy."

Not a chance. The more he saw of this room, the less he liked the situation. This was no hotel, but someone's private home. An extremely wealthy someone's private home. He rubbed his hands over his face and bumped a butterfly bandage stuck to his forehead. He ripped it off, tossed it aside.

"What the hell's going on?"

"Okay, okay. I'll explain everything, but…" She bit her lower lip and motioned a pressing gesture, urging him to calm down. "Don't freak out."

Oh yeah, he really wasn't going to like this. He shoved aside the blankets covering him only to discover he was naked underneath, except for a crisp white ace bandage wrapped around his bad foot. Well, fuck it. He'd planned for Audrey to see him naked sooner or later after this mess was over, when involvement with her wouldn't be considered unprofessional. Might as well be sooner, though this wasn't exactly how he'd imagined it going down. There was supposed to be kissing involved. Some licking. And groping. Lots of groping on both their parts.

And now would be a good time to put a kibosh on that kind of thinking or he'd only add insult to injury with a raging boner.

Audrey's eyes widened, but she didn't look away as he half-expected. He stood and put weight on his bad foot. Pain blazed up his calf, but the foot held, and he refused the crutches Audrey scrambled to retrieve.

"Where are my clothes?"

She sighed and returned the crutches to their spot in the corner of the room. "After Dr. Manello cut them off, I figured they were unsalvageable. But there are jeans and a T-shirt in the dresser for you."

Gabe stalked over to the bronze-finished wood dresser.

Those cargo pants had been his favorite pair, well-traveled and comfortably worn, and some doctor… Cut. Them. Off.

The fucker.

Scowling, fuming, he found clothes in the top drawer and yanked on stiff, brand new jeans in too dark a wash for his taste, forgoing both underwear and the soft red T-shirt.

"Uh, Gabe, maybe you should shower before—"

He sent a snarling, lethal glare over his shoulder that had quelled many a budding SEAL. But not Audrey. Her chin just hitched up in challenge.

"Well, sorry, but you look and smell like a caveman." Planting a fist on one jutted hip, she glared right back at him. "But that doesn't mean you get to act like one, too."

"Don't care. Now explain." He faced Audrey, crossed his arms over his bare chest, and waited. She mimicked his pose except she tapped her foot and sunlight glinted off the jewels decorating her sandals.

She met him stare-to-stare. "Not until you stop acting like an ass."

For some reason, instead of getting pissed at her defiance, Gabe found himself fighting back a smile. The woman had a backbone of pure steel. He really did love that about her.

Whoa. He backpedaled his thoughts, erasing that particular L word and replacing it with another. Like. Lust. He hadn't meant to think L-O-V-E.

"I thought you said I was acting like a caveman," he said.

"You are. A caveman's ass."

He snorted and rubbed his palm over his jaw to hide the laugh. Shit, he did look like a caveman.

"All right." Holding up his hands in supplication, he moved toward her and took a seat on the edge of the bed. Some victories just weren't worth the battle. "You're right. I was out of line."

She nodded once. "Always knew you were a smart man."

Gabe sighed. Fifty years down the road, he'll probably still be hearing about this argument. And for some reason, that thought didn't scare the holy hell out of him. In fact, he sort of looked forward to it. What kind of sick bastard was he?

"I was out of line," he admitted again, figuring a second time couldn't hurt. "But, Audrey, I do need you to tell me what happened, how we ended up here, and where here is."

After a second, her posture relaxed and she rolled her lower lip through her teeth. "Promise not to freak out?"

"I'll do my best." He held up a hand when she opened her mouth in protest. "That's all I can promise, Aud. I told you I don't break promises, so I never make ones I'm not sure I can keep."

But he had made one, hadn't he? Back in that jungle hut, after she'd kissed him senseless, he had promised to protect her. Yet he wasn't careful enough and now, despite their plush accommodations, she could be in more danger than ever. He had the sickening feeling he already knew where they were and who their *generous* host was, and ground his back teeth at the thought.

Striving for patience, he waited silently as she hesitated again. God, she was killing him.

"Audrey, talk to me."

"We're at Mena's estate in Cartagena," she blurted.

Gabe dropped his head forward and let out a long breath. Luis Mena, public enemy number one. Holy fuck. "How?"

"Those were his men that attacked the camp. But it's not what you think," Audrey rushed on. She knelt in front of him, bending to put her face in his line-of-sight. "Gabe, really. I talked to him over lunch and this isn't a bad thing."

Luis Mena, not a bad thing. That's like saying Hitler was misunderstood. And, whoa, she *talked to him over lunch*? She had to be out of her flippin' mind. "Do you have any idea what that man's done? What he's capable of doing?"

"Yes, I know. I've heard the horror stories same as everyone else in the Western Hemisphere. But he isn't our enemy."

He gave a humorless laugh. "He's everybody's enemy."

She pursed her lips. "Okay, I can't argue that. But you know that old saying about the enemy of my enemy. Will you just hear me out?"

"No." He abruptly stood. Audrey lost her balance and fell backward on her butt.

"Gabe!"

"Get up. We're leaving. Now."

"And you're more than welcome to," a pleasant, barely accented voice said from the doorway.

In one quick move, Gabe had Audrey off the floor and tucked safely behind him as he faced one of the most hated men in this half of the world.

Intel put Luis Mena close to seventy, but nobody knew for sure. Steel gray hair and a salt-and-pepper mustache showed his age, but he still had the toned body of a much younger man. Topping out at several inches under six feet, he was a thin man with stylish black-framed glasses and a surprisingly warm smile. He looked like someone's grandfather—and, in fact, he had several grandchildren and one infant great-grandchild—but that appearance belied his true persona. That of a stone-cold killer.

"We're leaving," Gabe said again.

Mena stepped aside and motioned to the open door. "As I said, you are more than welcome to go, but I would very much appreciate it if you and your lovely wife joined me for supper first."

Audrey shifted uncomfortably behind him at the word "wife." Interesting. But not important right now. "I don't think so."

"Pity." Mena waited until they were almost out the door before adding, "Because I think I know where to find Bryson Van Amee." He smiled when Audrey pulled Gabe to a stop. "That is, if you're interested, Commander Bristow."

Gabe kept his face impassive, but something—a flicker in his eyes, a tightening in his shoulders—gave away his surprise because Mena laughed.

"Yes, I know all about you, Lieutenant Commander Gabriel Bristow, former commanding officer of the American Navy SEAL Team Ten, bravo platoon, forced into retirement due to an injury sustained on your way to a training operation last year in Virginia." His smile took on an edge. "Training, I was told, that was meant to help you and your team take down my business."

How did Mena know that? Gabe managed to show no reaction, but—shit. The objective of that training mission had been highly classified information that most of his team hadn't even known.

Audrey looked up at him, worry in her eyes. He took her hand and gave it a light squeeze, still making sure to keep his body in front of hers. Which, naturally, drew Mena's attention right to her.

"I was quite surprised to find out you have a wife," Mena said. "None of the information I have on you—which really isn't much, I'm ashamed to say—mentioned a spouse."

"It's recent," Audrey blurted.

Jesus Christ, woman. Give him more ammo against us, why don't you? Gabe tightened his grip on her hand, hoping she got the hint to stay quiet.

This counted as a massive clusterfuck if he'd ever seen one. How they'd ended up married he had no idea, but it put her in even more danger than she realized. Married meant he cared for her — and, dammit, he did — which meant Mena could use her against him. If he'd known Mena thought they were husband and wife from the get-go, he would have treated her the way his father treated his mother, coldly and with disinterested tolerance. If he didn't care, she was not worth Mena's time. She'd be safe.

But the fact he still held her hand and used his body to protect hers nixed that plan. Any fool could see how much he cared.

"Recent, you say?" Mena's brows climbed toward his hairline behind his glasses. "I see. Well, I suppose congratulations are in order, then. We'll drink the finest bottle of Bordeaux in my collection with dinner to celebrate."

"We're not staying." The thought of sitting down to a civil dinner with this generation's Hitler soured his stomach.

Audrey tugged his hand. "Yes, we are."

"No." He tried to force patience into his tone and failed miserably. "We're not."

"Gabe! He wants to help us find Bryson. How can you refuse that?"

Because nothing Mena did came without a high cost. He wasn't offering to help out of the goodness of his heart — he didn't have one — and his motives were most likely pure as sin. "We'll discuss this later. My team — "

"Is no closer to finding him, I assure you," Mena said easily. "I've kept a close watch on all of you since your arrival in my country. As a precaution, of course. I had no idea you were investigating Bryson's disappearance until Señor Miller told me this morning when he brought you in."

"Is that why you had us followed?" Audrey asked, and no way could anyone miss the hope in her voice. "Just as a precaution."

"And my men ended up dead." His Cheshire Cat grin didn't waver. "However, let's not get into all that now. I think this conversation will be more palatable over good food with good wine, don't you agree?"

"Gabe, please," Audrey whispered behind him. "I need to find Bryson. Please."

Her pleading all but shattered his heart. He couldn't deny her, even though every instinct screamed to get her far, far away from Mena's lengthy reach. A deserted island might do the trick. Yeah, and then what? Stay there for the rest of their natural lives?

No, he wasn't a runner. He was a fighter, and if he wanted to keep Audrey safe, he had to face this threat head on. Alone. Unarmed. With a bum foot.

Shit, shit, shit.

Finally, jaw clenched, he nodded once. Behind him, Audrey let go a hiss of relief.

"Excellent," Mena said. "Dinner shall be served on the veranda tonight at six-thirty. I'll have appropriate attire sent up for you both." He eyed Gabe with a faint sneer of disdain, prince to pauper, and Gabe thought, *fuck you.* "You'll, of course, want to bathe before dinner, so I'll take my leave."

The door shut and Gabe heard the unmistakable snick of a

lock. Just a mind game since the balcony was wide open and a locked door wouldn't keep Gabe from leaving if he really wanted to go. Still, the sound of a lock closing off an exit always sent a quick skitter of panic down even the most trained operative's spine. It's human nature to want freedom. Mena's nature to take it away.

Audrey stared at the door in wide-eyed horror. "Why did he lock us in? He said we're guests. He—"

"Doesn't trust me." Gabe gripped her shoulders and gave her a little shake. "And you shouldn't trust a thing out of that man's mouth. He's more sophisticated and better dressed, but he rates right on level with Cocodrilo. Don't let him blind you to that."

"But…but he said he knows how to find Bryson."

"That's what he says. Is it true?" As tears filled her eyes, he let go of her shoulders to cup her face and brush them away.

"It could be," she whispered.

He sighed. "Audrey, don't cry. We'll find out what game Mena's playing during dinner. Until then, let's get some rest."

Because he needed time to strategize. A group of recon marines spent two months quietly scoping out Mena's home last year, and the DOD built a replica of the house and outbuildings in Virginia to run invasion scenarios with, so he knew the floor plan of this estate. Knew all the weak spots in the security system. Liam Miller, the British mercenary hired by Mena to oversee security, was good at what he did, no doubt about it. But Gabe and the SEALs were better, and if there had been no accident, if Operation Black Boa had gone down as planned, Mena would be sitting in an international prison right now awaiting trial. Not that he deserved a trial.

Gabe led Audrey over to the bed. She looked wrecked, exhaustion bruising her eyes with dark circles. Had she slept at all while he was unconscious? He'd bet not.

Truthfully, unconsciousness didn't count for sleep, either, and his own energy levels were also in the danger zone. He knew the fuzzy, disjointed feeling well, knew if he didn't catch a couple hours of sleep he'd crash out and be of no use to anyone.

"This is all so messed up," Audrey murmured, snuggling into the big bed on her belly, arms wrapped tight around a pillow.

"It is." He tucked the blanket around her. "SEALs refer to situations like this as fubar. Fucked up beyond all recognition."

Her lips curved in a hint of a smile, but it didn't last long. "I'm not going to sleep." Even as the words left her, she yawned.

"Try."

She yawned again. Now that she was horizontal, she was fading fast and fighting it. "I shouldn't have convinced you to stay here."

Gabe thought about telling her that despite what Mena had said, the drug kingpin wasn't going to let them leave until he was good and ready for them to go. Their surroundings were more comfortable, but substituting a castle for a prison doesn't change the fact it's still a prison.

Instead, he brushed back a lock of her hair. "Sleep."

"Hmm." Her eyes fluttered shut and a second later, she was gone.

Wishing he were that pillow she cuddled so close and cursing himself for the unprofessionalism of that thought, he sat on the edge of the mattress and watched her for a long time. Her braid had loosened, spilling pale golden brown hair over the paler gold blankets. Her eyes moved restlessly behind their lids, and every once in a while she made a small sound of protest and hugged the pillow tighter. He reached out, traced the curve of her cheek with one finger, and she settled again with a soft sigh.

Ah, hell.

He started to remove the pillow from her grip and caught a whiff of himself. Whew. He couldn't subject her to that stench. Shower first, then sleep—with Audrey tucked safely in his arms for a couple hours.

Sleeping together like that wasn't unprofessional, right?

CHAPTER FOURTEEN

When the bed sank and Gabe's muscular arm slid under her, Audrey woke. His skin was still warm and dewy from a shower, and he'd shaved. His hard jaw felt baby smooth as he nuzzled her ear. He pulled her close, his natural male spice and some kind of flowery soap scent enveloping her. Yum. She wanted to bury her nose in his shoulder and breathe in nothing else, but that would require moving, and she was quite comfortable now that he was in bed with her.

Except for the blooming ache between her thighs.

She smiled without opening her eyes. "You smell like a garden."

He grunted. "It's the shampoo. Some girly designer shit. I had no choice."

And he sounded really unhappy about that. Audrey stifled a laugh in the pillow, sure he wouldn't appreciate it. "It's nice."

"I'll be sure to order a bottle," he said, deadpan.

She huffed out a breath in exasperation. "Do you ever get sick of being so sarcastic?"

"Do you ever get sick of being so contrary?"

She elbowed him in the gut—and, ow! About like jamming her elbow into a block of stone. But she still heard a satisfactory *umph* in reply. "I am *not* contrary."

"Bullshit."

"Hey!" She moved to elbow him again, but he caught it and in one deft move had her on her back, pinned to the mattress with a big hand on each arm and one thick leg locked over both of hers.

With his pelvis pressed to her hip, she'd have to be a dolt not to recognize the bulge she felt there as anything less than carnal male interest. About freaking time. Despite their increasingly dicey situation, or perhaps because of it, she'd been dying for an opportunity to get her hands on him again. And this time, he wasn't going to talk her out of doing what she wanted to do to him.

"Stop. Hitting. Me," he said through his teeth.

Why? He needed to get hit every once in a while to remind him he was no superhero. But saying that aloud wouldn't improve her chances of getting him naked in the next five minutes, so she gave her most innocent smile instead. "Okay. How about I do this?"

With her arm still in his grip she couldn't move her hand far, but managed to wiggle it close enough to his crotch to cup him through his jeans. Pity he'd put the things back on after his shower.

No, on second thought, it wasn't. Now she'd have the great pleasure of stripping them off him.

The way he reacted to her touch, you'd think she prodded his family jewels with a branding iron. He jerked away and rolled to a sitting position on the side of the bed, his back to her. And what an amazing back, a perfect V of muscle that made her mouth water. She wondered if he'd flee in terror if she licked her way down the indentation of his spine.

Hmm. Only one way to find out.

Audrey crawled across the bed and placed an open-mouthed kiss on the back of his neck. On a groan, his head dropped forward. She took that as encouragement and experimentally ran her tongue along his spine, pausing long enough to give him a love bite on the elaborate tattoo covering his shoulder blade.

"Audrey, Jesus. Stop. We can't—"

"That's not what you said last night. Or this morning."

"I was trying to comfort you, give you something to focus on besides the guerillas and what they might do to us. That's all."

Oh, that hurt. But only for a second, because no way would he respond like this if that really was all.

"Liar." She shook her head and scooted off the bed to kneel on the floor in front of him. He gritted his teeth so hard a muscle jumped in his cheek and the fingers of one hand kept clenching and unclenching.

Good. She wanted him riled up. She wanted him to lose control. She just plain old wanted him. And she knew he wanted her, because the evidence was right there in that massive erection. So why did he keep fighting it, the stupid man?

She reached for the fly of his jeans, but he caught her wrist. "It's not right."

"Oh, yes, it is." She swatted his hand away and made fast work of the buttons.

Hallelujah, he'd gone commando underneath the jeans and she freed his erection. A bead of moisture appeared on the flared head of his penis.

And he claimed to not want this. Riiight.

Leaning over, she licked the drop away and grinned at the shudder that wracked his big body.

"Audrey…" His voice came out hoarse and he tried clearing his throat twice before continuing, "This is not professional. I won't take advantage of—"

"Looks to me I'm the one taking advantage right now." She blew on his glans, savoring the way his fingers tangled in her hair and the way his hand trembled. She could almost hear his mind frantically working to come up with a good reason to stop.

"We need to sleep," he said.

"This won't take long." To prove her point, she tongued him from base to tip and felt every muscle in his body go rigid. He let out a ragged groan and hauled her up by the shoulders to kiss her hard. His tongue invaded her mouth, the kiss stealing her breath.

Yes. She had him. Finally.

But then, panting, he ripped his mouth from hers. "No, goddammit. We're not doing this here. For all we know, Mena could have cameras—"

Oh no, he wasn't pulling back now.

"So we'll give him a show." She straddled his lap and pulled her dress over her head. He wasn't the only one going commando under his clothes and his gaze latched onto her naked breasts. He moistened his lips as if he wanted to bend over and taste her, so she threaded her fingers into his hair and urged his head down.

Oh, yes. He used his teeth to tug her nipple to a point and groaned in a half-desperate sound. Shocks of pleasure zinged from her breasts to the spot she really wanted him to kiss, the spot that already wept for him. But, dammit, she couldn't enjoy it yet, because the stubborn man had at least one hand still clutched on those reins of his control and was already starting to pull away from her again.

"C'mon, Gabriel." Audrey repositioned her body to rub against his length as she rocked her hips, teasing him with her heat, her wet desire. Leaning forward, she nipped his earlobe. "Walk on the wild side with me."

Ah-ha. That did it.

Gabe caught her mouth again in a hot, hungry kiss and stood, his fingers digging into her rear as she wrapped her legs tight around his middle. He had such big, masculine hands. They felt delicious on her flesh. She wanted them touching her everywhere.

He turned and dumped her on the mattress. She bounced and laughed until—

God, that expression on his face. He stood beside the bed, breathing hard, his lips swollen from their kiss, his hooded eyes drinking her in like he wanted to devour every inch of her.

Yes, yes, yes, she wanted to shout, but her breath stalled in her lungs. She shifted on the bed, letting her knees drop apart, allowing him to look his fill. And he did, studying her with a hot intensity that she'd never seen on another man's face before. If she were a match, his gaze alone would have set her aflame.

"Gabe," she whispered. His golden eyes flicked up to meet hers. She held out her arms. "Please. I want you."

Something stirred behind his eyes as he shirked his clothes in seconds and sank into a crouch at her feet. Reverence. Desire. Maybe a little fear.

She still wore her sandals and he kissed her toes as he

unbuckled each and tossed them aside. Then he kissed his way up
her body until they were nose-to-nose and she squirmed for more.

There. He was right there at her entrance and still resisting,
damn him. She hooked her legs over his hips and urged him closer,
dug her heels into his butt and lifted herself so that he had no
choice but to fill her. Hard. Again and again and again…

"Audrey," he breathed and gripped her hips, lifting her into
his thrusts. "You're—so hot. You're—God, baby, are you coming
for me?"

She was. Her head bumped the headboard with each powerful
thrust and she was flying apart underneath him. She had to clamp
her teeth onto his shoulder to keep from screaming and letting
everyone in the estate know exactly how incredible he felt inside
of her.

"Christ." Gabe stopped moving to stare at her. "You're like
nitro. One touch and boom."

She let go of his shoulder, soothing the bite with her tongue
before grinning up into his eyes. "Yeah, I'm a two pump chump."

He laughed. A real laugh, loud and rolling, the first she'd ever
heard from him. "I love it," he said and kissed her hard.

Then he moved again. Started slow, a long glide in and a
delicious slide out, until she was panting, so close on the verge of
another orgasm her fingers and toes tingled and she begged for
harder, faster…

He flung her into a whirlwind of sensuality she'd never
imagined and she soared, basking in the bliss of another release.
Oh God, the man had to be an angel, because she was in heaven.

When she floated back to herself a moment later, she opened
her eyes and there he was, her angel warrior, still surging over her.

Sweat rolled down his temple and his jaw clenched. With one final deep thrust, his head fell back and his mouth opened on a ragged moan as he shuddered with his orgasm. Just as she'd once mused, he was beautiful when he let go and lost control like that.

Gabe collapsed on top of her, but only for a second. She didn't mind his weight, but protective man that he was, he was probably afraid of squishing her. He rolled to his back, switching their positions. His eyes closed, his breathing settled into a nice, even rhythm, but Audrey knew he wasn't asleep. His fingers stroked up and down her arm in the lightest of caresses.

Silence descended, but it wasn't at all uncomfortable. Amazing that she didn't feel the need to fill it with cooed oh-it-was-so-goods and other inane ego stroking. Gabe was a man comfortable with his body, comfortable with a woman's body, and comfortable with sex, and he knew all too well he'd done it right.

Boy, had he ever done it right.

Audrey smiled to herself and propped her weight on one elbow to study him. His body fascinated her now more than ever. Wide, heavy arms and shoulders, and an honest-to-goodness eight pack with ridges between each muscle group that arrowed into a sharp V at his hips. His nipples were like copper pennies, his navel such a shallow innie that it was almost an outie. And how adorable was that?

With a smattering of dark hair, his chest was the most defined she'd ever seen, but he still wasn't body-builder bulky. Maybe he wore all that muscle so well because of his height.

A set of dog tags rested on a ball chain between his pecs. Audrey had felt them, cool against her skin, when he was on top, had seen them swinging when he propped himself up on his big arms to thrust deeper. Now she picked them up to read the engraving.

BRISTOW, GABRIEL M

938867004USN A NEG

NORELPREF

"These look new," she said. No scuffs or dings, still shiny. She didn't doubt that Gabe, meticulous man that he was, would keep them in mint condition. Still, it seemed like they'd be a little beat up if he'd had them since he was seventeen. "Are these new?"

"Hm?" Gabe looked up, spotted the dog tags dangling between her fingers, dropped his head back to the pillow and shut his eyes again. "No. I just didn't start wearing them until last year."

"Why not?"

"Wearing them on ops was more of a risk than not. Last thing I wanted was to let the enemy know I was a SEAL. And now…" He opened his eyes again and took the tags from her, rubbing his thumb over his name. "I can't seem to take them off."

She smiled at the pensive note in his voice and thought about the tattoo on his shoulder. Two battle-dressed skulls faced off while an eagle carrying a trident wrapped in an American flag flew over the design. Across the bottom stretched a banner with the famous SEAL motto: *The only easy day was yesterday.*

She bet he got that tattoo around the time he started wearing his dog tags. "You miss the Navy, huh?"

He stayed silent for so long, she didn't expect an answer. Then he surprised her with, "I really do, Audrey. It's where I belong. Not here, working as a private contractor."

She so didn't agree, but decided to keep her protests to herself.

For now. "What does the M stand for?" she asked instead, rubbing her thumb over his name.

"Matthew."

"Named for an archangel and a saint," she mused. "My mama would have loved that. The only reason I didn't end up Mary Something-or-Other is because Daddy was a huge Audrey Hepburn fan. Are your parents very religious people?"

He grunted. "They like to appear that way. Truth is, we never went to church."

Audrey nodded and pointed to the last line on the tag. "Hence your lack of religious preference?"

"Yup."

"My mother was extremely religious," she said and weaved the chain between her fingers. "She raised me to be, too, but…well, I've never really fit into the mold my parents cast for me."

"I don't think any children do," Gabe said, again surprising her. Who'd have thought him such an insightful man? His voice softened. "Parents need to be able to accept their children for who they are or not become parents at all."

Ah, she got it now. He was thinking of his brother. Knowing what she knew of his father, Raffi's coming out of the closet must have been a hellish event in the Bristow household. She imagined young Gabe torn between the love he had for his baby brother and the loyalty he felt toward his tyrant of a father—and fell hopelessly in love with him because he'd chosen Raffi.

Not that she'd had very far to fall.

She replaced the dog tags and soothed a hand down his chest. "You'd make an excellent father, you know." When every muscle in his body went tight underneath her, she laughed. "Just an observation, sailor."

"Jesus Christ, Aud. That's seriously not great post-sex conversation." He groaned and slapped his forehead with the palm of his hand. "And we didn't use anything. Fuck!"

"Yes, that's what we did."

He shifted to face her, his gaze a little bit wild. "I didn't... I never... Are you...?"

Stuttering. The big bad SEAL was stuttering! Audrey thought about goading him on, but he looked so genuinely distressed that she didn't have the heart.

"Relax, Gabe." She patted his cheek. "We're safe. I'm on birth control."

"You haven't been able to take any—"

"Since I'm too forgetful to take a pill every day," she interrupted, "I switched to the shot, which is good for three months, and my next isn't due until July. So relax before you hyperventilate."

"Okay." He ran a hand over his eyes, heaved out a breath. "Okay. You should know I was clean last time I got tested. And I haven't slept with anyone since before the car accident."

That long ago? Wow. He was practically a monk. A very sexy, very very *talented* monk. And, yeah, the dirty little fantasy that just popped into her head of dressing him up in a Franciscan robe while she wore a school girl outfit probably just secured her seat in Hell. Mama would be so ashamed.

Gabe was watching her, waiting for a reply to... Um, what were they talking about? It definitely wasn't Franciscan monks.

Oh, right. Him being disease free. "I had no doubts about that, Mr. Responsible."

He lifted his head to scowl at her. She rolled her eyes and added, "I'm clean, too. I don't take those kinds of chances. I don't sleep around."

"Good."

Was that possessiveness she heard in his voice? Oh, a girl could only hope. She snuggled into his side and savored the feel of his heavy arm around her. His lips brushed her temple.

"Get some sleep, honey. We're going to need it."

She tried. She truly did, but as soon as she shut her eyes, she saw her brother's face.

Was he still alive? If he was alive, was he in one piece? Had his captors beaten him or starved him…or worse? And even if they get him back, would he still be lost to her? She wasn't a dummy. She knew what a traumatic experience like this could do to a man.

Did Mena really know anything about Bryson? She didn't see how, and Gabe didn't think so, but she felt like they were out of options. No telling when the FBI would try to exchange money for Brys, and although Gabe never said so, she knew he thought paying the ransom was an all-around bad idea. The captors would have no reason to keep Bryson alive after that. And sixty-five million reasons to kill him so he couldn't identify them.

"Audrey," Gabe whispered in her ear then moved over her. His mouth found hers in a sweet, gentle kiss that was more about comfort than sex. "I can hear your mind churning from over here. Shut down, honey."

"I can't," she confessed. "I'm scared."

"I told you I'd let nothing happen to you."

Cocky man. But she believed him. He was more than capable of keeping her safe. "I'm not scared for us." She raised a brow, his expression patient but dubious, and she sighed. "Well, okay, I am. But I'm more worried about Bryson. What if—"

"No, no. Never play the 'what if' game. You'll drive yourself nuts."

She bit her lip. "But what if we don't get to him in time? They'll kill him, won't they?"

Gabe rolled over onto his back again and stared up at the ceiling. "If we can't get to him in time, my team will find him," he said after a moment and squeezed her against his side. "Don't worry. Quinn knows what he's doing."

CHAPTER FIFTEEN

Quinn had no fucking clue what he was doing.

Since leaving the guerilla camp, Jesse and Ian had been at each other's throats constantly, still bickering over Ian's treatment of Cocodrilo, who was now a "guest" in one of the bedrooms at base camp. And since Quinn had all but sanctioned Ian's actions, Jesse shared the love with him. Jean-Luc sided with Jesse, and Marcus sided with Ian once he found out what was going on. Harvard tried to mediate, but the poor guy got crushed between both sides.

This mission was turning into a snafu for the record books.

Quinn sat at the table while the guys raged around him. He studied maps of the city and outlying areas that highlighted known EPC strongholds, but what he really wanted to do was bang his head against the table until he passed out. Because that would probably be more productive since, according to Cocodrilo, the EPC knew exactly squat about Bryson Van Amee's abduction. They had nothing to do with any of it, and if Jacinto Rivera was involved, it was without his brother's or the EPC's blessing.

So who the hell took Bryson Van Amee? And who attacked Cocodrilo's camp and presumably took Gabe and Audrey? He imagined it was the same person or organization that got into that shootout with the EPC on the jungle highway, but the license plate numbers Jean-Luc had taken down after finding Gabe's Jeep shot to hell had come back stolen.

Back to square one.

Quinn pushed aside the maps and sat back in thought. They still needed to find Jacinto Rivera, their only solid lead to Bryson. And that warehouse still needed to go *boom* at some point, or else he wouldn't be able to sleep soundly at night knowing he left a bomb-making factory in the hands of the baddies.

Mostly, the team needed to pull the fuck together or nothing would get done.

How would Gabe do it? Quinn had no clue. Gabe just had a natural aura of authority that made people follow him without question. Quinn didn't have that, but he did know one surefire way to whip the guys into line. He may not be a great leader, but he was one helluva drill instructor.

Quinn stood up fast, letting his chair clatter to the floor. "Ten-hut!"

It would have been amusing to watch the former soldiers in the group snap to automatic attention if he wasn't so pissed. Once a soldier, always a soldier.

Marcus, the fucking fed, just crossed his arms and scowled. "You military dudes really say that?"

"Yeah. Really. And if you guys have enough energy to bitch at each other like a bunch of nagging housewives, you have enough for some PT training. On the deck. Now!"

To Quinn's complete surprise, the first to drop was Ian. The rest followed in grumbling succession—Marcus with a roll of the eyes—until only Jesse was standing and Harvard still sat at his computer.

Jesse said, "This is bullshit."

"On the deck."

"Screw you."

"You're not my type. Drop, Warrick."

Jesse leaned forward, eyes narrowed. "Make. Me."

In a quick succession of moves, Quinn snapped Jesse's Stetson off his head, slugged him in the solar plexus, the gut, and the side, bending him double, then elbowed him between the shoulder blades. Jesse went down to his hands and knees, gagging. Another blow to his lower back sent him sprawling on his face.

"Jesus Christ," someone whispered in awe.

Quinn straightened, tossed the Stetson in front of Jesse, and looked around at the men lying flat on their bellies like an angler's catch of the day. "*Don't* fuck with me, guys. Since this isn't the military, I don't have to play nice anymore, and I'm done with you assholes jerking me around. From now on, listen to me and do what I say without question or you'll all get to know the deck as personally as Warrick just did. Got it?"

A round of muttered yeses.

"Yes, what?"

"Yes, sir." It came in succinct unison this time.

"All right. One-hundred push-ups. Now. You stop, you falter, you start over. Go!" Quinn pinned Harvard, who was still at his computer, with a hard look. "You, too."

Swallowing hard, Harvard dropped out of his chair like a rock.

Satisfied, Quinn righted his own chair and sat down, planted his feet on the table, and snagged Harvard's laptop. He wasn't as good at research as their resident genius, but he had sources that needed checking. He began a search for Jacinto Rivera's current whereabouts while the guys called out each push-up in resounding unison.

One. Two. Three.

Like ticking off seconds on the clock.

Jesus.

. . .

A knock on the bedroom's door jolted Gabe out of a dead sleep. He launched from the bed and reached for his firearm, only to realize he was buck ass naked. Evening spilled vibrant colors into the room and tortured his pounding skull as the sun sank over the peaceful slice of ocean outside the windows. He groaned and squeezed his eyes shut.

The knock sounded again, impatiently this time, and Audrey sat up with a gasp, her hair a wild cloud around her pale face. "What's that?"

Gabe scrubbed his face with both hands, trying to rub away the fog of sleepy disorientation, and found his jeans on the floor. "It's okay. Probably a butler with the *proper attire* Mena mentioned."

Sore and stiff from the beating he took that morning, followed by the fantastic way he'd spent the afternoon, he stuffed his legs into the jeans and crossed the room while buttoning the fly. He glanced back at Audrey to see her wiping her eyes like a drowsy child—but she sure as hell didn't look childlike with her small breasts bare, pale peach nipples perky in the air-conditioned coolness of the room.

Yeah, he definitely didn't want whoever was now pounding on the door to see her like that. "Cover up, Audrey."

"Huh?" She yawned, then looked down at herself. "Oh!" She scrambled for the sheet and clenched it to her lovely breasts. He liked the flush that climbed up her chest into her cheeks. It reminded him of how she looked when turned on, when he was moving deep inside her.

Wouldn't it be nice to crawl back into bed with her and forget everything again?

He sighed, turned the doorknob, and found Liam Miller with his fist raised in mid-pound.

"Liam," Gabe said and leaned against the doorframe, arms crossed, to block his view of the bedroom. "Still got a temper on ya, I see."

Liam's upper lip curled. "Gabe Bristow. Imagine my surprise when my men dragged you unconscious from that poppy field. Lost your edge, I see."

Gabe eyed the garment bags Liam carried. "And you, playing butler for the scum of the earth. I don't know why I'm surprised."

"I go where the money is. As a mercenary now, it's something you'll learn fast." He gave a bitter laugh and shoved the garments toward Gabe. "The infamous Commander Bristow, a mercenary. It still tickles my funny bone to say it. My, how the mighty do fall."

"My, how the spineless do flee. Tell me something, have you pried that tail from between your legs yet?"

Liam's teeth gnashed together. "I *had* to flee. I had no choice because of you, you self-righteous prick."

"Hm. Hey, Liam." Gabe made a brushing motion near his

nose. "You got a little something…"

Liam raised a hand halfway to his nose before he caught himself. Eyes spitting fire, he said, "Back up."

Unperturbed, Gabe pushed away from the doorframe and stepped back. Liam slammed the door and the lock snapped into place again.

"Whew," Audrey said on an exhale a few seconds after the door closed. "That's some bad blood there. I take it you know each other."

Gabe nodded and laid out a plastic-wrapped dress on the end of the bed for her. He opened his own garment bag to study the contents. A freaking tux and dress shoes. And here he was hoping for cammies and combat boots.

"Let me guess," Audrey said when he stayed silent. "Long story?"

"Yes and no." He pulled out the crisp white dress shirt and slid into it, but left it hanging open, unbuttoned. "If you want to know the bare bones, I got the bastard kicked out of the British Special Forces during an op a couple years back, and he's had it out for me ever since. It's a mutual hate-hate relationship. Now get dressed, hon."

She pushed aside the garment bag, ignoring the plum-colored gown inside. "Kicked out? What did he do?"

Gabe started to say, "That's classified," out of habit, but caught himself. Considering he'd spent the afternoon inside Audrey, making love to her, she deserved more than the rehearsed response he reserved for SEAL wannabes and frog-hogs. And, technically, Liam's disgrace was public knowledge—or at least it was in Great Britain. He sat beside her on the bed and pulled her into the crook of his arm, savoring the softness of her skin under his hand.

"Liam Miller—which is not his real last name; he went by Collington back then—was one of the British SAS officers helping us to locate a CIA operative who…" He trailed off. Insurgents had held the CIA operative captive in a training camp near the Turkey border. By the time the SEALs located him, he'd been skinned alive. With no way of knowing how many classified secrets he spilled, orders came down from on high to neutralize the camp. Including the women and children.

Um, yeah, Audrey didn't need to know the nitty-gritty. And he didn't much care to relive the experience.

Gabe cleared his throat. "That part's not important. But during the mission, I caught Liam snorting something. Come to find out later, it was coke. That put my team and his in danger, so I reported it to his superiors and they jettisoned his ass so fast he probably still has road rash."

"Sounds like he deserved it," Audrey said.

"He did and then some. The drug use wasn't the whole of it. A couple days after his replacement arrived, we discovered he'd been stealing and selling ordnance to terrorists for years."

Her eyes widened. "And he was never arrested?"

"He bolted and found himself a comfy position as Mena's right-hand man. As long as he stays here and Mena stays out of prison, he's safe."

Part of the draw of taking down Mena had been the opportunity to get Liam Collington-slash-Miller behind bars as well. It had been Gabe's pet project right up until the car accident that stole his career. Throughout the many tedious hours he'd spent in the hospital, he often wondered if the accident was more premeditated than accidental. The driver of the pick-up that had caused the crash was never located, and with Gabe out of the teams, the operation came to a dead halt. As far as he knew, nobody had revived it.

He gave Audrey a light squeeze. "Liam's a dangerous man. He's extremely well-trained and very unstable. Watch your back around him tonight, okay? He might try to hurt you."

She flinched. "What? Why? I don't know him. I had nothing to do with what happened between the two of you. Why would he want to hurt me?"

"Because you're mine."

Her eyes lifted to his, filled with a soft something that looked a lot like hope. "Am I?" she whispered. "Yours?"

Jesus Christ, he wanted her to be in the worst possible way. It wasn't professional, it crossed every line of honor he'd ever drawn for himself, but there it was.

Still. Now was not the time to fight an emotional battle with himself. Now was the time to focus. She couldn't be his if either of them wound up dead.

"Liam thinks you are, and that's all that matters." He knew the instant the words left his tongue that it was the wrong answer. The hope in her eyes faded to disappointment, though she looked away quickly to try and hide the reaction.

"I, um, should shower before dinner." She pulled out of his embrace and scooted to the edge of the bed, trailing that pale gold sheet behind her to the bathroom.

Gabe let her go. Hurting her feelings hadn't been his intention, but that's exactly what he'd done, and he felt powerless to fix it without admitting things he couldn't afford to admit yet.

He *hated* feeling powerless.

Cursing, he pushed to his feet and strode toward the bathroom door, but paused before barging inside. What if she was using the toilet or something? Muscling his way in when he knew damn good and well she wanted private time would be just plain rude—he could almost hear her scolding for his lack of manners and dropped his hand away from the doorknob, raising it to knock instead.

"Audrey?"

The shower turned on, but she didn't reply.

Gabe sighed and rapped his forehead lightly on the door, once, twice, which did nothing to help his headache or the blooming ache in his chest that made it hard to breathe.

"You are mine," he muttered into the wood, although he knew it was a little too little, a little too late.

• • •

Am I? Yours?

Ugh. Gabe was such a dunce. Audrey might as well have spilled her heart out to him with those three words, and it went completely over his head.

Okay, so that wasn't entirely fair. He was focused on keeping them safe, getting them free, finding Bryson. He had a lot more on his mind than their budding intimacy. Really, she should, too, but even thoughts of Bryson couldn't keep her from reliving this afternoon in vivid detail as she soaped herself. She ached in all the most delicious places, her breasts plump and tender from Gabe's affections, her thighs shaky, her core all but rubbed raw from the friction of his thrusts, and it felt wonderful.

She wanted more. So much more.

She just had to convince Gabe he wanted the same.

Feeling better, Audrey shut off the water, reached for a towel, and noticed the dress she was supposed to wear hanging from a hook on the back of the bathroom door. She'd left it in the other room, so Gabe must have put it there sometime while she was showering. She never heard the door open, but knowing Gabe, she wouldn't have. For a big man, he moved with eerily light feet.

The silk, plum-colored cocktail dress clung to her in all the right places, with a plunging V neckline that showed a tantalizing glimpse of cleavage. It wasn't even close to her style, but how disturbing was it that Mena had so accurately guessed her size? She had to fight the urge to rip the awful thing off, shred it into expensive, itty-bitty scraps, and flush it down the toilet.

She left her hair down to air-dry and hoped the heavy mass covered some cleavage. In her everyday life, she liked wearing as few clothes as possible and had no problem with flashing a little skin—but not with men like Mena and Liam around. No thanks.

She opened the bathroom door and spotted Gabe staring out the balcony windows at the sunset. Or at least she thought it was the sunset he watched with such unwavering intensity. Either that, or he was scoping Mena's security set-up.

Sadly, that was more likely.

All Gabriel Bristow saw when he looked at a sunset was a tactical advantage or disadvantage. He wasn't the type to take a minute to admire the world's natural beauty, to soak in a pretty moment. She'd have to change that.

Gabe made such a striking picture standing there in the dying sunlight, dressed in a tux with his bowtie undone around his neck and a fatigued expression of pure concentration on his face, that she wished for her paints. She let her eyes roam over his hard body, committing every detail to memory so she could transfer it to canvas as soon as she got back to work. His military-erect posture, feet braced apart, hands folded behind his back. The way the sunlight set sparks of gold and red off his dark hair. The play of light and shadow over his features. His caged intensity, pitiless focus. She'd capture him in acrylic with stark lines, dramatic contrasts, and call it, *The Only Easy Day Was Yesterday.*

God, he was beautiful.

A modern avenging angel.

As if sensing her gaze, he turned away from the window slowly, gold eyes focusing all that intensity on her. If she didn't know any better, she'd think that jerk of his shoulders was his breath catching. Maybe the dress wasn't that awful after all if it elicited such a reaction.

Goading him a bit, she did a little turn and prompted, "So?"

"You look…" He seemed at a loss for words and rubbed a hand around the back of his neck. "Beautiful."

The sincerity in his voice stopped her mid-twirl and pleasure warmed her blood like a shot of good Southern whiskey. He might not be ready to admit they had something more than sex, but the emotion behind that one simple compliment came close. "Thank you. Now, do you need help with that bowtie?"

He shook his head and asked softly, "Are you still angry with me?"

How one man could be capable of the cold ferocity she witnessed at the guerilla camp and also such childlike sweetness, she couldn't begin to fathom. But, Lord, was it endearing to know her SEAL was not always one-hundred-percent sure of himself.

"Oh, Gabe." She crossed to him and soothed her palms over the lapels of his jacket. "I was frustrated, not angry, and it was over nothing you did. It's the situation."

"It is a sucky situation," he agreed.

"It is, but the shower helped relax me." And so did the look on his face when he saw her in the purple prom bomb of a dress. If she could have captured that on canvas, she'd call it, *Lovestruck*.

Silly man just didn't realize he was a goner yet.

She knotted his bow tie, then stood on her toes to kiss him as the door popped open. No semi-polite knocking this time. Liam Miller stood there with a scowl fit to kill. "Out."

Gabe tucked her in close to his side and together they left the tenuous safety of the bedroom to dine with the devil himself.

CHAPTER SIXTEEN

"So how is Bryson doing?" Despite the phone conversation going from strained to explosive in a matter of heartbeats, Danny Giancarelli kept his voice as even and calm as a late-night radio announcer urging people to enjoy some smooth jazz as they drifted to sleep.

The HT, who wanted to be called Angel, had not liked it when he demanded to speak to Chloe Van Amee and Danny answered instead. He'd liked the suggestion that he let Bryson talk again even less.

"He's fine," Angel said in thickly accented English. "But he won't be if you keep stalling."

"Nobody is stalling, okay? We're working as fast as we can to raise the funds for Bryson's release, but it is going to take some time."

Angel swore in Spanish. "You're lying. He's rich. The money is already there."

"He has money, yes," Danny conceded. "But Chloe can't just walk into the bank and withdraw such a large sum from his accounts. The bank has rules and regulations that need to be followed."

"What about his insurance? The insurance company can pay."

Insurance. How could the HTs possibly know about the kidnap and ransom insurance policy? Danny gazed up at Frank Perry, who looked completely befuddled. Useless. The insurance rep wasn't in the room at the moment, and O'Keane gave him a nudge in the side and mouthed, "I'll find out more about it."

Danny nodded and sidestepped the insurance question, saying instead, "We're working as fast as we can through all the regulations, okay? But while we're doing that, I need to know Bryson is still alive. Can I please talk to Bryson again?"

"No. I'm done with this. You will pay the ransom tomorrow at noon or else I will kill him."

"I understand, but tomorrow is Sunday and it's a holiday weekend here in the States. The banks won't open until Tuesday."

"It will be tomorrow or never. I have no problem killing him, Agent Giancarelli. I can find another family that is willing to pay."

"Okay. None of us want that. How about you let me speak to Bryson? I only want to hear his voice, Angel. You can understand why I want to make sure he's still okay, right? I simply want to ask him some questions."

"Ask me."

Danny snapped his fingers for the list of proof-of-life questions that O'Keane and Chloe Van Amee had spent the last hour working on. They had to be very specific, uncomplicated questions, with an easy answer that the HTs wouldn't be able to guess. Coming up with a viable list was always a lot harder than it at first seemed, especially in today's technological world where a quick computer search could turn up loads of personal information.

Someone slid the paper across the table and he scanned the list. The first two questions about Bryson's sons' middle names and birthdays were far too easy, but the third should work. "All right. Are you still there? I need you to ask Bryson what name he wanted to use if his son Ashton had been a girl."

Silence.

"Can you do that for me, Angel? Go ahead and ask him for me. I'll wait."

Dial tone.

Danny sat back and blew out a breath that puffed up his cheeks. His heart was hammering, adrenaline surging through his veins like a nitrous injection, leaving his engines revving and his hands shaking. He knew from experience it'd take hours to come down if he just sat here, so he pushed away from the table.

"I'm going for a run. Call me if they get back in the next hour." He doubted it, though. He wouldn't hear from Angel again until later tonight at the earliest.

He made it about a block before his phone, tucked in the zippered pocket of his running shorts, rang. The HTs got back that fast? Well, color him surprised. He skidded to a halt underneath a palm tree, dug out the phone, and lifted it to his ear.

"Giancarelli," he answered.

"Danny. Uh, hi."

For the space of three heartbeats, Danny struggled to make sense of the voice he knew, but hadn't heard in years. He pulled the phone away from his ear and looked at the number. It wasn't a

Los Angeles number, wasn't even a U.S. number. "Marcus? Where the hell are you?"

"It's…" Marcus Deangelo sighed. "I can't talk about it right now."

A skitter of fear worked down Danny's spine. "Are you in trouble?"

"No. I'm working a case."

"You got a new job? For the government?" Yeah, he doubted that. Marcus and the government hadn't parted on the best of terms.

"No. I went into the private sector," Marcus said. "I'm working a hostage case and I need a favor."

Danny looked at the number on his phone's screen again. Fifty-seven. It started with a fifty-seven, which was Colombia's country code. The HT's number started with the same.

And he knew.

"Jesus Christ. Don't tell me you're working the Van Amee case. Who hired you?"

Marcus evaded the question beautifully. After all, the man hadn't been one of the FBI's top negotiators for nothing. "It's not important. Bryson is what's important here, and in order to help him, I need any information you can tell me about the case."

"Whoa, whoa, whoa." Danny shook his head. Marcus wanted him to do *what*? "Hold up. I don't hear a word from you in nearly two years. Nada. How hard is it to pick up the phone and say, 'yo, I'm still alive. How's *la famiglia*? By the way, I've found a new job'? And now you want me to forget that and do you a solid by giving information on a case I'm working? Info you know— *know*—I cannot divulge."

"So you're the negotiator?" Marcus asked, completely undaunted.

Danny shut his eyes. Dammit. "I can't talk about this."

But Marcus either didn't hear him or ignored him. "Why are you going through with the ransom payment? Is Bryson's business partner or wife pushing you to it? What happened to the whole the-U.S.-doesn't-negotiate-with-terrorists thing?"

"You know that's more of a theory than practice." Danny turned and started back up the street toward the Van Amee house. "And I'm just the mouthpiece in this. Perry the Prick's in charge."

"Shit." A moment of silence. "Can you just—I'll take whatever you can give me. You *know* paying the ransom will all but sign Bryson's death certificate."

Marcus had a point there. This case was bound for tragedy if they didn't get control of the situation. And fast.

"C'mon, Dan," Marcus said. "Help me out. We're poking around in the dark down here."

Up ahead, O'Keane stepped out of the house and waited there, arms crossed. Danny slowed his pace. "Listen, Marcus. I can't promise anything, but... I'll call you back." He hung up and broke into a jog for the hundred or so yards of driveway. "Did the HTs call again already?"

"No." O'Keane arched a brow. "The wife still mad about you canceling the family vacation this weekend?"

For a second, Danny didn't get it. Oh, right. Marcus' phone call. O'Keane thought he'd been speaking to his wife.

"No," he answered. "Leah and the kids went out to the coast without me." He looked at his phone. Goddamn Marcus. He shook his head and pocketed it. "She was…just checking up."

CARTAGENA, COLOMBIA

"Bryson works for me," Mena said and sipped his wine, taking a moment to let that news flash hit home.

No. Even as her mind instantly rejected his words, Audrey's throat tightened. He wasn't lying. Why would he? Except maybe to play with her and Gabe, but hadn't he already gotten his fill of that through the long, agonizing first two courses of the three-course meal? He'd refused to talk about Bryson through the lemon dill crab cake appetizers, or the stuffed veal chops main course. He'd ignored Gabe's repeated demands for answers and instead rambled on like they were old friends catching up as each new dish arrived. The food had tasted like wood to her, was about as appealing although Mena most certainly had only the best of chefs in his kitchen, and she spent more time pushing it around her plate than eating.

Finally, when the classic Colombian dessert of *pastel de tres leches* arrived, Mena dropped his bomb and then sat back with that Cheshire Cat smile, scrutinizing her face for a reaction.

Unable to swallow, she returned her wine glass to the table with a hand that shook. Gabe's solid hand landed on her thigh and squeezed in a silent "I'm here" reminder.

That small gesture meant more than any words of reassurance he could have spoken. She grasped his hand under the table and met Mena's amused gaze. "What does my brother do for you?"

"Little things." He flashed a grin. "Nothing too...*involved*... yet, I assure you, although I admit I was working him up to it."

Oh God, Bryson. "Why?"

"He was very good at what he did, moving merchandise efficiently in and out of countries. Truly the best I've ever met, and I only deal with the best. I cannot suffer fools, which is why I was extremely displeased when Bryson never showed for our afternoon meeting on Thursday. I never thought him a fool, but I started to wonder if I had miscalculated with him and sent people to...find him."

"So the day Bryson was taken," Gabe clarified, "you two had a meeting. Here in Cartagena or in Barranquilla?"

"Here, of course."

The itinerary, Audrey realized. Gabe was trying to pin down Bryson's plans for that day, trying to figure out who he had dealings with and who might want him out of the picture.

She sat forward. "Do you know why Brys planned to go to Barranquilla before meeting you?"

Mena gave her an indulgent smile that said he thought a woman didn't belong in this conversation. Yes, well, to borrow a phrase from Gabe's book, fuck him. Woman or not, she deserved to hear all the details.

"It was not for me," Mena finally answered when she didn't back down, his smile straining a little around the edges. "Perhaps he had other business to attend to there. Bryson was a busy man, and as long as his other business did not interfere with mine, I saw no need to keep tabs."

Uh-huh. Somehow, Audrey doubted that. And it didn't escape her notice that Mena kept referring to her brother in the past tense. "You said you know where he is. Did you kill him?"

"I said I might know." He sent an aggravated look toward

Gabe. "Really, Commander Bristow, you should muzzle your wife until she learns some tact."

Outrage burned through Audrey. She opened her mouth to give him a piece and a half of her mind, but Gabe squeezed her thigh hard. She closed her mouth and looked over at him. His expression was dark and shuttered as he leaned toward Mena.

"She's far more tactful than I am. Now answer her question. Where is Bryson?"

Mena's jaw slid to one side. Then he motioned to Liam with a flick of the wrist.

Gabe tensed up beside her, readying for who knows what, but Liam simply laid a map out on the table and went back to skulking in the corner like a good little minion.

"I don't have an exact location," Mena said and poked a finger at the map. "But I think he might be here."

Heart hammering, Audrey stood to get a better look at the street map of Bogotá. Mena's finger rested on an intersection in a well-to-do part of the city barely a mile from Bryson's apartment.

Gabe also stood and leaned over the map. "What makes you think he's there? And why haven't you gone in after him if you want him back so badly?"

Both good questions. Audrey had a feeling he smelled a trap. In fact, even her untrained nose caught a whiff of one.

Mena lifted a negligent shoulder. "Politics, mostly. I do want Bryson back because, despite what you and your government think of me, Commander, I'm not a monster without friends. I like him, consider him a good friend, and I want him safe again. I also want his captors punished for making me lose hundreds of thousands of dollars a day by taking him from me.

"However," he continued, "I have a rather tenuous relationship with the EPC's generals. If I send men in after Bryson, and the EPC is involved, the damage to that relationship could be irreparable, thus making me lose more money."

Gabe's eyes narrowed. "If you're so worried about your relationship with the EPC, why send Liam and his men in to destroy Cocodrilo's camp?"

"I did no such thing."

"Hm. So where exactly do you think he found us?"

Mena stared at Gabe for a long moment, then turned that lethal gaze to Liam, a vein bugling in his temple. "Is this true? Did you *attack* Cocodrilo against my specific orders to leave him alone?"

"I did what I had to do," Liam said. "He killed four of my men in that shootout on the highway, including Estaban's baby brother. He was not going to get away with that."

Mena pinched the bridge of his nose and waved a hand as if shooing off a pestering fly. "Get out of my sight. We'll discuss this insubordination later."

"Sir—"

"Leave," Mena said and pulled a gun from under his suit coat. He pointed it directly between Liam's eyes. "Or die. Your choice, Señor Miller. I do not care either way."

Liam backed up a step. Then another. After shooting a hate-filled look at Gabe, he disappeared into the house.

"Imbecile." Mena replaced his gun and returned to the conversation as if he hadn't just threatened a man's life. "As I said, my ties with the EPC are tenuous—even more so now—and to keep them from attacking my business, I need to stay on their good side. I'm not convinced they are involved, because this scheme is a little too advanced for them. They are uncouth, uneducated brutes. Still, I did not want to take the chance of sending my own men in to find Bryson."

He sent Gabe a sly smile. "But, you, Commander. I have no qualms about sending you. In fact, if the EPC kills you in the process, they will have removed a massive thorn from my side. It will effectively kill two birds with one stone, as you Americans like to say."

Gabe straightened away from the table. "Sorry to disappoint, but that's not happening."

"All's the pity."

"And until you give me one good reason why you think Bryson is held there, I'm not sending my men within ten blocks of that neighborhood."

"So cautious. An admirable quality in a mercenary." He returned to his seat, picked up his wine, and studied Gabe over the rim. "Truthfully, you put Señor Miller to shame; have made me see his unreliability. His job will be opening up very soon. I don't suppose you would be interested…"

"No." The finality in Gabe's voice left no room for argument and Mena laughed.

"No, I didn't think so. All right." Finishing his wine, he stood again and motioned them to follow him through the veranda doors into the library. He crossed to a huge, glossy desk and opened a drawer, drew out a file.

"This contains everything I know about Bryson's abduction, from my own research and from keeping tabs on your team, Commander—and I might add your second-in-command, the invariable Travis Quinn, has been struggling to hold them together in your absence."

Gabe's face gave away nothing, no flicker of surprise or another emotion, but Audrey felt him tighten up at her side. Much like he'd done for her earlier, she reached down and grasped his hand in reassurance. He gave hers a small squeeze in return, but then let go and crossed his arms over his chest.

"Get on with it," Gabe said, ice in his voice. "Stop yanking my dick and tell us what you know."

"Ah-ha. I do love your frankness," Mena laughed. "On with it, then. I know your team, such as it is, is searching for a man named Jacinto Rivera. I know they found nothing at his last known address, and have no idea where else to look. I also know where to find him." He tossed the file on his desk and it skated across the polished wood.

Gabe caught it before it slid off the edge. "Where?"

"Patience. First, you need to know something about Jacinto Rivera. He is the younger, even less cultured brother of Angel Rivera, the EPC general of the Andean region, and their family tree reads like a horror story of depravity. Their father was a drunk that got himself killed in a bar fight ten years ago. Their mother was a whore murdered by a client a year after that, and their sister, also a whore, disappeared six years ago. God only knows what became of her.

"Their uncle was a disgusting rapist interested in small boys, and his son, Rorro, finally took revenge for all of Papa's late night visits last year. Rorro's fifteen and he sliced his father up, the likes of which I haven't seen since La Violencia. He's a mean little brat, not to be underestimated, and he's attached to his cousin's hip.

Wherever Jacinto goes, Rorro's not far behind."

"So what does this have to do with Bryson?" Audrey asked.

Mena pointedly ignored her, instead addressing Gabe as he motioned toward the Bogotá map still laid out on the table on the veranda. "That house belonged to Rorro's father. Your team cannot find it because Rorro's father, in addition to being a pervert, was also a very accomplished racketeer and money launderer. Nothing he owned is in his name. Even for your analyst, Señor Physick, whom I'm told is one of the best available, it'll take days to wade through all the paperwork, and that is only if your team is looking in Rorro's direction. We both know Bryson doesn't have days. As soon as they get the money, they will kill him. That is what I would do in their place."

Audrey recoiled in disgust. He spoke of murder like you would crush a cockroach, without a second thought or regret. She looked at Gabe to see his reaction, but he was nodding in agreement.

God. Sometimes, when he was in war mode, he truly scared her.

Gabe opened the file in his hand, leafed through, closed it again and, to her surprise, passed it to her. She opened it and found all the pages written in Spanish. Ah, that explains it.

She shook off her horror and translated without waiting for him to ask. "It's papers pertaining to the house's ownership and bank statements for both Rorro and Jacinto. Rorro, a.k.a. Rodrigo Salazar Vargas, is very well off. Jacinto, not so much, but there has been a flurry of activity on his card in both Bryson's and Rorro's neighborhoods." She found a picture dated last night of Rorro leaving a disco and showed it to Gabe.

"Huh," was all he said.

"There's also a charge for a limo rental on one of Rorro's cards the day Bryson was abducted," she told him. "It's not an unusual charge, but there's a note here saying he never returned the car to the limo company."

"I believe you wanted a good reason to approach Rorro's house," Mena chimed in. "There you go. One very good reason."

"Yeah, it is." But Gabe didn't sound happy about it. He looked at Mena and ground his molars for a moment of pure frustration before biting the bullet and asking, "Can I use your phone to contact my team?"

That Cheshire Cat grin flashed again. "Oh, that was painful, wasn't it? Asking me for a favor."

"You have no idea," Gabe said. "But, you're right, Bryson doesn't have much time, and I won't waste it by nursing a grudge."

"You are so noble. Really, I find it sickening." He sat in the leather chair behind his desk and waved toward the phone. "It's all yours, but keep in mind they will not be able to trace the number."

Audrey stayed where she was, looking through the file, but watched Gabe dial out of the corner of her eye. He stood with all his weight on his left foot again and looked so far beyond fatigued that he was freefalling into exhaustionland.

Poor man. He'd had…what? Not counting his bought of unconsciousness, he'd had about four hours of sleep in the past forty-eight. She had squeezed in a little more than that and still felt dead on her feet, so she couldn't imagine how he was still going.

Maybe she shouldn't have pushed him so hard to have sex earlier. Even as much as they both wanted it, and she'd *needed* it, she should have let him sleep instead. The short afterglow nap obviously hadn't been long enough to do him any good.

"Quinn," he said into the phone, and Quinn's exclamation of surprise was so loud she heard it from across the room.

Gabe made a gesture of impatience and raised his voice in a drill sergeant's command: "Listen up. You need to destroy your phone as soon as we disconnect."

Mena lifted his brows at that, but said nothing, smile still in place.

"Then scramble the team and recon this address." He gave the address in some sort of military code Audrey didn't understand. "Our principle may be inside. I'll be—"

Gabe stiffened and turned toward the library doors a second before they burst open and Liam Miller strode in with a gun and a wild, hyped look in his brown eyes. He grinned and shut the doors soundly behind him.

Several things happened at once, so fast Audrey's mind raced to catch up. Liam raised his weapon to Mena and said, "I quit," the same moment Mena started to rise and reached inside his jacket for his own gun. Gabe stood directly between them, caught in the crossfire, and could only drop the phone and twist partially out of the way before Liam's bullet ripped through his side and struck Mena in the face, taking off the back of his head and spraying brains over the back wall. Mena's finger tightened reflexively on the trigger as he slumped sideways in the chair and the shot went wild. Audrey felt the burn of it slice through her upper arm.

"Gabe!" Shaking, terrified for him, she lurched over to where he had crumpled in front of the desk, but he was already army crawling under it, scrambling for the gun Mena had dropped.

"Hide!" he shouted. "Take cover!"

She couldn't. There was no place to go, so she lunged toward the phone several feet away. If she could get it, she could tell Quinn where they were and—

Liam plucked the phone out of her hands and dropped it into its cradle. "No calling for help."

Dismissing her, he shoved her aside and kicked at Gabe's bad foot before it disappeared under the desk. "We have a score to settle, Bristow. Stand up!"

To her utter horror, Gabe did just that. He rose from behind the desk, limping as his weight settled on his feet, and raised hands covered with blood in surrender.

"I'm unarmed, Liam." He caught Audrey's gaze and tilted his head ever so slightly to the right. She looked over and down and saw Mena's gun had landed closer to her than him.

No. Oh, God, no. He couldn't expect her… She met his gaze again and shook her head once. He just stared back, expression composed, gold eyes grim.

When violence is the only language your enemies know, you gotta learn to speak it, too.

He said to Liam, "There's no honor in shooting an unarmed enemy. Is that really how you want this to end?"

"Yeah, mate." Liam smiled and leveled his gun on Gabe's chest. "It is."

• • •

Tough love worked. Who'd have thought it?

After Quinn's beat down of Jesse and the hundred push-ups, the team stopped bickering and treated him with a little more respect. Which was a nice reprieve. He'd been so, so tired of battling them.

Now, an hour later, they stood around the table, throwing about ideas, trying to plot their next step.

"I don't think that will do us much good," Harvard said in response to an idea Jesse had tossed out. "We might as well go door to door to Jacinto Rivera's neighbors and ask if any of them have seen him or Bryson Van Amee."

"Not in that neighborhood," Marcus said, and others murmured agreement. "Nobody's gonna say shit to us."

"They're more likely to shoot us," Ian added. "And what are we doing about that warehouse? I vote we make it go boom before the bad guys move it on us."

"You always vote to make things go boom," Jean-Luc said with a friendly elbow nudge in Ian's side, and Ian didn't rip his head off for it.

Quinn, still in the chair with his feet on the table and a computer on his lap, was feeling rather proud of them all when his phone rang. All eyes turned toward him and the room went so silent you could hear the proverbial pin drop from a block away. Everyone who would be calling him was present in the room—minus one—and they all knew it.

He slowly lowered his feet to the floor and sat up, checking the phone's screen.

"Restricted," he said. "Probably won't get a trace."

"We can try. I'm on it. Give me a sec." Harvard shot over to his computer, fingers flying across the keyboard with the grace of a concert pianist. After another ring, he put on a set of headphones and looked up. "You're good, boss. Answer it."

Quinn drew a fortifying breath and raised the phone to his ear. "Yeah?"

"Quinn," Gabe said.

And his composure soared right out the window, leaving him mired in a mix of relief and worry. He surged to his feet. "Holy shit! Gabe, where are you? What the hell happened? Is Audrey okay? Are *you* okay?"

"Listen up," Gabe snapped out in his no-nonsense voice, and Quinn realized he was babbling. He ground his teeth and strived for calm again.

"I'm listening."

"You need to destroy your phone as soon as we disconnect."

He squeezed his eyes shut. Yeah, this can't be good. Gabe would only ask him to destroy the phone if he was afraid someone on that end would try to trace the call back to him. "Aye aye."

"Then scramble the team and recon this address." He gave the address in code. Another bad sign and Quinn committed it to memory. "Our principle may be inside. I'll be—"

He broke off.

Disturbed by the sudden silence, Quinn said, "Hello?"

Bang!

One gunshot, followed by the soft *umph* of a body hitting the floor.

Bang!

A second, and Audrey screamed, "Gabe!"

"Hide!" he shouted. "Take cover!"

The call disconnected and Quinn spun toward Harvard, who removed his headphones and shook his head. The kid looked as ill as Quinn felt.

"Signal was too scrambled, boss. I'm sorry, but it was bouncing me all over the globe and I couldn't lock on."

"Goddammit!" Quinn threw the cell phone as hard as he could and it crashed against the wall, leaving an indention in the cheap plaster before clattering to the floor in pieces. Then he went so numb he didn't even feel Jesse's hands on his shoulders, shoving him into a chair, until the medic knelt in front of him with a penlight.

Gabe was in trouble. And he couldn't do a damn thing to help.

As soon as the light hit his eyes, he snapped back to himself and pushed Jesse aside. "Get away from me. I'm fine."

"Uh-huh," Jesse said, but packed up his bag and stood. "Still haven't seen those medical records, Quinn."

Christ, he was sick to death of doctors. And cowboys who wanted to be doctors. "A little busy here, Jesse."

The address, he thought. He may not be able to help Gabe now, but he could damn well follow orders. He shoved to his feet and rifled through the papers on the table, looking for—

"What did Gabe say?" someone asked softly behind him. It sounded like Marcus, but he was so focused on finding a street map of Bogotá under all the papers that he didn't turn to look.

"He gave us orders." There it was. Finally. He spread the map out and found the correct coordinates at an intersection a mere mile from Bryson Van Amee's apartment. He tapped the spot with his index finger. "He said Van Amee might be at this location and we need to check it out."

"But what about Gabe and Audrey—"

This time he did look up to spear Harvard with a hard stare meant to shut him up. The others didn't need to know the details of what they'd heard over the phone or he might have a mutiny on his hands, despite the team's newfound cohesiveness.

"Gabe's got it handled." He hoped. "The best thing we can do for him now is follow his orders."

CHAPTER SEVENTEEN

The gun went off and Gabe thought, *Oh shit.*

Only he never felt the impact of a second bullet ripping another hole in his body. He felt blood trickling from the one already in his side, but no new damage that he could tell.

In the silence that descended on the room, he looked around, trying to get his bearings. The adrenaline surge burned off, leaving him muddled and shaky, and for a long second, he couldn't figure out where the gunshot had come from. Or where it had gone.

Across the room, Liam's eyes widened in shock and pain as blood bloomed on his chest and his gun fell from his hand. With blood bubbling from his mouth, he took two lurching steps toward Audrey—who held Mena's gun in a perfect stance, ready and willing to fire again.

Gabe circled the desk and caught Liam around the middle, tackling him to the carpet. He went down easily, already half-unconscious, and choked on his own blood as his eyes rolled back into his head.

"Did I kill him?" Audrey whispered.

Yeah, she probably had, but Gabe wasn't about to tell her that. Hearing the telltale wheeze of a sucking chest wound, he pushed himself upright and stared down at Liam's graying complexion. Audrey had gotten the bastard square in the lung.

He looked up. Her complexion matched Liam's, except without the blue cast of approaching death.

"I had to. He gave me no choice. I had to. I had to." She still held the gun clenched in her shaking hands.

Gabe swore and shoved Liam up onto his injured side to protect his good lung from filling with blood. The guy deserved to rot for the rest of eternity in the innermost layer of Hell, but Audrey wasn't going to be the one to send him there. The guilt of killing a man would crush her.

Liam moaned in pain.

"Shut up." Ignoring his own wounds, he stripped out of his jacket and made a compress. "Audrey, honey, snap out of it and search the desk. Find me something plastic or something else I can use to seal the wound. Scissors, tape."

She blinked and finally lowered the gun. "Wh—what? Why?" She looked at Mena's corpse in the desk chair, then at Liam, struggling to breathe and spilling blood onto the Aubusson rug. "We need to leave!"

"He'll die if we do."

"I don't care." Color rushed back into her cheeks. She hurried to his side and tried to tug him to his feet. "Better him than you. You're bleeding everywhere. You need medical attention. Let's go!"

Gabe grabbed Liam's gun and lumbered to his feet. Shit, he was weak as a kitten from blood loss, and getting weaker. Still, he met her stare, wanting her to understand. "If we leave and he dies, you'll have killed him. Are you prepared to live with that?"

Her chin hitched up. "I wouldn't have picked up the gun if I wasn't."

So strong. He flicked away one of the tears he didn't think she was even aware were running down her cheeks. "I wish I could have gotten to it first."

"But you didn't. I did, and then did what I had to do to keep us both alive."

"And you're okay with that?"

She hesitated, gazed down at Liam, then firmed up her trembling lips and nodded once. "You were right. Sometimes, with people like him, violence is the only option. Now, let's go before someone comes looking for one of them."

God, he adored her. He gripped that stubborn chin and lifted it, giving her a quick, hard kiss. "All right. We're outta here."

Grasping her hand, he pulled her toward the door, but his legs went out from under him after the first step. One minute he was on his feet and the next, his hands and knees. His mouth felt like cotton and tasted like blood, and his visual acuity was way off.

Oh man, he was crashing. Pushed himself too far for too long.

He shoved away Audrey's helping hands. "Go."

"Are you insane?"

He let go a huff of laughter. "Only around you, honey."

"This isn't a time to joke." She yanked hard on his shirt and managed only to tear it. "C'mon, Gabriel. Move."

He tried, but his head suddenly weighed a hundred pounds, each of his limbs at least a couple thousand a piece. He collapsed and, hard as he fought it, consciousness became nothing but a good memory.

That is, until her palm connected smartly with his cheek. He jolted awake to find her in his face, eyes sparking with fear-fueled anger.

"Don't you dare do this to me, sailor," she said through her teeth as tears choked every heated word. "I killed a man for you, and you are *not* going to make me leave you behind. You are going to pick your sorry ass off this floor and get us to safety."

Yeah, forget adoration. He loved this woman.

"Yes, ma'am." Weakness plaguing his every movement, he struggled to sit and managed to get upright. Sitting there on his butt, panting and shivering, with sweat dripping off his temples, the realization struck that he couldn't do this under his own steam.

He looked up at Audrey. So tough, so stubborn, and almost as demanding as he was.

He held out a hand. She released a huge breath of relief and clasped his palm. "On the count of three, big guy. One, two, up ya go."

With her help, Gabe hauled himself to his feet. He staggered a little, and took a moment to draw a deep breath and regain his bearings. He touched his fingers to the seeping wound in his side.

Messy. A lot of torn flesh and a whole lot of blood, but he didn't think anything vital had been hit and, with adrenaline coursing through his system, he couldn't feel the pain. Yet. But that would change real damn fast, and they had to be well away from Mena's estate when his brain caught on to the fact he was probably bleeding to death.

"We need to bandage you," Audrey said when his fingers came away smeared red.

"Later." Nausea threatened to choke him, but he swallowed it down and shuffled to the door. "Search the desk, their pockets. We need money, car keys, an AK-47. Anything that will help us get the fuck out of here."

"Okay," Audrey said.

As she scrambled through the desk drawers behind him, he cracked the door open enough to peek into the hallway. Two guards stood there with their backs to him. They must have been told to expect gunshots, which played to his advantage, bought him some time to strategize. Too much longer, though, and those guards might start getting antsy.

Gabe quietly shut the door, leaned his forehead against it, and thought back a year to all of SEAL Team Ten's plans for raiding Mena's estate. They'd had intel on the servants' and the guards' shifts, on the placement of all the cameras and motion sensors. He knew the house, the grounds, and the security system's strengths and weaknesses like he knew his own name. Escape would have been difficult if he was in prime condition and had his SEAL teammates for back up. Escape while seriously wounded with an untrained woman in tow…

Fuck.

Audrey returned to his side with a roll of Colombian bills. "No keys."

"Doesn't matter," he said and shoved the roll into his pants pocket. "We can't get to the garages from here. Hallway's guarded."

"What are we going to do?"

Gabe pushed away from the door and, ignoring his lightheadedness, weaved across the library, out onto the terrace, all the while scanning, searching for an out. Hallway was a no-go unless he took out the guards, but where there were two, there would be more. Could he take them all in his weakened condition? Maybe if he got lucky. Was he willing to risk Audrey's life like that? No fucking way.

So his only option was the terrace. He leaned over the railing and scanned the ground below. The pool glowed a soft blue-green two stories down, but jumping was out of the question. The terrace overlooked the pool's shallow end, and any miscalculation on his part would send him slamming into the concrete deck. He was already in enough pain and didn't need to add the possibility of breaking every bone in his body to the equation.

"What's that up there?" At his side, Audrey pointed to the roof one story above them. He straightened away from the railing and gazed up.

Well, shit. Why didn't he think of that? They might just have a shot at escaping yet.

"Mena's chopper." He grinned and grasped Audrey's face in his hands, planting a hard kiss on her open mouth. "You're brilliant, honey. Can you climb?"

She gave him a look that said *duh* and started unbuckling the straps on her high heels. "Can you fly?"

"It's been a while."

"Good enough for me." She handed him her shoes and stood on the balcony railing to grip the edge of the flowered trellis overhead. In one smooth move, she pulled herself up and flattened herself to the wood, then stretched out her hands to help him. He climbed onto the railing and, reaching up for the trellis, he sucked in a fortifying breath.

This was going to hurt like a bitch.

CHAPTER EIGHTEEN

The address Gabe had given them was a hideous two-story house shaped like a sideways T with balconies at each of the three ends. Sure, it screamed money, but it also shouted, "no taste." Quinn was no architect, but even he knew the Greek-like columns out front clashed horribly with the post-modern vibe of the rest of the house.

It sat on a fenced-in property surrounded by foliage. A gated entry to the brick driveway provided some security, but it was mostly for show, because Quinn and the team got through without breaking a sweat. The back yard boasted a BBQ pit and bar on a tiled patio shaded by a wood pergola. A sunroom entirely made of glass opened up to the patio from the back of the house and shielded a Jacuzzi, which was currently in use by a scrawny kid of about sixteen and a very *friendly* older man. The man disappeared under the water and the kid sat back with a look on his face that only came from oral sex.

"That is disgusting," Marcus whispered beside him.

Laying belly to the ground in the bushes at the edge of the property, he frowned, thinking of Gabe's brother. "Keep your derogatory comments to yourself, men. I have friends that are gay."

"Not that." Marcus sounded completely insulted. "What do you think I am, a far right wingnut? I don't care they're gay. More power to 'em. I meant that kid's not even close to legal. The guy's what, at least forty? *That* is disgusting."

Quinn focused his night vision goggles on the hot tub again and winced. Things had progressed past oral and into BDSM territory. Yeah, it was disgusting and disturbing, but with the brutal way the kid acted, he was obviously the dom in the relationship.

And where in hell were the kid's parents?

"Man," Marcus muttered. "I can't sit here and watch this. I'm gonna sneak around front, see what I can see."

"Careful," Quinn warned. He couldn't watch what was happening in the Jacuzzi either, so he scanned over the upper floors of the house. The lights were out and he didn't see any movement inside. Had to wonder if there was a basement. Gabe sounded very sure when he said Bryson Van Amee might be inside this address.

"Incoming," Jean-Luc said. Stationed by the front gate as a lookout, he rattled off the details of the approaching vehicle. "Red four-door Mercedes convertible. Bogotá license plate, mike-xray-uniform-two-niner-eight. One occupant."

"Copy that," Quinn replied. "Visual on his face?"

"Negative. The top's up—wait. He's opening the door. All right. Got visual confirmation. The driver is Jacinto Rivera. Repeat, I have visual confirmation on Jacinto Rivera, and he is armed."

Excellent. A thrill chased through Quinn's blood. Finally, they were getting somewhere. "Hold your positions. Let's see where he goes."

. . .

Jacinto Rivera shoved through the front door of his cousin's house, cursing. That stupid negotiator Giancarelli was jerking him around by the *cojones*, claiming they needed more time to secure funds. What bullshit. The funds sat right in Bryson Van Amee's bank account, ripe for the taking. He knew. He'd seen the bank statements.

They also wanted more proof of life or they were calling the whole deal off.

And if that wasn't bad enough, Rorro, the perverted little fuck, had been wandering about the city doing God knows what to God knows who instead of watching Van Amee. Anyone could have strolled right in last night and plucked their golden goose out from under their noses.

Jacinto cursed and stalked through the house. First thing, he crossed to the basement door and flipped on the light. The ripe odors of shit and urine and unwashed man assaulted his nose as he descended three steps. Van Amee sat up from the cot in his tattered, bloody business suit and blinked owlishly at the light. Several days' worth of beard covered his jaw, and his black and purple left eye had swollen shut. He looked and smelled more like a street bum than the owner of a multi-million dollar empire.

"Water," he whispered through cracked lips. "*Agua. Por favor.*"

"What did you want to name your son if he was a girl?" Jacinto asked in Spanish and then again in English.

Van Amee blinked his one good eye. "Please. I need water."

"Answer the question."

"I—I—don't know. Which son?"

"Ashton."

"I—God, I can't remember. It was…something Susan. After my mother. Uh, Adelaide. Addie Susan." He winced. "Please, I need something to drink."

Jacinto shook his head and went back upstairs to the kitchen. Trusting his cousin to help with this had been a stupid idea from the start, but he couldn't have asked his brother without getting the EPC involved. The plan was only to make it *look* like the EPC was involved. They took enough people hostage that sliding one more under their belt shouldn't raise suspicion.

Or so Claudia said.

She said if they made it look like their brother's doing, nobody would cast them a sideways glance. He wasn't sure about that, because if Angel found out they were setting up him and the EPC, kin or not, he'd kill them both and lose not a wink of sleep over it. Angel Rivera was one scary *cabron*, and Jacinto wanted nothing more than to be free of him.

Soon. Once they got the ransom money, he could go somewhere Angel would never find him. Hollywood, maybe. He'd live the good life with women and booze and drugs. Maybe act in a movie or two. All he needed was his cut of Van Amee's ransom.

Jacinto found a bottle of water in the fridge, crossed to the basement door, tossed it down, and heard a scramble of limbs. Like a rat. That's all Van Amee was. A wealthy, well-dressed rat, who didn't need even half the money he had. Claudia said so. But even rats had to drink, and it'd do no good if he died of thirst before they got their money.

Jacinto shut and locked the door and, hearing sounds on the back patio, headed that way. He had to talk to Rorro, though he really didn't care to see the little pervert going at it with his flavor of the day.

And wasn't it interesting that this flavor was a younger replica of Jacinto's uncle, Rorro's not-so-dearly departed father? No wonder the kid was being especially brutal tonight. Jacinto could hear the flesh on flesh action from the kitchen and waited outside the solarium doors until the sounds faded into heavy breathing. Then there was a gasp, a gurgle, and it was over.

Jacinto stepped into the room and tried his hardest to keep his eyes off the battered man hanging limply over the side of the Jacuzzi. Blood dripped from his throat onto the tiled patio. Rorro sat in the bubbling water, smoking a joint and looking very satisfied with himself. The knife he'd used to slit the man's throat lay near his elbow on the edge of the tub.

Bile rose in Jacinto's throat. He'd never had the stomach for murder, which was part of the reason he'd called Rorro in the first place. Bryson Van Amee had seen both of their faces, knew at least his name if not Rorro's, and had to die tomorrow after they got the money.

"What did you do to Van Amee?" he asked, remembering the man's black eye.

"Had a little fun."

Jacinto held back his wince. He was always torn between disgust and sorrow when it came to his young cousin. Rorro seemingly had it all: money, intelligence, movie star good looks, privileges and opportunities other children in Colombia would kill for—but all that glamour hid horrible secrets, ones that made Jacinto's dysfunctional home life look like a fairy tale. Little wonder the kid turned out as *loco* as he was.

"I told you," Jacinto said as gently as he could manage. "You cannot have him until after we get the money."

Rorro flopped a hand in the air. "He tried to escape. I had to punish him."

"*What?*"

"Last night. No, don't look at me like that. It wasn't my fault."

It most certainly was his fault, but Jacinto wasn't in the mood to argue. "Did he get far?"

"Only to the patio."

At least he hadn't made it off the property, onto the street where anyone could have spotted him.

Jacinto shot a look at the dead man, who was starting to stink with the release of bodily gases and fluids.

"You're staying in tonight, Rorro. I mean it. We can't risk him trying to escape again." And the clubs downtown would be much safer with the little shit tucked away at home. "This will be all over tomorrow."

Rorro flashed a smile that was all boyish charm, a hint of the kid that Jacinto had once adored like a little brother. "Then we'll leave here?"

"Yes," Jacinto said. "We'll leave."

He felt only the tiniest prick of regret for lying as he walked inside the house and started upstairs. He had no intention of going anywhere with his psycho cousin. Once this was over, he wanted to be able to sleep soundly at night without the fear of ending up with his throat slit open like that poor bastard stinking up the hot tub.

Jacinto stepped into his bedroom and shot home the deadbolt lock on the door.

. . .

Gabe passed out on her three times. Twice at the small airfield after he landed the helicopter, and once in the taxi from the airport to the safe house.

The first two times Audrey was able to wake him. This time, he was out cold, and she had no idea how to get his big body from the taxi into the house. She'd hoped to find Quinn and the rest there waiting for them, but no such luck. The place was dark and silent.

C'mon, Gabriel. Wake up again for me.

She tried tugging on his arm, but that only succeeded in making him slouch sideways in the taxi's backseat. The driver eyed her in the mirror.

"He's drunk," she explained in Spanish and then sized up the driver. He was a big guy, more fat than muscle, but moving Gabe would be much easier with his help.

"I'll pay you extra," she said when he balked at the suggestion.

Grumbling, the cab driver slid from behind the wheel, and together they managed to half-carry, half-drag Gabe as far as the front entryway.

Ah, the power of the almighty peso.

Audrey didn't dare turn on any lights, having no idea what the cab driver might see inside the room, so she fished in Gabe's pants pockets, paid him with every bill left there, and ushered him out as fast as possible. She helped Gabe down to the floor and went to the window to make sure he was gone before hitting the overhead light.

Harvard's computer hummed on the table in the corner. Marcus's fedora hung forgotten from a lamp. A box of cold pizza with one measly slice left sat on the table in the center of the room on top of a map, which had a circle around the address Mena had given Gabe.

So they hadn't abandoned the house. They'd followed Gabe's orders to check out the address.

Frantic, Audrey searched for Jesse's medical bag. She'd seen him retrieve it from a bookshelf…

Gone.

Of course the medic wouldn't leave home without it, but was it too much to ask for him to leave a scrap of gauze behind?

Behind her, Gabe groaned and she spun to find him up on his hands and knees. She'd once teased him about being the Terminator, but, God, he really must be. She hurried to his side and soothed a hand over his head.

"Shh, shh. Lay down, sailor. We're safe. You got us home. We're safe now."

Either he wasn't fully conscious or he took her words to heart, because he collapsed back to the floor without a word of protest. The too-small coat he'd found on Mena's helicopter bunched up around his shoulders and she saw that he was bleeding again, blood soaking through the bandages and the side of his dress shirt.

All this time, during the whole four-hour flight from Cartagena to Bogotá, he'd been bleeding when she thought she'd patched up his wound. Duh, of course he'd be the color of flour and as weak as a newborn. He'd lost most of his blood.

She wanted to cry. Hot tears even leaked from her eyes, but a sobbing fit wasn't going to help him so she dashed them away. Spotting Quinn's coat on the back of a chair, she figured he wouldn't mind her ruining it if it saved Gabe's life and bundled it into a compress. Gabe sucked in a sharp breath when she pressed it to his wounds, which was a good sign. She hoped. She remembered an episode of *Grey's Anatomy*—or was it *House, M.D.*? Whichever, she remembered them saying that if a patient responded to painful stimuli, they were not in a coma.

So now what?

Audrey had no clue what else to do for him, so she sat on the floor, keeping pressure on the compress with one hand, stroking his hair with the other. And she talked to him.

"You stay with me, Gabriel, you hear me?" She tried to keep her voice strong, commanding, positive, but her tears spilled over in earnest and choked the words. "You need to stay here so you can save my brother and protect the world from the bad guys like Cocodrilo and Mena and Liam and—and you're going to come to Costa Rica and swim with my dolphins. Your men need you to stick around, too. Quinn… God, he really needs you, you know? He seems like a very sad, lonely man and he…he just needs you. And so do I."

Gabe didn't move, didn't acknowledge that he'd heard her in any way, but she kept talking. "You hear that? You have to stay with me because we all love you. *I* love you, and I'm not ready to lose someone else I love. I'm still grieving for my parents, and I might have to grieve for my brother. Please, please don't make me grieve for you, too. Please, I—"

A phone vibrated somewhere in the room and Audrey shot

to her feet. She hadn't thought to look for one, figuring everybody had taken their phones along, but hallelujah, someone had forgotten theirs.

She found the source of the *bzz bzz bzz* under the pizza box and a stack of papers and flipped it open. It was Marcus's phone—she could tell from the internal wallpaper of a surfer catching an enormous wave. She reminded herself to plant a big, fat, wet kiss on him when she saw him again.

Marcus had a text from someone named Giancarelli, but she ignored it and called up Quinn's number. Dumped straight into voicemail. Next, she tried Jesse and got the same. So she called Harvard's number, thinking he was the most likely to be somewhere he could answer. Beethoven's Fifth swelled from the bedroom off the living room. She shut Marcus's phone and pushed open the bedroom door.

Harvard.

Skinny, tousled, and sleepy-eyed, he sat on the edge of the bed in only a pair of white briefs, fumbling around for his phone. When it stopped ringing before he got to it, he groaned, gave up the search and flopped back to the mattress.

She'd never been so happy to see anyone in her life. "Harvard!"

He bolted upright. His dark hair hugged his head on one side while the other stuck up in a near mohawk. "What?" He squinted at her, then scrambled for his glasses and put them on crookedly. "Audrey? Christ, is that you?"

"Gabe's hurt," she said. There would be time for lengthy explanations later. "Do you have any way of getting hold of Quinn?"

"Uh, yeah. Yeah, of course. Uh…let me…it's here somewhere."

He groped around in the bed for a radio and hit the talk button in Morse code. Three short bursts, three long, three short.

A moment later, Quinn responded in a whisper. "This is Achilles. Go ahead. Was that a S.O.S. call?"

"Affirmative." He looked at Audrey, realized his glasses were askew, and straightened them. "Stonewall is home."

Pause. "Say again."

"Stonewall is home and needs medical attention ASAP."

Another pause. "Aye aye." Quinn's voice was tight with emotion. "ETA fifteen minutes. Out."

Relief washed over Audrey in a great wave that took the last of her energy reserve with it. Safe. Finally. Gabe would get the help he needed and she could relax, breakdown, throw a tantrum—everything she hadn't had the luxury of doing in the past thirty-six hellish hours. She slumped against the door's frame, suddenly so very weak.

Harvard, sweet man, was right there, propping himself under her arm. He hid surprising strength in that rangy body, taking her weight easily, but he still wore only his briefs and looked like a whitewashed broomstick in underwear.

Audrey had to laugh at that mental image, though it came out sounding more like a sob. "You always did strike me as a tighty-whitey guy."

"Yup, that's me." He either didn't care that he was nearly naked in front of her or hid his embarrassment well. Back in the living room, he guided her to a chair. "Boring as vanilla pudding."

"I like vanilla pudding."

"Sit down," he coaxed. He spared Gabe's motionless form the briefest of glances before focusing all of his attention on her. "Are you hurt?"

"No. No, I—I—I'm bruised and blistered, but—just help him. He's been shot. Please. I don't want to lose him."

Harvard's eyes widened behind the lens of his glasses and she realized how telling that statement was. Well, they'd all find out sooner or later.

She met his gaze with a challenge in her own. "Yes, I'm in love with him." At Harvard's disbelieving laugh, she nibbled on her lower lip. "Is that a problem?"

"Nope." He grinned, but sobered up fast. "Not for me, at least."

Meaning some of the others might take issue with their relationship. Namely, Quinn. "Do you think it'll cause problems?"

"Can't say. If it does, they're both professionals. They won't let it get in the way of finding your brother."

"God. Bryson." She rubbed her forehead. "Is it horrible of me that I haven't thought about him in hours?"

"Not at all, sweetie," he said, but she knew he was just trying to comfort her.

CHAPTER NINETEEN

Gabe's eyes felt like someone had hot glued them shut by the lashes. It took three tries to pry them open, and then he had to blink several times before he got a load of the white plaster ceiling overhead and a line of florescent lights turned on low. Bags hung on a pole to his right, one filled with a clear fluid and the other with a dark red substance that could only be blood.

Hospital.

Hello, déjà vu.

Except this time, unlike when he woke in the hospital in Virginia after the car accident, he remembered exactly where he was and what happened to him. Colombia. Shot.

Audrey.

He searched the small room for her with his eyes. Nothing but a visitor chair, TV, and dresser.

Okay. He refused to panic and squashed the instinctive surge. If he made it to a hospital, she's the one who got him here. Good chance she was also here somewhere, unharmed. Maybe off getting food and a cup of coffee or having whatever minor injuries she had tended.

God, he hoped they were minor. His were serious enough for the both of them.

Speaking of, time to take stock of his condition. Gabe drew a breath and shifted in the bed, expecting pain, but instead got little more than a numbed-out tugging sensation in his side.

Not bad.

His foot hurt more than the bullet wound. A pull on the sheet covering him showed it wrapped in an ace bandage and caught in a splint. Crutches leaned against the wall across from his bed. And he was not naked or in a johnny gown, thank God, but dressed in hospital scrubs. Perfect.

He swung his legs over the side and sat up. Dizziness swamped him, but only for a second, and he studied the IV pole when his double vision merged back into one picture. A painkiller, no doubt. Saline. Both of those he could do without and pulled the tape, sliding the needles out of his arm. Machines started beeping and he jabbed the off button. Last thing he wanted was for some pushy nurse to come running.

Gabe hesitated over the bag of A neg still hanging from the pole. It was almost gone, but he'd bled hard and probably needed every drop of the transfusion. Instead of unhooking it, he grabbed the bag and took it with him. His foot held okay, so he ignored the crutches and peeked out the door.

In the dimmed hallway lights, a clock jutting from the wall halfway down the corridor said 2300. With everyone tucked into bed and the staff whittled down to the skeleton night shift, that made things extra convenient. Should be no problem to find

Audrey, get back to his team, and finish this whole goddamn catastrophe of a mission.

He slipped into the hallway and—shit, footsteps coming his way. The fast, sure, quiet stride of someone on a mission. He faded back into his room and waited for them to pass, but the steps slowed as they reached his door.

Yeah, figures. He knew it was too easy.

He pressed his back to the wall at the left of the door. Across the room, his bed, in plain view of anyone in the hallway, was a rumpled mess and obviously empty, but there wasn't much he could do now to disguise that fact. Besides, if those heavy footsteps belonged to a nurse doing nightly rounds, he'd eat his dog tags.

Possibilities raced through his mind. One of Mena's men come to get revenge? Or one of Cocodrilo's men? Or, hell, with the rotten luck he'd had lately, it could be someone totally unrelated to this whole mess yet just as dangerous.

The man paused outside the door, then stepped quietly into the room. He moved two steps before he realized the bed was empty and started to turn, but Gabe was already on him, an arm around his neck in a hold meant to put him to sleep in less than a minute. The guy tensed in automatic reaction like he wanted to fight back. His arms even came up, but then he relaxed and his hand tapped out against Gabe's arm in a very familiar way.

"Gabe," he choked.

Quinn? Gabe spun him around by the shoulders. Dim light spilling in from the hallway cast deep shadows around his nose and eyes. Exhaustion, worry, and relief ravaged his normally stoic features, his gray eyes red-rimmed and haunted.

Gabe clasped Quinn's head in his hands, just to make sure this was real, make sure he wasn't still unconscious and dreaming of his best friend. He wasn't. Quinn's head was a solid mass under his hands, skin warm, beard stubble abrading the cuts on his palms.

He let out a relieved breath. "I can't tell you how happy I am to see you, bro."

"Same here, man. When I heard that shot over the phone—" Quinn's voice came out thick and he paused to clear his throat. Then he drew Gabe into a hard hug.

Gabe wasn't a big hugger by nature, but with a brother as physically affectionate as Raffi, it was something he'd gotten...well, if not comfortable with, than tolerant of over the years. Still, he didn't know who was more stunned by the contact: him or Quinn, who abruptly released him and backed up, looking anywhere but at him, uncomfortable with even that small amount of affection.

Well, shit. Audrey was right. He had never paid attention to it before, but Quinn was one very sad man. Lost. Drifting. Alone.

And days ago, someone might have used the same words to describe him. Not sad, because while he was no roses and sunshine optimist, he'd always done his best to retain an ounce of humor even when his world looked the bleakest. But drifting, lost, and alone? Oh yeah, he'd been the poster child.

Until Audrey. Odd that he'd find such a solid anchor in a woman most people considered flighty.

Of course, her anchoring effect was only temporary. Despite her confession of love—yeah, he'd been out of it, but he'd heard that nonsense loud and clear—he had no illusions that whatever he and Audrey had would last past the end of this mission. They hadn't talked of a long-term commitment, or short-term for that matter, and even if they wanted to give it a go, she lived in Costa

Rica, which was three-thousand-plus miles from his home in D.C. How would *that* work?

Quinn cleared his throat, wiped a hand over his face, then finally looked at Gabe. "You should be lying down."

"Nah. I'm fine."

"Gabe, you were shot."

"Believe me, I know. How bad was it?"

"All considering, Jesse said it should have been worse. It tore up some muscle, but missed all your vital organs and only needed stitching. You got lucky. An inch over would've been a direct gut shot. His biggest concern was the amount of blood you lost, which is why you need *this*."

Quinn grabbed the bag of blood from Gabe's hand and returned it to the IV pole. He eyed the two other disconnected IV lines, but said nothing about them. "So don't fuck around with this until it's gone."

Hearing how close he came to death, Gabe sat on the edge of the bed. Better not to press his luck any further. "Where's Audrey?"

"She's in the waiting room down the hall. She didn't want to leave your side and threw one hell of a hissy fit until Jesse poured a mild sedative into her."

Ha. He'd have paid to see his men handle one of Audrey's hissy fits.

Quinn was looking at him with an odd expression. He shoved aside thoughts of Audrey. "What's wrong?"

"You." He frowned. "You're…different."

"I've been hiked all over Hell, beat to a shit, and shot. Yeah, I'm not exactly in top form."

"No. You're…" He made a rolling motion with his hand as if looking for the right word, but then gave up and glanced toward the hallway. "What's with you and her?"

Ah. That's what this was about. Probably should have seen it coming. Since he hadn't, he'd blame whatever was in those IV bags for addling his brain. "Nothing."

"Did you fuck her?"

"Jesus Christ." Anger exploded inside Gabe, so hot, so primal, that it took him by complete surprise. He didn't get angry. Or if he did, he converted it into cool motivation. Always calm, unflappable, a rock, a stone wall.

But he definitely wasn't feeling very stone-like right now and rolled his hands into fists in the sheet on either side of his hips to keep from hitting something. Or someone.

"Don't go there, Q."

Quinn stared back, unrepentant. "It's a legit concern. For all we know about her, she could be behind her brother's kidnapping."

"That's bullshit and you know it."

"No, I don't. And neither do you."

Silence stretched taut between them. Gabe didn't care what Quinn thought. He knew down to his bones Audrey didn't have it in her to mastermind something like this, nor did she have the connections to do it, and he was not budging. Neither, it appeared, was Quinn. So they could sit here trying to stare each other down and waste time, or move on to another more relevant topic.

Gabe bit the bullet and spoke first, even as he inwardly continued to seethe. "Are we in Bogotá?"

After a second more of stubborn silence, Quinn nodded. "Affirmative."

"The address I gave you. You check it out?"

"We have visual confirmation that Jacinto Rivera is staying there with an as-of-yet unknown kid of about sixteen," Quinn said, sliding flawlessly from the role of concerned best friend to XO giving his superior officer a sitrep. "Harvard's checking into the property, but he's running in circles chasing aliases and dummy corporations. Whoever owns that house does not want it known. We never would have found it. We just don't have good enough equipment. Or enough manpower."

Something Gabe planned to fix. If they were going to do this whole private contractor thing, they were going to do it right from now on. No more of these half-assed, trial-by-fire missions.

"The kid's name is Rodrigo 'Rorro' Salazar. Jacinto's cousin," he explained. "His deceased father owned the house. Did you see any sign of Bryson?"

"No visual confirmation, but when Jacinto arrived he went into a basement. There's a small rectangular window on the south side of the house and Marcus saw the lights come on. By the time he got to the window, Jacinto had shut them off again, but he saw movement down there. They are definitely holding someone. What are the chances it's not Bryson?"

Slim, Gabe thought. Everything they had pointed to Jacinto Rivera as Van Amee's hostage taker. Were the chances good enough to risk his team in an extraction operation? He wasn't sure. But did he really have a choice? No. They were out of time. Bryson was out of time.

"Is the team around?" he asked.

Quinn nodded. "Jesse's in the waiting room with Audrey, and Harvard's still back at the safe house. Marcus and Ian were heading to the cafeteria for coffee and snacks when I came down to check on you. I left Jean-Luc at Jacinto's house. He reported in about ten minutes ago. All's quiet."

"Good. Leave him there, but get him on the phone and everyone else in here for a briefing. We need a plan."

"Hooyah," Quinn said.

• • •

Once everyone crammed around Gabe's bed in the small hospital room, he gave them the rundown of what he knew about Jacinto and Rorro. He left out that he'd gotten the information from the now deceased Luis Mena since it would only cause a stir. He also left out his run-in with the probably deceased Liam Miller-slash-Collington because Quinn had more of a personal beef with the guy than he did. There would be plenty of time for those war stories after they got Bryson Van Amee home safe.

The guys then briefed him on what they knew. He agreed that the bomb-making factory they had stumbled over in their search for Jacinto Rivera had to be decommissioned, but it wasn't a priority now.

It came as no surprise when they told him Cocodrilo claimed the EPC had no knowledge of Van Amee's abduction. The more Gabe learned about the situation, the more he thought Jacinto and Rorro were acting on their own. The team also apparently had Cocodrilo held as a drugged and bound "guest" at the safe house, though there was some disagreement over what they should do with him.

"Turning him over to the authorities won't do shit," Ian said. "He'll be free and back terrorizing people before breakfast."

"What do you suggest we do with him?" Jesse drawled. "Oh, wait, we all know the answer to *that*."

Interesting. Gabe studied the pair and made a mental note for future reference to keep them apart since they seemed to be about as compatible as fire and gasoline. He'd eventually have to work out that animosity between them. Just one more problem in a long list he had to deal with if this team was going to function smoothly.

"Easy, gentlemen. Let's focus on Bryson right now. *He* is what's important here." He shifted in bed to pin Ian and then Jesse with silencing stares. He hated that he couldn't do this standing up, but his strength was fading fast and he needed to conserve every ounce of energy. He regretted ripping out the IV pain medication, which Jesse had blasted him about as soon as the medic stepped into the room. Pain flared through his side every time he moved, and much to his annoyance, he couldn't sit up straight without the head of the adjustable bed to support him.

With the pair grudgingly subdued, Gabe focused his attention on Marcus. "What can you tell me about the FBI agent in charge of Bryson's case?"

"You want my professional opinion, boss, or personal?" Marcus asked.

"They're different?"

"Only in that my personal is much lower." Marcus snorted. "Frank Perry's a know-it-all jackass who actually doesn't know squat about shit. And, yes, that *is* my professional opinion. Perry's a wannabe hotshot who rides on the coattails of everyone around him until all the hard work is done. Then he's suddenly front and center to get all the credit. Or, if it goes to shit, he fades into the background and lets everyone else take the blame. Believe me, the Van Amees did not win the FBI agent lottery with him. He's known around the office as Perry the Prick."

"So he won't be willing to work with us."

"Not on your life."

So much for that idea. "We'll have to come up with another—"

"But," Marcus interrupted, "the lead negotiator, Danny Giancarelli, is a good friend of mine. Or, uh, was. He has no more love for Perry than I do, and I'd bet my left nut he's bound in so much red tape right now it's driving him crazy. I've spoken to him once already, and I believe he's frustrated enough to help."

"Get him on the phone," Gabe said. "We need to know anything he can tell us about the ransom demand and the instructions for the drop. Once we know the specifics we can coordinate our rescue operation to go down before any money is exchanged."

• • •

"Who are you?" Agent Danny Giancarelli had a smart and no-nonsense voice tinged with the barest hint of his Italian roots. Gabe liked him instantly. "What exactly is your stake in this?"

"Same as yours," Gabe said. "I want Bryson Van Amee home with his family, safe and sound. Name's Bristow. I'm CO of HumInt Consulting, Inc's hostage rescue team."

"Who hired you? Not the family," Giancarelli said without a shred of doubt.

"No, not the family, but I can't divulge my client's name."

And he didn't particularly want to admit Van Amee's greedy insurance company hired him because they didn't want to pay out the kidnap and ransom insurance that Van Amee no doubt paid a ridiculous premium to have. Especially not with Audrey sitting right beside him, listening intently to every word. She'd come into the room midway through the team's briefing, looking tired, tousled, and worried, and sat beside him like she had every right to be there. Which she did.

A few eyebrows arched when he laced his fingers with hers and unsubtly raised her hand to his lips, staking his claim, but everyone kept their mouths shut. Smart men.

At first, her presence had been a comfort, a balm soothing the distress he hadn't realized he'd been feeling since he woke. Now, as he spoke with Giancarelli on the phone, having her beside him felt more like a heavy weight on his shoulders. It was stupid, but he kind of liked the knight in shining armor fantasy she'd built up around him and hated to tarnish it, but he couldn't mince words with Giancarelli either. Not if he wanted to get the information he needed to save her brother.

"And my client doesn't matter," he added. "Our end goal is the same."

Giancarelli said nothing.

Since he didn't hang up, Gabe took that as agreement and continued, "You don't believe paying the ransom will save Bryson's life any more than I do."

Giancarelli sighed. "What I believe doesn't matter much around here."

"It does on my end."

"Yes," the agent answered after a second's pause. "I think Marcus is right. By sending that money to the HTs, we're condemning Mr. Van Amee to death."

"If you give me whatever information you can about the HTs and the ransom, I'll make sure that doesn't happen."

Another pause. "Put Marcus back on."

Gabe handed the phone to Marcus, who raised it to his ear and said, "Danny." Then, "Uh-huh. Uh-huh." He glanced up at Gabe then said definitively, "Yes," probably in answer to a question about Gabe's legitimacy. He listened some more. "Well, funny story there. When I'm stateside I'll buy you a beer and tell ya all about it." After a moment, he nodded and handed the phone back to Gabe. "He's willing to hear you out, boss."

Giancarelli said, "What do you want from me?"

"We're about ninety-five percent sure where Van Amee's being held." Gabe relaxed against the tilted head of the hospital bed. His stitches pulled as he reached for the notebook Harvard had brought him and flipped to a clean page. "We just don't know what we're dealing with as far as opposition and what our timetable looks like. You've been in contact with the hostage takers, correct? What can you tell me about them?"

"I've only talked to one," Giancarelli began. "He has me call him Angel."

Gabe wrote "Angel" in the notebook and circled it twice. As in, Angel Rivera, Jacinto's brother. Was Jacinto just using his brother's name, or was the FBI dealing with the man himself? If Angel was involved, things could get messy fast. Jesus Christ. "What's his state-of-mind like?"

"He puts on a good front," Giancarelli said, "but you ask me, he's nervous. He doesn't strike me as a professional."

Which didn't jibe with what they knew about Angel Rivera, who had at least ten kidnappings under his belt that Harvard had been able to dig up, and possibly more that hadn't been attributed to him.

Gabe added a question mark next to Angel's name even though he was now about ninety-eight percent sure that Jacinto was acting on his own, using his brother's name. "What about accomplices?"

"Thing is, I've only heard one other voice in the background…"

"But," Gabe prompted, because he heard it in the dot-dot-dot Giancarelli put at the end of that sentence.

"But nothing. I've heard only one other voice and it's… high pitched. Like a woman's or a boy's. Probably more boy than woman because it has that squeaky adolescent sound to it, know what I mean? I've never been able to make out enough of what he says to translate."

Gabe bet that squeaky adolescent voice in the background was Rorro. "When exactly is the ransom exchange supposed to go down?"

"I've managed to push it back until Tuesday. I'm going to try and talk them down another couple mil and get them to postpone again next time they call, but I don't know how successful I'll be."

"Have they given specific instructions for the exchange yet?"

"Well," Giancarelli said on a drawn out sigh, "it's not a dead drop. As inexperienced as I think they are, the HTs were smart about that, at least. They want the money transferred to an offshore account."

Where they probably had someone waiting to launder it till it shined, Gabe thought. Not a big stretch of the imagination if Rorro kept his racketeer father's connections.

"Once they confirm the transfer," Giancarelli continued, "they *claim* they'll send Bryson in a taxi back to his apartment."

"Yeah?" Gabe finished writing the information down, ripped

out the sheet, passed it to Quinn, and made a motion that he circulate it throughout the room. "That's putting a helluva lot of faith in the bad guys."

"Yep. And I told Perry that, but he's convinced we're dealing with professionals. I don't know how much you know about international hostage negotiation—"

"Not a lot," Gabe admitted. "I was a SEAL. I usually came in after negotiations failed."

"All right. Quick and dirty lesson," Giancarelli said. "If you have to get taken, you want it done by professionals, because you're more likely to come out alive at the other end. It's nothing more than a business transaction to them. Professionals don't want to kill anyone. In fact, they go out of their way not to kill. It'll hurt their reputation if they become known for not upholding their end of the bargain.

"The EPC," Giancarelli continued, "has a reputation for returning hostages unharmed, and Frank Perry thinks we're dealing with the EPC."

"But not you."

"Let's just say I'm not convinced and leave it at that. I have no proof I've been talking to someone other than Angel Rivera. It's just my gut reaction."

"So because of the EPC's rep, Perry wants to trust that the HTs will return Bryson alive after they get their money." Gabe shook his head. That wasn't a good idea on so many different levels. "I can see why you'd have a problem with that, Giancarelli."

"And unfortunately, my hands are tied. It makes me sick that two little boys are about to become fatherless and it'll be the FBI's fault, *my* fault, but I still can't do a damn thing to stop it." He hesitated. "Marcus says I can trust you, and I trust Marcus. If you promise you can stop it, I'll believe you and do whatever I can to help."

Gabe looked up and met Audrey's eyes, saw the hope and fear there, and squeezed her hand. "I can and will stop it," he told them both softly. "I promise."

CHAPTER TWENTY

If a man sound of mind, if not of body, wants to walk out of a hospital, they should damn well allow him to without all this hassle. Gabe scowled at the powerhouse of nurse blocking the door of his room, speaking in rapid-fire Spanish. He didn't need Audrey to translate. The woman's posture and tone said it all. You. Are. Not. Leaving.

Ha. He'd like to see her stop him.

The nurse and his doctor were not happy. Hell, Jesse and Audrey were not happy either, but, dammit, he was going to be in on the raid. Period. He'd spent too many hours these past two days planning this raid, and had gone through too much shit this past week in the name of saving Bryson Van Amee's life. Bitter or sweet, he would see this snafu through to the end.

Finally, the nurse backed away. Despite the language barrier, he understood Audrey had talked her down. Had to admire the woman. She had a knack for people. For talking and listening and truly caring about what they had to say. Left to his own devises, he would have steamrolled over the nurse, but man, this made things so much easier.

Audrey stood with her back to him and stared at the now empty doorway. She wrapped her arms around her middle, hugging herself as if chilled, and Gabe ached to hold her, even took two steps toward her before he caught himself. If he held her in his arms right now, there was no guarantee he'd let go, and he had a job to do. She had distracted him enough already. To the point that he'd almost gotten himself KIA'd not once, not twice, but three goddamn times.

Audrey drew a breath, let it go in a rush, and faced him. "She's gone to get the paperwork stating you've refused medical treatment."

"All right. Now we're getting somewhere." He'd been in the process of changing into an olive green t-shirt and cammies when the nurse interrupted, and finished now, skimming the hospital scrub bottoms down his legs. It hurt to bend over and pull them off, but he clamped his teeth together and worked through the pain.

Pain was a SEAL's best friend.

Audrey made an exasperated sound. "Oh, for God's sake. Sit down before you fall down."

"I'm fine."

"Yeah, that's why you're weaving on your feet."

Shit, he was, wasn't he? He made himself stand still by force of will and the room started spinning around him. Two days flat on his back in bed may have helped his healing side but had done shit for his equilibrium.

Audrey planted a hand on his shoulder and gently pushed him

down. The fact that his legs buckled under such light pressure did *not* hurt his ego. Much. But the fact that she was now undressing him like a mother did a baby, with nothing sexual to it at all, smarted big time.

"I can do it."

She slapped away his hands then reached over to yank the privacy curtain shut around the bed. "No, you can't. You were *shot* less than forty-eight hours ago."

"Yeah, I remember," he said mildly, but Audrey seemed not to hear him.

"Jesse says you're an idiot for not letting yourself recuperate and I agree, but you're too much of a pigheaded jerk to listen to either of us!" She pulled his shirt off over his head. "You need to be careful not to rip out your stitches or you'll start bleeding again. You don't need to lose any more blood. And that splint on your foot is going to limit your movements. You won't have the mobility you're used to, so no running or jumping out of freaking airplanes or whatever it is you do on these insane missions."

Was she…? Shit, she was. Crying. Fat tears pouring down her cheeks.

"Whoa, whoa. Aud, stop." He reached for her, but she jerked out of his grasp and refused to meet his eyes. Damn, she might as well have shoved a stake through his heart. Would have hurt less. He rubbed the center of his chest. "I'll be okay. It's okay."

"No, it's not." With jerky movements, she flicked away tears before yanking off the scrub pants and throwing them aside. She snapped up the cammies and stuffed his feet into the holes. Even as angry as she was, she was careful not to jar his bad foot. "You shouldn't be going anywhere in your condition. Especially not out after dangerous terrorists."

"My condition?" He almost laughed, but wisely choked it back. "C'mon, this is nothing. I've done far more in far worse shape."

"I'm sure you have."

The bitterness in her voice surprised him. "Audrey, I'm trying to save your brother. Don't you want him home safe?"

"Of course I do." She stopped trying to dress him and laid her head on his bare thighs, wrapping her arms around him. Her tears felt hot on his skin, her sobbing breaths tickling his leg hair.

God, she had to notice the way his body, battered as it was, responded to her touch. How could she not? His erection was at half-mast, right there by her cheek, straining toward her, all but begging her to turn her head and—and, oh baby, she did.

"But not at the expense of losing you." Her breath whispered over his flesh before she kissed him, a light caress of her lips down his shaft. The contact jolted and sizzled through his nerves like electricity. As she opened her mouth and took him in deeper, it nearly broke every careful link of control he'd spent his life forging. Again. He couldn't afford that, not now when everything was situation critical, not when it left him feeling so raw and exposed afterward.

He gripped the back of her neck, intending to pull her away but managing only to draw her lips up to his. She hiked up her skirt and fumbled to straddle him.

"Audrey," he groaned and gripped her rear, guiding her down.

She gasped and her head fell back in pleasure. The ends of her hair tickled his legs. "Oh, please, Gabe. I need this. I'll be careful not to hurt you."

Gabe snorted a laugh. "You're not going to hurt me. The nurse—"

"Two pump chump, remember? I won't last."

God, he realized, neither would he.

Her eyes, still spilling tears, never left his, and he saw her heart there, his for the taking if he wanted. He did. Christ, did he ever want it, want her. So much that he ached with a sweet need to make her his forever. But he couldn't. It was impossible. He couldn't be the kind of man a woman like her wanted for the long haul.

Then she started to move against him and Gabe strived for control even as coherent thought fled and sensation engulfed him. Every lift of her hips off his cock was a slow, painful death, and he felt the loss of her warmth in even the darkest pit of his soul. Every languorous slide down was his salvation.

Control. Yeah, right. With her, it was nothing but a pretty illusion, and he was already lost. In her eyes. In her body. In her soul. He'd never had any control when it came to her.

Then it was over, the aftermath as crushingly silent as the joining had been sudden and intense, leaving them twined together, boneless and gasping, his face buried in the crook of her neck, her cheek resting on top of his head. He could hear her pulse thundering, matching his beat for beat, and closed his eyes.

Yep, he was raw again. As much as he enjoyed sex with Audrey—and, God, did he ever enjoy it, enjoy *her*—he did not like the way he felt right now. Like a throbbing, open wound. If she wanted, she could easily pour salt into him and scar him for life. And he had enough scars, thanks.

It was too much.

"Promise me you'll come back safe," she whispered against

his hair.

He refused to open his eyes, afraid of what he might see in her face, but even more afraid of what *she* would see in *his*. "I'll do my best."

"No. You *promise* me, Gabriel. I love you, and I can't lose you."

All right. He'd known this conversation was coming. He could handle this, tell her like it is. Despite the cold, hollow ache that flash froze into a lump of ice in his chest.

"Audrey." He touched her cheek and waited until she met his gaze with red-rimmed eyes. "You don't love me. We've been through hell, and in order to survive, we've had to rely on each other in ways most never have to rely on another person. It's natural to feel the way you do now, but it's not love. Believe me. I've been here before."

Christ, he hoped that little speech hadn't sounded as canned and phony to her as it had to his own ears.

But she seemed to believe him. The hurt of it shone in her eyes. "So you always sleep with the women you help?"

No, you were the first. The only. You were…so much more.

Ha. Like he'd say that little gem of a thought aloud and kibosh his whole argument. Sure, she was special to him, and he had a feeling she always would be, but what he felt didn't matter. A month, six months, a year from now, when the fear and adrenaline faded to nothing but bad memories, she wouldn't feel the same about him anymore. He just knew it. If he hung around, if he let her continue thinking she was in love, it'd put them both in an awkward place when she realized she wasn't. Better to extract himself now, before they reached that point.

Jesus, he never should have let things go this far between them to begin with, never should have allowed himself to give in to how much he wanted her.

"Sometimes," he said slowly, searching for the right words to let her down easy without crushing all that wild spirit he admired so much. "Sometimes when you face a deadly situation, the natural reaction is to want to experience life. Sex is one of the good parts of life."

Scoffing, she shoved him. Not hard, but enough that he knew she was seriously pissed. She stood, giving him her back, and he thought—hoped—maybe she'd see the logic and let it go without a fight. Then she whirled to face him and—surprise!—indomitable woman that she was, she called him out.

"You are such a jerk." She jabbed a finger at his nose. "This between us is more than sex and we both know it. I've never felt this way about anyone before, so you can't tell me—"

"It'll fade."

She shook her head. "No. I know myself better than that. Why are you trying to push me away?"

That was the question. The more he talked, the less he believed his own bull. God help him, he wanted her even though it made him feel so exposed. Maybe he loved her, he didn't know. Never had any experience with the emotion to know if that's what all the roiling, turbulent feelings of admiration, joy, fear, and lust meant. Even if it was love—not that he was ready to cop to that yet—but hypothetically, even if it was, they couldn't…*He* couldn't…

This was all too much. She was too much. And he was not nearly enough for her.

Okay, his thoughts were rambling, not making a whole hell of a lot of sense even to him. He rubbed the center of his forehead and then did something he'd never done before in his entire thirty-three years of life: he stood, pulled up his pants, grabbed his shirt, and chickened out.

"Audrey, I have to go."

Standing in front of him, arms crossed over her chest in a stance that was both defensive and vulnerable, she squeezed her eyes shut. "Don't. Please, Gabe. Stay here and let your team handle it."

He couldn't. Why didn't she get that? He wasn't one of those commanders that sat safely behind the battle line while ordering his men to charge into the fray. Injured or not, if they had to put their lives on the line for the mission, he'd be right there with them, fighting shoulder to shoulder.

Not that he expected that kind of opposition today. If all went well, his team should be in and out with Bryson before anyone was the wiser. If all went well, the entire op should last no more than ten quiet minutes.

If all went well.

That thing called Murphy's Law might try to turn it into a clusterfuck, but they were prepared for that, too.

Audrey stared at him, waiting for an answer, and he just shook his head.

"I'm sorry." Feeling like an utter coward, he edged around her and out the door. "I…gotta go. I'll call you when we have Bryson."

CHAPTER TWENTY-ONE

Dawn broke over Bogotá with no fanfare whatsoever. Low-hanging clouds kept the streets dark longer than normal—a few measly streetlamps tried and failed to beat back the oppressive grayness, their yellow glow dampened by the light morning fog, making for excellent cover. Gabe couldn't have asked for a better morning, though he could do without the persistent, drizzling rain that froze him to the bone.

Then again, maybe that icy cold was from the conversation—argument—whatever he'd had—with Audrey in the hospital.

No, he couldn't think about that. He had to stay one hundred percent focused on the here and now. Block out the pain in his heart, the pain in his side, the throbbing in his foot. Focus on the bite of cold, thin mountain air filling his lungs; the manicured lawn cushioning his body as he crawled toward the house; the earthy scents of mud and wet grass stodgy in his nose; the rifle's familiar feel in his hands; the easy rhythm of his heart in the muffled silence of the morning.

Easy, at least, until he heard the trilling whistle of a birdcall and his heart kicked up. Harvard, acting as lookout, had found a hide in a tree in the side yard that provided a perfect eagle-eye view of both the front and the back of the house. The call signaled trouble.

Gabe looked toward Quinn and Jesse, lying belly to the ground at his right, Jesse's medical bag a dark lump between them.

They waited.

Harvard gave another call. Three short trills.

Someone was coming. Or, more to the point, three someones. Then five more whistles from Harvard indicated five more approaching. Eight total, which tipped the scales a little too much for Gabe's liking. Ten baddies including Rorro and Jacinto to his six undertrained men.

Shit.

He gave his own call, a sign that the men should hold their positions, Marcus in the woods bordering the south side of the property, Jean-Luc on the north side near Harvard, and Ian in the southwest corner.

Quinn scooted across the foot of grass that separated them and put his lips close to Gabe's ear. "What are you thinking?"

Gabe shook his head. "Don't like these odds."

"You wouldn't think twice if these guys were SEALs."

"Yeah, but they're not." And, God, how he wished they were. "We're moving to plan bravo."

Plan B was a blitz attack, using the element of surprise to their advantage. Overwhelm the tangos, distract them by making them think more soldiers waited in the woods than there were, and slip Bryson out from under their noses while they panicked.

It involved more inherent risk, which was why it was their backup plan. But with the arrival of the new tangos, Gabe calculated it had a better chance at succeeding than their original stealthy plan to slip in and out unnoticed while Jacinto and Rorro slept.

Quinn's lips thinned. He glanced over at Jesse, who gave a grim nod, then met Gabe's stare again. "We can still—"

"Negative. Too risky." Especially for Quinn and Jesse, and they both knew it. Even though he wasn't going to let it happen, it did him proud that they were willing to stick to the original plan and take that risk. He patted Quinn on the shoulder to get his attention, then reached for his weapon. "Go in hot on my signal."

"Hooyah," Quinn said.

· · ·

Gabe moved fast, staying low as he flanked the north side of the house and made a beeline for his linguist's position. Jean-Luc, laying in a stand of bushes, raised an eyebrow in question when Gabe settled in next to him, but didn't say a word, which was probably a first for the man.

Gabe took a moment to survey the situation from this angle. The eight new bad guys had arrived in two vehicles. They looked like members of a local gang, dressed in jeans, T-shirts, and bandanas, carrying Uzis, most of them barely old enough to take a legal drink. And that was saying something, since the legal age in Colombia was eighteen. Jacinto probably recruited them in preparation for the ransom exchange.

Four of the kids now stood around in the driveway talking, while a fifth headed toward the front door with purpose in his stride. The other three still sat in the closer of the two vehicles, smoking something. From the sweet scent on the air, he'd guess pot. That evened the odds out some, but still not enough for his liking.

"We need to take out some of these guys," he whispered. "Can you get to that car?"

Jean-Luc nodded. "Gotcha. I'll go have a nice chat with our friendly Colombian gangbangers."

"Don't get killed."

"Wouldn't dream of depriving the world."

Damn, but you couldn't dislike like the guy. Gabe smiled and watched him crawl toward the car before turning his gaze to study the four gangbangers still standing in the driveway. He calculated several options and discarded them all with no small amount of frustration. A flashbang would be great right about now. So would hands-free radios.

A shout drew his attention back to the driveway. Several of the tangos spoke in rapid Spanish and ran across the pavement toward Jean-Luc's position. Dammit, someone had spotted him. So much for taking out a few covertly before the action began.

Gabe lifted his rifle to his shoulder, took aim, and put a bullet through the neck of the closest man. Even before the dead guy collapsed, the others peppered Gabe's hiding place with bullets and forced him to hit the ground behind the bushes for cover. He felt the heat of one round zing alarmingly close to his temple and Audrey's voice whispered through his mind.

Promise me you'll come back safe.

"I will," he vowed into the dirt. Better late than never.

Gabe rolled away from the shower of bullets, gained his feet, and took off in a zigzagging sprint toward the back of the house as Jean-Luc and Ian engaged the remaining tangos. Their window of opportunity to get in, secure Bryson, and get out was now very, very slim. They had to go now, while everyone's attention held firm on the firefight out front. He calculated fifteen minutes, max, before a neighbor alerted the authorities and all hell came crashing down. Once the authorities knew, the EPC would know. If they were involved, they'd send in reinforcements. Even if they weren't involved, they might still send reinforcements solely because of Jacinto's family ties to one of the head honchos.

Gabe hoped to be long gone—with Bryson Van Amee in tow—before that happened.

With a series of quick hand movements, he told Quinn and Jesse to go. In the original plan, he was supposed to stay outside and keep the backyard, their evac route to the helo, secure. Couldn't do that now. The danger inside the house while they were in the basement was too great to leave the door unprotected, so he made eye contact with Marcus and motioned him over to the patio.

"Keep this area clear," he ordered over the bursts of gunfire. Marcus nodded and took up the position as Gabe ducked into the house.

The kitchen reminded him of a morgue—vast, with a lot of cold stainless steel and black marble. He wouldn't have been surprised to see a wall of drawers on the other side of the endless center island, but there was only a heavy door with a massive padlock holding it closed. Quinn hunched over the lock, muttering between his teeth as he tried to finesse it open.

Jesse stood to one side, medical bag slung across his chest. He peeked around the wall into the corridor that led to the action at the front of the house. "How we doin' back there?"

Quinn cursed and smacked the lock. "Can't get it. We need Marcus."

"No," Marcus, standing half in the kitchen, half on the patio, said. "Ian will do it faster." And he sprinted across the yard.

Quinn straightened away from the door and grabbed his rifle. "You got this?"

"Yeah." Gabe nodded. "Go help the men out front."

Weapon raised, Quinn sprinted down the hallway off the kitchen.

A moment later, Ian came running, stumbling as a stray bullet ricocheted off the patio table and nailed him in the shoulder. Gabe laid down cover fire and Ian scrambled inside. He leaned on the island for a second, holding his shoulder, his lips pulled back in a grimace of pain. Jesse took a step forward to help, but Ian waved him away.

"Don't touch me."

"Okay?" Gabe asked.

"Yeah." He straightened. "You needed me? *Sir.*"

Gabe ignored the contemptuous tone—for now—and motioned to the lock. "Blow it."

Even with blood dripping down his arm and his mouth still drawn tight in pain, Ian eyed the lock like it was a woman he wanted to lick from head to toe. "With pleasure."

He made short work of it, taking a brick of C4 from his pack and stuffing a small amount in the keyhole. He inserted a blasting cap, twisted off a length of fuse, lit it, and crouched behind the island with the rest of them.

"Fire in the hole!"

The lock blew. The door popped open.

"Nice," Ian said, admiring his handiwork.

"Get to the helo and stop that bleeding," Gabe told him. "We've got it from here."

"Yeah, right." He snorted, grabbed his pack and rifle, and charged toward the front of the house. Away from the helo and into the fray.

Way to follow orders, Reinhardt.

Jesse disappeared down the dark, yawning mouth of the stairs. Gabe prowled the kitchen, checking windows and doors for threats. A gangbanger bolted from the hallway into the kitchen, spotted him, and raised a pistol. Gabe didn't give him the chance to get his finger anywhere near the trigger. The gut shot dropped the guy where he stood, and Gabe strode over to kick the gun out of his reach. Just in case.

"Boss." Marcus popped his head inside, sweat pouring off his face. "I gotta help Jean-Luc. They have him pinned."

"Go." He confirmed the yard was still clear as Marcus disappeared around the side of the house, then shouted down the stairs, "We're outta time!" as another baddie ripped through the front door, bolted across the hallway and up the foyer stairs to the second floor. Ian, the crazy bastard, was right on his heels.

Gabe moved away from the basement door to the set of stairs on the other side of the kitchen, thinking the guy might try to come down them and escape. The stairwell curved and he could only see as far up as a landing. He put a foot on the bottom step, intending to clear the area, when he heard rustling behind him.

Jesse emerged from the basement carrying Bryson Van Amee in a fireman's carry.

"How bad?" Gabe fell into step beside him as he humped his

unconscious cargo across the kitchen.

"He's severely dehydrated and tachycardic," Jesse said. "Another day of this and he'd be in serious trouble."

Gabe held up a hand before they reached the patio and scanned the yard again. A body lay cooling at the edge of the patio, blood soaking through the front of his hoodie sweatshirt, his eyes frozen half open. Otherwise, the yard was empty and silent, the pop of gunfire coming more sporadically now.

"We're clear. Go!"

Jesse took off like a swimmer from the block, jarring Van Amee, who moaned with each rattling bounce. They made it across the yard and vanished into the trees at the edge of the property. From there, it was only a short jog to the helo in a clearing on the next property over. Gabe could already hear the rotor powering up.

Almost home free. Time to round up the rest of the guys and beat feet out of there.

Gabe pivoted to go find Jean-Luc—and his bad foot went out from under him. Goddammit. With adrenaline firing his system, he hadn't realized how bad the pain had gotten, like someone had repeatedly stabbed a knife in between his toe bones and then left it there. One second he was up on his feet, jogging toward the side yard. The next, down on his hands and knees in the dewy morning grass with a scream lodged in the back of his throat.

And that's when he saw them. Jacinto Rivera and Rorro Salazar creeping through the trees, trying to escape.

For all of point-oh-three seconds, Gabe considered closing his eyes, turning away, and pretending he hadn't seen them. Capturing them wasn't part of the op. In fact, as far as his client was concerned, it was mission complete. Bryson Van Amee was safe in friendly hands. No ransom exchanged. No money lost for Zoeller & Zoeller Insurance. Handshakes and cigars all around.

He didn't have to bring Jacinto and Rorro to justice. He didn't have to risk himself or his men like that. But it went against every fiber in his being, every code of honor he'd ever set for himself, to let them get away.

Then there was Audrey to consider. He thought about the pain and worry and fear these two asswipes had caused her over the past few days. And it wasn't over. Bryson was safe but had a long road to recovery, and Audrey was going to worry for him, fear for him, for a long time to come. Especially if his captors were still free. For that reason alone, Jacinto and Rorro needed to pay.

Gabe groaned and limped to his feet, commanding his bad foot to hold. It did. Barely. He took off at a hobbling run, very aware that if Jacinto and Rorro continued circling the property like they were, they would run directly into the helo.

"Hey!" he shouted.

Rorro raised an assault weapon, peppering him with bullets, and his foot gave out again as he pivoted to find cover. Cursing, he hit the ground and rolled behind a decorative brick wall before returning fire in short bursts. Rorro grabbed his older cousin, used him as a living shield at the same time as a bullet came from nowhere and skipped off the top of Jacinto's head. They both collapsed.

Gabe peeked over the wall to see who had saved his neck. Quinn stood not twenty feet away at the edge of the yard, pistol in hand and a quirk on his lips. He holstered the weapon, closed the distance between them, and held out a helping hand.

"Man, you ever get tired of me saving your ass?"

Gabe clasped the offered hand and climbed to his feet. "Never."

Another bullet ripped into the earth near Quinn's boot and he stumbled backward with a shouted curse as Rorro, covered in his cousin's blood, crawled out from under Jacinto's body and fired wildly in their direction. Gabe let loose a short, controlled burst from his own weapon and Rorro crumpled face-first into the blood-soaked ground.

"Okay," Quinn said and huffed out a breath. "Now we're even."

"Never," Gabe repeated. "I'll always have your six, buddy."

All around, the gunfire came to an abrupt halt, a chilling silence spreading out in its wake. Gabe whistled between his teeth and waited, praying....

Five whistles bounced back and he breathed a soft sigh of relief. His men had stopped firing because the tangos were dead, not because they were. Now, as per the plan, they'd rendezvous at the helo.

Quinn slung an arm around his waist. "C'mon."

He hobbled across the yard with Quinn's help, met the rest of the team at the edge of the neighboring property, and performed a quick head count as everyone climbed aboard the helo. Yeah, it was very Mother Hen-ish of him, but it made him feel better to know Marcus, Ian, Jean-Luc, Jesse, and Harvard were safe and sound.

Gabe shut the door behind him and circled a finger in the air. "Let's go." He moved through the crammed confines of the helo's belly and crouched down beside Jesse, who was still working over

Bryson Van Amee. "How's he doing?"

"He's awake," Jesse said. He had started an IV and squeezed the bag every few seconds, pumping fluid into the drowsy man's veins.

"Yeah?" Gabe pulled out his cell phone and dialed. "Mr. Van Amee, can you hear me?"

Bryson's brown eyes, so very much like his sister's, focused blearily on Gabe. "Yes." His voice was barely a whisper of sound, and hearing him over the rotor was impossible, but Gabe nodded.

"All right. You're safe now, and someone really wants to talk to you. Audrey," he called into the phone over the noise of the helo. "Say hi to your brother."

CHAPTER TWENTY-TWO

It was over.

The call came in that Bryson Van Amee was safe and headed back to the States as soon as doctors stabilized him, and a cheer rang up from all the federal agents in the room. They high-fived, congratulated each other and Frank Perry like they'd all had a hand in the op that saved Van Amee's life.

Danny Giancarelli just shook his head and pulled on his coat. He had no doubt Perry the Prick would make sure his face was all over the top media stations today, basking in the glory of the success.

Well, let him.

Gabe Bristow and his men sure didn't seem like media whores, and all Danny wanted was to spend the final night of his so-called vacation with his wife and kids.

He passed his partner in the foyer.

"Gonna try to make it to the coast?" O'Keane asked.

"Yep."

"Traffic will be a bitch."

"Probably."

O'Keane looked toward the great room, where the other agents were packing up equipment. "Crisis averted. That was something, wasn't it?"

Danny didn't bother pretending he had no clue what O'Keane meant. "Yeah. Something."

"Can't help but wonder," he mused. "All those phone calls you made last night? They wouldn't have had anything to do with this privately funded rescue operation…"

Danny gave him a friendly thump on the back. "See ya Tuesday, buddy."

"Uh-huh. That's what I figured." He lowered his voice. "Whatever you did, you saved the man's life. Good job." As another agent walked by, he plastered a smile on his face and said normally, "Give Leah and the kids my love."

Giancarelli stepped outside. The morning air was crisp and cool, the sky a gorgeous cerulean with feather-like wisps of clouds. It promised to be a beautiful day, perfect for stretching out on the beach with his wife while his kids played in the surf. He couldn't wait.

His mind was already running ahead, a hundred miles down the highway, pulling up to the cabin with his kids squealing in delight at his arrival, and he almost tripped over Chloe Van Amee. She sat on the front steps, hugging herself.

"Whoa, hey. Sorry."

She blinked up at him, and he'd have to be blind not to see the glazed expression of shock in her dark eyes.

"Mrs. Van Amee, are you okay?"

She nodded, but it was an obvious lie. Sighing inwardly, Danny postponed his trip for another few minutes and dropped to the step beside her. Yes, he wasn't her biggest fan, and he especially disliked how little she had to do with her sons, but he couldn't leave her sitting here like this, alone and in shock. He put an arm around her shoulders. She felt tiny and fragile, Barbie meets china doll.

"It's over, you know?" he said. "Bryson is safe now. He's coming home to you and your sons in a couple days."

"I—I know. I know. He's okay. In the hospital and he's… okay." She sounded like she was trying to convince herself and raised shaking hands to cover her face. "I just—what about the men that took him? What happened to them? Are they…still out there somewhere?"

"I don't know. Would you like me to find out?"

She looked at him, studied him with eyes far too world-weary to belong on the face of a selfish, pampered socialite like Chloe Van Amee. "Is it bad of me to hope they're dead?"

"I'd be surprised if you didn't." He gave her a light squeeze then stood. "Lemme make some calls, okay?"

BOGOTÁ, COLOMBIA

"We have the final casualty report."

Gabe turned from the ICU room's observation window as Quinn approached.

Please, he thought, *say all ten tangos are dead.* Then he could call Giancarelli with the news and tell Audrey—

Scratch that, *he* would not tell her anything. It was easier on them both if he just faded away now. But he'd make sure the news got to her that it really was over, that the threat was completely neutralized.

If the threat was neutralized.

He studied Quinn's impassive expression and swore under his breath. "How many got away?"

"The police reports Harvard hacked into only list nine casualties of the 'gang fight'. Rorro Salazar's unaccounted for."

"No, they have to be wrong. I hit him in the chest. It was a kill shot."

"They found a Kevlar vest near Jacinto's body. Bullet still lodged in it."

"Goddammit." He looked through the window again. Audrey slept fitfully with her head on Bryson's bed, his hand gripped in both of hers as if she was afraid to let go of him. "The little shit should be dead."

"Agreed. The men are packing up to go home, but we can stay a few more days if you want to go after him."

Tempting.

Very, very tempting.

Except he was exhausted past his limit and so were his men.

And he had to get away from Audrey. The longer he stood here staring at her, the harder it was to leave. He had to put the safe distance of a continent between them before he did something stupid, like beg her to come with him when he knew she wouldn't.

He rubbed a hand over his face. "No. Everything we have on

him says that without Jacinto, he's not much of a threat. Let's chalk this up as a win and get the hell out of here."

Quinn nodded, but hesitated and looked through the window at Audrey and Bryson. "Are you going to say goodbye?"

"No." Turning away, he fell into step beside Quinn without a backward glance. It was the hardest thing he'd ever done in his life, and his chest burned with the pain of it.

It *was* easier this way.

Quinn stayed silent until they reached the parking lot and climbed into the 4Runner. He started the engine, but then sat there, hands on the wheel, gearshift still in park. Then he turned in his seat and opened his mouth as if to say something.

"Don't." Gabe shut his eyes, blocking out the concern so evident in his best friend's usually stoic expression. "What did you do with Cocodrilo?"

Quinn shut his mouth with a click of his teeth, then gave a resigned sigh. "We handed him over to HumInt, Inc. They'll make sure he's passed to the right agency for prosecution."

"Good. Then let's get outta here."

Quinn still didn't shift into drive. "Gabe, man, you can't leave her like this without—"

"Just drive."

• • •

Audrey felt eyes on her and lifted her head. The observation windows across the room were empty, nobody out in the hallway. She must have been dreaming, caught somewhere between wakefulness and sleep, because she swore she'd heard Gabe's voice just a moment ago.

Unlikely. She hadn't heard a word from him since he called to tell her Bryson was safe.

Sitting up, she rolled her neck around on her shoulders and tried to stretch the crick out of her spine. Goodness, she needed a real bed and about twelve hours of uninterrupted sleep. Then after a good meal and about a gallon of coffee, then maybe she'd have the strength to face Gabe again.

She wasn't about to let the stupid man push her away out of some misguided sense of honor. What they had was not a fling—she'd had enough flings in her life to know that for sure—and what she felt for him was not a fluke of the circumstances. It was real and deep and, truthfully, a little bit frightening.

Bryson's hand shifted in hers. She gazed down at him and her eyes filled with tears yet again. Crap. Hadn't she cried enough today? First out of relief, then out of sorrow when she finally saw Bryson. With his left eye sealed shut, his lips cracked and bleeding, he looked like he'd gone several rounds with a heavy-weight boxer and lost every one. His skin was papery and so pale his veins stood out in stark contrast on his arms and the backs of his hands.

How could they do this to him, a man who never even raised his voice in anger?

His hand shifted again and she realized he was squeezing her fingers. Was he awake? She studied his face. It was hard to tell with everything so swollen, but his one good eye was definitely open.

"Brys?"

"Hi, sis," he whispered.

If those weren't the two most beautiful words anyone had ever said to her. She couldn't hold the tears back any longer. They poured down her cheeks, soaking into his hospital johnny as she hugged him as tightly as she dared.

His hand settled on her head. "Don't cry. Please."

"Sorry. Can't…stop." But she managed to choke back the sobs. "I thought I'd never see you again. I thought I'd never be able to tell you I love you and I'm sorry I'm not the sister you want me to be and—"

"Shh. You are, sweetie. I wouldn't change you for anything."

"But the condo and the money and my paintings—"

"Audrey, I was wrong about all that. I just wanted you to be happy."

"I am." She thought of Gabe and smiled. "Brys, I've met someone. One of the men that rescued you. He's—well, I love him."

"The big guy out in the hall?"

She sat up, but the hallway was still empty.

Bryson made a sound that might have been a laugh. "He's not there now. He left, but he stood there for a long time just staring at you."

"He…left?" She shook her head, eschewing the doubts before they entered her mind. Gabe probably just went to help his men do whatever they did after a mission. Debriefing or whatever. He'd be back. He wouldn't leave without saying goodbye.

"Does he love you, too?" Bryson asked.

She smiled. "I think so, but he's being stubborn about it."

"Hm." He closed his eye and was silent for a long time. She almost thought he was asleep, but then he asked softly, "Want me to kick his ass for you?"

Audrey laughed at the absurdity of that mental image. "Thank you, Brys, but how about you relax and work on healing first? The doctors say you'll be okay enough to travel to a hospital in the States tomorrow. Chloe and the boys will be waiting there."

"My boys." A tear trickled from his good eye. "I've been such an idiot. I kept thinking I'd never see them again and they wouldn't even remember me as anything but a—a sperm donor. Do you think they'll forgive me? I've missed so much."

"That's the great thing about kids." She tucked the sheet around her brother's shoulders and leaned over to kiss his bruised forehead. "They're remarkably better at forgiving and forgetting than adults."

• • •

Bone-deep tired, his side aching from the hole in it, heart aching because, God, he really did not want to leave Audrey, Gabe hobbled aboard the plane with Quinn to find his team already there. He'd expected a rowdy celebration with lots of noise and possibly alcohol, but the whole lot sat quiet as churchgoers. They must all be as exhausted as he was. He nodded at them and took his seat, leaned his head back, and shut his eyes.

"Bristow," Ian said in his usual caustic tone. "There's something I need to say to you. *Sir.*"

He groaned. "Save it. I'm not in the mood, Reinhardt."

Clothing rustled behind him, a lot of moving and shifting of bodies. Jesus, what was the guy doing now?

Gabe glanced over his shoulder. Ian stood in the center of the aisle, one arm in a sling, the other raised, his hand forming a blade across his forehead.

As one, the rest of the men stood and saluted.

Gabe looked at Quinn in surprise, but he was also standing.

"Sir," Ian said without the slightest hint of mockery. And was that…respect…in his dark eyes? "We're glad to have you back."

Humbled, flattered, Gabe pushed to his feet and returned their salute. "It's good to be back. At ease, gentlemen." When they didn't lower their hands or sit down, he smiled. "Relax, guys. Hit up the bar in the back. You deserve it. You did good. *We* did good."

"No, Sir," Marcus said.

"Our mission's not over," Ian said. "With your permission, we'd like to finish it."

The warehouse, Gabe realized. After everything, they still wanted to get rid of that damn warehouse. Well, why the hell not? "You up for it?"

"Yes, Sir," they said in resounding unison.

He studied them. Bruised, battered, but not beaten. Never beaten. Pride swelled in his chest. All this time he had wished for his former SEAL teammates when he had a group of men who were just as good, just as loyal, and just as honorable at his command. Maybe even more so.

"All right." Grabbing his cane, he gimped toward the plane's door. "Then let's give the EPC a giant FU and blow that puppy from the map, gentlemen."

CHAPTER TWENTY-THREE

It should be raining. Hell, it should be storming with how wretched Gabe felt, but Mother Nature had blessed the Capital with a gorgeous start to summer. The nice weather served as a stark contrast to his mood and, honestly, kinda pissed him off.

Yet here he stood, barefoot and shirtless on his balcony, watching the sun drop below the city's horizon, exactly as he had every other night for the past month. Reds, golds, and purples splashed across a sky so pale blue it was almost white—so hopeful, bright, and a little wild. Like one of Audrey's paintings.

Like Audrey herself.

Gabe squeezed the balcony's railing so hard his knuckles cracked. Called himself a thousand kinds of fool. He had to stop thinking about her. Had to stop standing out here every night, watching the sunset and pining for what could never be. Had to put her out of his mind and focus on what was important: the team and their training.

A knock sounded at his front door and Gabe forced himself to let go of the railing and go answer it. He made it halfway across the living room before a key rattled in the lock and Quinn stepped inside.

"Hey," Quinn said and held up a grocery bag. "Brought some Natty Boh."

Gabe shook his head and about-faced, going back to the window as Quinn headed toward the kitchen with the beer. For a second there as the doorknob turned, he had this stupid notion that Audrey had come to Washington and…

Yeah. Completely stupid. He'd known Quinn was coming over, so why was he so damn disappointed to see him?

"I don't feel like drinking," Gabe said.

At the kitchen counter, Quinn paused halfway through opening a second bottle. "You sick?"

"No, I'm not sick."

"All right." He popped the cap and tossed it and the bottle opener in the sink, then brought the two beers back to the living room. He held one out. "You look like you could use one. Have you slept since we left Colombia?"

"Of course I have." Gabe snatched the bottle since Quinn was just stubborn enough to stand there, holding it out to him forever.

"Uh huh," Quinn said and wandered around the room. "This place smells like a gym locker."

"Haven't done laundry."

"Or dishes. Or shaved. Or showered." He stopped beside the desk, littered with pizza boxes and empty bottles of beer and water.

Gabe thought he should be embarrassed by the state of his

apartment, but couldn't find the motivation for even that. Maybe he was sick after all. He never used to have a problem motivating himself. "I've been busy."

"Doing what, internet stalking?" Quinn said and spun the computer monitor around.

Shit, he'd left Audrey's website up on the screen.

"I'm checking up on a client." He crossed to the desk in three strides and swatted Quinn's hand away from the monitor. When he tried to close out of the site, he found he couldn't do it. Again. Audrey's face smiled out at him from the page and he just… couldn't. He switched off the monitor instead. "That's all."

"You miss her," Quinn said. "You should go see her, talk to her. Who knows? Maybe she'll even forgive you for being an ass."

"Wait." A sneaking suspicion crept through the fog of depression hanging over Gabe's mind and he narrowed his eyes on his best friend. "Is this an intervention?"

"No. But, c'mon, man." Quinn encompassed the apartment with a sweep of his arm. "This isn't you. What the hell?"

Gabe felt a muscle tick under his eye and loosened his clamped jaw. "Can we talk about something else? Like the reason you're here."

"Yeah, but you're gonna listen to me first. I know it's none of my business, but I have to say this. I've known you for twelve years, and in all that time, I'd never have dreamed of calling you a coward. Until now."

Gabe ground his teeth as the blow hit exactly where Quinn had calculated it to: his pride. He was *not* a coward. "Noted. Now can we get to work? You wanted to talk to me about the team."

Quinn took a long drink from his beer, then sat on the arm

of the couch. "That mission in Colombia could have gone much worse."

"No shit."

"We were undertrained, underequipped. We put our team in danger."

"Yes, I know." Gabe couldn't keep the heat out of his tone. *He* had put *his* team in danger, all because he had wanted back into the action. "And I've been working around the clock to rectify those problems."

"When you're not moping," Quinn muttered, but then held up his hand. "Sorry. Low blow. I know you've been working your ass off here, but there is one problem you haven't addressed yet."

Gabe sat down in the chair across from him. "And what's that?"

"We don't have enough men."

"I've been looking at dossiers."

"We need a sniper."

Hell, no. Gabe saw where this was going and frowned. "I know what you're thinking, Q. Didn't I already make that decision?"

"Yeah, but we need a sniper. A good one, at that. Seth Harlan's one of the best and he wants on the team. He wants a second chance."

Second chance.

In a flash of understanding, Gabe suddenly knew how the sniper must feel. In fact, hadn't he felt the exact same way only a month and a half ago as he stood in his parents' house in his dress whites, dreading his future? HORNET had given him and all of the other guys another shot. What was stopping him from doing the same for Seth Harlan?

What the hell. Not like his team wasn't a ragtag bunch already. Why not add a potentially traumatized sniper to the mix?

And, speaking of second chances, maybe Quinn was right about other things, too.

Gabe picked up his beer, drained it on one breath, and stood. "All right, I'll give Harlan a call, but he's going to be your responsibility, Q." With that, he strode toward his bedroom. He needed a shower, a shave, and to pack a bag.

"Where are you going?" Quinn called.

Gabe stopped just outside his bedroom door and glanced back at his messy apartment, curling his lip in disgust with himself. Why the hell had he let it get this bad? "I'm not a coward."

Quinn raised his bottle in salute. "Hooyah."

DOMINICAL, COSTA RICA

If someone had told Audrey this morning that she'd come home from a lunch meeting with her manager in San Jose to find Gabriel Bristow swimming in her slice of the Pacific, she would have called them crazy.

"Gabe?"

She walked out to the end of the dock, sure she was dreaming. She had to be. He'd starred in her dreams every night and they all began like this. She'd come home to find him begging forgiveness for being a class A asshole, then one of two things would happen. One, she'd yell at him, call him a bunch of creative four-letter words, and then kick him out with the righteousness of a woman scorned. Or two, she'd fall into his arms and make wild, passionate love to him for hours before they lived happily ever after.

It was still a toss-up which dream she liked better.

Maybe she fell asleep on the bus ride home? But she didn't feel like she was sleeping. This was all too vivid, and as good of an imagination as she had, she didn't think she could conjure up the feel of the salty ocean breeze playing with her skirt or the hot sun burning her cheeks. Plus, if she was dreaming, the air, soupy with summer humidity, would not be making her dress stick to the sweat rolling down her spine and her hair would not be a frizzy mess right now.

So he really *was* here.

"Gabe?" she said again, so stunned she couldn't find any other words for a solid five seconds. She shook her head. "What are you doing?"

Treading water, he looked up at her. His hair was slicked back, his long eyelashes spiked around wary golden eyes. "Well, uh, I'm swimming."

"You came all the way to Costa Rica for that?"

Rata playfully bumped his side, and the smile that spread over his face was so genuine it melted the ice wall she'd tried to build around her heart to ward off his memory. He stroked the dolphin's head, and then took hold of a rope and ball dog toy she'd never seen before and chucked it into the waves. With a happy chirp, Rata dove after it.

"Had to," Gabe said. "There are no dolphins in D.C. You promised me a swim with dolphins, woman."

She choked, caught somewhere between tears and laughter. And here she'd thought he was too out of it to hear anything she said during that long, horrible night. "You remember that?"

"Hmm. Vaguely."

Her heart did a back flip that would have made her dolphins proud, but she couldn't bring herself to relive that night and dredge up all the bad memories. Not yet. Not when seeing him again, alive and well and *here*, made her so freaking happy she struggled to hold back tears.

Instead, she took off her sandals, sat down on the end of the dock, and dangled her feet in the water. She watched her dolphins fling their new toy around with so much excitement she feared it might break.

"You brought them a toy." And if she wasn't already in love with him, she'd have fallen hard just then. "Thank you for that."

Gabe swam toward her, strong arms slicing through the waves with ease. Goodness, he was even more graceful in the water than out of it, fast and lithe like her dolphins.

Reaching the dock, he folded his arms on the edge and kept his lower half submerged, but he was definitely sans swim trunks under the water.

"Well," he said with a mock-serious expression, "this amazing woman I once knew told me—several times—that I needed to learn manners. Apparently, it's rude to come calling without a gift."

"Very true." She smothered a laugh. "Gabriel Bristow, are you skinny dipping?"

"Like I said." He grabbed hold of her legs and pulled her over until he was propped between her thighs. His hands slid under the skirt of her sundress, kneading her soft flesh. "It's rude to show up without a gift. The dolphins got the toy. You get me."

Oh, that did it. The tears she'd been fighting spilled over and she threaded her fingers through his wet hair. "I do, huh?"

"For as long as you'll have me. I'm in love with you, too, Audrey. Have been practically since minute one."

"Then why did you walk away?" *And hurt me so badly.* Although she didn't say that part aloud, it was there, hanging in the air between them, palpable as if she had said it.

"Hell, I don't know. Stupidity?"

"I won't argue that."

"And, uh…" He hesitated and cleared his throat. "And fear."

Her SEAL, afraid? Somehow, she found that very difficult to believe. "Nothing scares you, sailor."

"You do. Or what I feel for you does. It makes me raw. Exposed in ways that… God, I can't even put it into words. I was terrified of keeping you. Terrified of losing you. I, uh, still am." He lifted a hand to show her the slight tremor in it. "I've never been so goddamn frightened in all my life, but I couldn't stay away. I've been miserable."

Really, she shouldn't be so petty that his confession made her giddy with a spiteful kind of glee. But she was and it did. He'd been just as miserable this past month as she had, which almost made all the tears she'd spilled over him worth it.

Almost.

But she'd need ice water in her veins to stay mad at him after a confession as sincere and heartfelt as that.

"I tried to find you," she told him. "When Bryson got out of the hospital, I went to D.C., even attended one of Raffi's plays in New York, hoping he'd tell me where you were. He wouldn't, but he did say he'd have a talk with you."

"*Talk?*" Gabe snorted. "That's what he called it? Man, he reamed me a new one for walking away from you."

"Hm. I like Raffi even more now than I did. And I liked him a whole lot before."

"I knew you would. But it was actually Quinn who gave me the push I needed."

Audrey didn't bother hiding her disbelief. "Really?"

"He called me a coward and he was right." He pulled himself up further to wrap his arms around her waist and laid his head in her lap. "I wanted to come right away, but I had to take care of some business things first. I wanted at least a solid week with you without interruptions."

God, that sounded like heaven.

"How's your brother doing?" Gabe asked.

She sighed. "He's back to normal, throwing himself into work. I suppose I shouldn't complain. He does make a conscious effort to be there more for his sons. And for me. He even came to my show. But…. I don't know. After everything, I expected more of a change, I guess."

"Change is a hard thing to do."

"Yes," she agreed, "it is." And yet Gabe was willing to change his life by letting her into it. Oh God. She was not going to cry again.

Not. Going. To. Cry.

Instead, she forced herself to sound casual as she said, "Raffi mentioned word's getting out about your team's success."

Gabe winced and nuzzled her leg. "I wouldn't call it a success. We still don't know who was pulling Jacinto's strings. No way he came up with the abduction all on his own—he really was an idiot. But the EPC has publicly denied involvement and so have the other guerilla organizations."

"But you got the bad guys and saved my brother and started making a good reputation for your team. I'd call that a success."

"Yeah, guess so." He didn't sound convinced. "We've been flooded with contract offers. Mostly private security gigs, but I haven't accepted any yet and won't for a while. The guys are going through some serious training first. They're all at SERE school right now, except for Quinn. He's setting up our new office in D.C."

"SERE school?" She lifted an eyebrow at the relish in his tone. "Do I even want to know?"

"Survival, Evasion, Resistance, and Escape training," he explained.

"Oh, that sounds…horrible."

"It is. The guys'll hate every second of it, but it will make them stronger as individuals and a team."

She poked his side with her index finger. "So why aren't you there with them?"

"Been there, done that, got the T-shirt, and sure as hell don't wanna do it again."

"Says the oh great and fearless leader."

He made a noncommittal sound and nuzzled her thigh again, kissing her through the skirt of her dress. "Besides, I have other things to do."

"Hm." She couldn't wait to hear this. "Like?"

"Like comb through the flood of resumes I've gotten for new guys, figure out an easy-to-remember name for the team—I'm *not* going with HORNET—and set up an international office."

"Oh." Didn't that just deflate her bubble? She'd thought for sure he was thinking more along the lines of taking her to bed for the next, oh, fifty years. "Well. I like HORNET."

He lifted his head to give her a dark scowl. "You would."

She bopped his forehead with her palm, intending to shove him back into the water, but with his arms still wrapped around her, the jerk dragged her in with him. She broke the surface sputtering, cursing him in English and Spanish. He laughed, and the man who didn't know how to cut loose yanked her under again.

Having not taken a decent breath before going under, she struggled to get to the surface, but he held her tight and his mouth covered hers. He gave her his air, then licked the inside of her mouth, igniting sparks of pleasure in her belly. Hooking her legs around his waist, she found him fully erect. All it took was a shift of her dress and a wiggle of her hips and—oh, yes, he filled her up until she gasped into his mouth.

Gabe walked toward shore, careful not to break the contact of their mouths or bodies, and each step pushed him deeper, deeper, deeper. They broke the surface together, gulping air before their mouths fused again with urgency. He dropped to his knees in the surf and the skirt of her dress floated out around them in a pale yellow cloud.

"God, sweetheart," he groaned and rolled his hips in a torturous sweet and slow rhythm that matched the beat of the waves. "I've missed you. You feel…so…good."

Audrey nuzzled his neck, opened her mouth over the strong beat of his pulse. His skin tasted like salt and sand and her man, and she adored the way he shivered when she kissed him there. Unlike the other times they'd made love, the build to climax happened slowly, and the release, when it came, stretched out into oblivion, soft and lovely, like floating on a cloud. Gabe tangled his fingers in her hair to tilt her head up and kiss her forehead, her nose. Before taking her lips, he pressed deep one last time and moaned with his own climax. Audrey held him through it and laughed. Her heart felt so full it was either that or cry again.

LOS ANGELES, CA

"Danny? Honey, what are you still doing up?"

Danny Giancarelli looked up from his laptop and managed a smile for his sleepy-eyed wife despite the headache pounding directly in the center of his forehead. She wore a ratty USMC T-shirt from his military days, which he'd given her before his deployment after 9/11. Leah said she'd worn it to bed every night for the entire year that he was gone and even now, all these years later, it was still her favorite nightshirt. His, too. She'd been wearing it the day he'd arrived home when he, knowing without a doubt at the ripe old age of twenty that she was the woman for him, popped the question. She'd worn it on their wedding night, and it was sexier than any of the lingerie her girlfriends had bought her for her bridal shower. She'd also worn it the night they'd made their first baby, and every subsequent baby thereafter.

And it still looked sexy as sin on her.

"Come here." He held out a hand, his wedding band glinting in the soft glow of his desk lamp. When she set her hand in his and he pulled her onto his lap for a kiss, he thought, not for the first time, that he was the luckiest S.O.B. alive.

Leah drew back and soothed her thumb down the crease between his brows. He'd been noticing more and more of those creases in the mornings when he gazed into the mirror to shave.

Around his eyes. His mouth. His forehead. He looked more like his father every freakin' day. Luckily, he hadn't started losing his hair yet like Pop, but it still made him feel old, especially when his wife was as hot at twenty-nine as she'd been at eighteen.

"What's wrong?" she asked. "Is the Patterson case bothering you?"

"No."

One brow arched the way it did when the kids told a lie, and she gave him a dubious expression.

"Yeah, okay," he admitted, "it's bugging me."

His last case, a local hostage situation involving a girl named Sylvia Patterson and her ex-boyfriend, hadn't had the same happy-ever-after as the Van Amee case, ending in a murder-suicide.

"But not how you're thinking," he added. "I did everything in my power to save that girl. It wasn't enough, but that's part of the job. You accept it and move on. You have to or you'd drive yourself insane with guilt."

"Like Marcus did," Leah said.

"Yeah, like Marcus." He sighed. "I am sad the girl died, but dwelling on it won't change that, so I've put it out of my mind."

"Then why are you sitting here in the middle of the night, looking up"—she leaned over to get a peek at his computer screen—"whatever it is you're looking up. Is that in Spanish?"

"Yeah."

She blinked. "When did you learn to speak Spanish?"

"I can't speak it," he said. "I can read it okay, enough to get the gist, anyway."

"Huh. Just when I think you can't surprise me anymore. What are you reading about?"

He hesitated for a heartbeat before answering, "The EPC."

She huffed out a breath. "*That's* what you're still hung up on? I thought the Van Amee case was one of your success stories."

Not really his. It was Gabe's, Marcus's, and the rest of their team's. If it wasn't for them, he had no doubt Bryson Van Amee would be dead and Jacinto Rivera and Rorro Salazar would be in the wind somewhere, millions of dollars richer. Okay, technically Rorro was still in the wind, but the little shit wasn't considered much of a threat since the supposed brains of the operation, Jacinto, was dead.

Except, Jacinto wasn't known to have brains, was he?

Man, his head hurt. Danny shut the laptop with a slap of his palm and rubbed his temple.

"Honey," his wife soothed and laid her head on his shoulder. She smelled good, like the raspberry body wash she used. "Let it go. That case was a win. I don't understand why you're still obsessing over it a month later. This isn't like you."

"God, Lee, I know. But the whole thing stinks and I can't figure out where the smell is coming from."

"Okay." She scooted off his lap, grabbed the ottoman from in front of his easy chair across the room, and sat on it cross-legged so that she faced him. "Maybe you need a fresh nose."

Danny smiled. "Have I shown you lately how much I love you?"

"No, but we can get to that later." She gestured a c'mon motion with her hand. "Lay it out for me, G-man."

"All right." He opened the laptop and called up the Word file he'd been keeping since the end of the hostage situation. Then he laid it all out for her. Everything from the abduction of Bryson

Van Amee in front of his apartment right on through to the rescue by Gabe and his men.

"Everything we know about Jacinto Rivera says he was a thug, plain and simple," he told her. "He couldn't have masterminded something as sophisticated as rigging a limo with ether gas to knock Bryson unconscious. Someone had to have been pulling his strings, but according to the website I was reading, the EPC has denounced Jacinto for the ransom attempt and claims no responsibility."

Which was not their modus operandi. And *that* was bugging him.

"They *like* people to know they are capable of snatching anybody from anywhere," he continued. "Angel Rivera *likes* propagating that reputation, but yesterday, again according to that site, he publicly disowned his remaining family."

"Wait, wait." Leah raised her hands to stop him. "'His remaining family.' Are you sure that's what it said? You didn't mistranslate?"

He opened the laptop, called up the website from the browser's history, and reread the paragraph. "No, that's exactly what it says."

"Well, that's an odd word choice, don't you think? I mean, wasn't Jacinto his only brother?"

"Yeah, he was. Maybe it's a cultural thing?" Danny mulled it over for a second, spinning his wedding band around on his finger. "No, wait, I think there was a sister…" He called up another file and scanned over the information. "Claudia Rivera. She's been missing since August of '05, presumed dead."

Leah opened her mouth, but froze before uttering a sound and her eyes went huge behind her glasses. She scrambled off the ottoman and out of the room.

"Um, Lee?"

She came back, flipping through an old baby name book they'd bought five years ago when they discovered they were expecting the twins.

"Jesus, Lee. You still have that thing?"

"It's fun to look at. Besides," she said and sent him a sly sideways smile. "You never know when we might need it again."

"Oh, no." He held up his hands. "We agreed to stop at three."

"Actually it was two, and the third was a surprise. I'm not entirely against a fourth, but it'll have to be before I turn thirty-five." With that, she turned her full attention to the book, leaving him sitting there catching flies with his mouth.

"Lee, c'mon, I'm getting too old to do the whole newborn thing again. The twins practically killed us, remember? You can't drop that bomb on me and expect—"

She slapped the book down in front of him and pointed to a name. "Look. I found your bad smell."

He picked up the book. Read the passage once. Twice. And— holy shit—suddenly saw the whole case in a new light. "Yeah, baby, I think you did."

DOMINICAL, COSTA RICA

For a man who didn't know how to cut loose, Gabe was doing a very good job of it. She'd never seen him so laid-back, so relaxed, so...content. He lay stretched out beside her, his scarred leg draped over both of hers, his eyes closed. If it wasn't for his fingers combing idly through her hair, she'd think he was asleep, he was so utterly limp.

She propped herself up on one elbow to gaze down at him. He looked like a happy, well-satisfied man, and it gave her a little thrill that she'd had a hand in putting that expression on his face. She wanted to paint him like this with the moonlight spilling through the windows, sparking off his dog tags.

Her wounded warrior. Her strong SEAL. Her muse. Her love.

God, did she love him.

She smiled and poked him in the ribs until he groaned and opened one eye. "What is it, woman? I want sleep. You wore me out."

"Earlier, you mentioned an international office. Where?" She hoped not on the other side of the world, or else she'd never see him.

Both eyes open now, his expression turned serious. "Well." He moistened his lips. "I was thinking here in Costa Rica."

"Not Europe?"

"We might open one there eventually, but no. Not Europe."

"Because of me?"

"There were several reasons. Pricing, location, local laws… But you were the biggest factor in my decision," he admitted and rolled over so that they were nose to nose. He curled one arm up underneath his pillow and traced a finger down her cheek with his free hand. "I know you love it here and couldn't ask you to move. So I'm coming to you. I, uh, hoped—I was going to ask you—"

Gabe stopped short, drew a breath. She'd never seen him look so nervous, and a little thrill jittered around her belly.

Was he going to…?

No, she wouldn't even think it yet, too afraid she'd jinx herself.

"Audrey," he said softly, "will you move in with me?"

Okay, as far as proposals went, it wasn't quite what she'd been hoping for. But it was a start. A very good start. She'd have to warm him up to the idea of marriage, because she fully intended to be his wife before the year's end.

She leaned in to kiss him. "Technically, you'll be moving in with me."

Relief filled his beautiful golden eyes. "Is that a yes?"

Silly man. Had he honestly thought she'd turn him down? "Of course it's a yes."

With a hoot of triumph, he rolled her underneath his body and kissed her dizzy. His hand stroked the curve of her waist to her hip and dipped between her thighs, nudging her legs apart as his knuckles brushed her most sensitive spot. She was tempted—oh, wow, especially when he did *that* with his fingers—to let him keep going, but a knock sounded at the front door.

She slapped her hands against his chest. "Hold up, bub. Someone's here."

"Ignore it," he murmured and scooted down her body until his lips grazed her inner thigh, his tongue snaking out to tantalize the sensitive flesh there. "I have plans for you."

Her belly muscles clenched at the thought. Maybe…

The knock sounded again, more persistent than polite this time. Damn. She squirmed out from underneath him. "They're not going to leave."

"Audrey…" Left balancing on his hands and knees on the mattress, he hung his head and heaved a long-suffering sigh.

"Oh, poor baby got his favorite toy taken away." She smacked his very fine butt. "We'll play later. Get dressed."

"Naked's more fun."

"Also inappropriate for company." She found her discarded sundress wrinkled and still a little damp from their earlier swim, but it'd do. She pulled it over her head and started toward the bedroom door.

"Audrey, wait."

She turned at the odd note in his voice. "What's wrong?"

Back was the tension the day had bled out of him. Very slowly, moving like a cat stalking its prey in the moonlight, he slid out of bed. "Look at the clock. Who would be visiting at this time of night?"

She shrugged. "Maybe it's a neighbor. I do have them, you know." Except the closest one was a mile down the road, and Gabe was right, midnight wasn't a normal time for an old-fashioned neighborly visit.

"Stay here." He leaned in and kissed her soundly before she could protest. "Please. This doesn't feel right. Let me check it out first."

She swallowed hard and nodded, her own anxiety spiking at the worry she saw in his eyes as he pulled on a pair of cargo shorts. "Be careful."

"Always." After another quick, reassuring kiss, he disappeared down the hall with his gun in hand.

She waited.

And waited.

Heard nothing and her heart kicked into high gear, drumming a cumbia beat out on her ribcage until she couldn't stand it anymore. She peeked out into the hall and saw Gabe standing at the screened front door, scowling at a dark shadow on the other side.

"Audrey?" the shadow called. "Is that you? Who is this guy?"

At the familiar voice, she let out a breath of relief and walked to Gabe's side. He gave a slight nod, conceding to the false alarm, and holstered his weapon.

Jesus, she was going to kill him for scaring her like that.

She hit the porch light, illuminating her sister-in-law's face. "What are you doing here, Chloe?"

CHAPTER TWENTY-FOUR

Goddamn Gabe Bristow. And Quinn. And their team-fucking-building.

Marcus dropped his bag inside the door of his condominium and shuffled on legs that felt like Twizzlers as far as the oversized leather couch before collapsing face down into the cushions.

Bruised. Blistered. Sunburned. Parched. Dirty.

His aches had aches.

And he was pretty sure his aches' aches were reproducing like rabbits. But, hey, at least he got to come home and sleep in his own bed tonight, unlike the rest of the guys, who were stuck in a hotel near the naval base.

SERE training. Ha.

They might as well call it break-you-till-you-cry-for-your-mommy training. Welcome-to-the-ninth-circle-of-hell training. Expose-and-exploit-your-every-weakness training.

But he hadn't cracked. None of them had, not even scrawny

little Harvard. They all bent to their limits and past, but they hadn't cracked. As soon as his body stopped throbbing, Marcus thought he might find some pride in that.

Take that, Navy SEALs.

Marcus jolted awake to the sound of his cell phone vibrating near his head. He hadn't been aware of falling asleep, but he'd rolled off the couch and now lay with his head partly under the coffee table. When he pried his eyes open, he saw the cell doing a jig across the glass top. He could even see the caller ID.

Giancarelli.

If it was anyone else, he'd ignore it, drag himself into the shower and then pass the fuck out in his king size, sleeping-on-a-cloud memory foam bed for three days. Or four. Hell, a whole week.

But it was Giancarelli. His best friend. The guy he'd ditched for nearly two years without so much as a see-ya-later because he'd been feeling sorry for himself.

Marcus groped around the edge of the table until he got hold of the phone. He didn't have the energy to sit up. "Yo."

"Shit, don't tell me you're drunk," Danny said.

Drunk? Yeah, probably sounded that way, Marcus realized. "No. Overtired. What's up?"

"I need to get a hold of Gabe, but I don't have his number."

"Can't. He's in Costa Rica with Audrey." The fucker. Living it up with his woman in a tropical paradise while his men were all but tortured by his SEAL friends.

'Course, Marcus had to admit, the man did deserve some down time after being taken hostage, beaten to hell, and shot.

"What about the other guy? Quinn?" Danny asked.

The urgency in Giancarelli's voice penetrated the fog in his brain. He finally scooted out from under the coffee table and propped his back against the couch. "What's going on?"

"I know who was pulling Jacinto Rivera's strings. I know who was behind the abduction plot. The FBI won't give me the time of day until I have the proof, but Bryson Van Amee needs protection ASAP."

Marcus snorted and tried stretching out his legs. Christ, even his bone marrow ached. "Protection? From who, his airhead wife?"

Giancarelli's silence spoke louder than anything he could have said and Marcus sat up straighter. "That was supposed to be a joke."

"Do I sound like I'm kidding?" Giancarelli said. "It's Chloe. Which my extremely beautiful and intelligent wife realized is a nickname for Claudia. As in, Claudia Rivera, who disappeared from Bogotá in August, six years ago. And guess who popped up in the States in September, six years ago. Chloe Smith, who became Chloe Van Amee about three months after that."

Jesus Christ. If Giancarelli was right….

Marcus hauled himself to his feet and powered up his laptop. When the internet came up, he wasn't surprised to find Harvard online and tucked the phone into his shoulder to type out an instant message: *H, GOT A ? 4U.*

As he typed, he asked, "How sure are you about this, Dan?"

"Pretty damn. I know it in my gut."

And Danny had a good track record with gut feelings. "Okay. Hang on." He set aside the cell and typed another message.

CAN U DO A BCKGRND CHK 4 ME?

Harvard was quick to respond: *NAME?*

CLAUDIA RIVERA SALAZAR.

ALREADY HAVE IT. DO YOU WANT ME TO SEND IT TO YOU?

Marcus smirked at Harvard's need to use proper English, even in instant messages. *PLZ & THX.* He picked up the phone again, but set it down and typed, *HAVE CHLOE VAN AMEE 2?*

NO, Harvard answered. *NEVER SAW THE NEED TO LOOK AT HER.*

PLZ CHK HER 2 PDQ & SEND INFO 2 ME.

The computer beeped with an incoming email. He brought up Firefox to access his inbox and raised the phone to his ear again. "Danny, you still there?"

"What did you find out?" he asked.

"Harvard sent me an email. Just a sec." He read it over, swore loud and long, and opened the picture attachment just as his IM dinged with another message from Harvard: *HOLY SHIT.*

The pic opened and Marcus stared into the face of a teenage Claudia Rivera. IM dinged with another picture, one of Chloe standing next to her husband.

IS THIS CHLOE VAN AMEE? Harvard asked.

YEP, he typed and said to Danny, "Just got a picture of Claudia and one of Chloe and I'm looking at them side-by-side. I think you're on to something. Chloe's about fifteen pounds lighter, has bigger boobs, fuller lips, a straighter nose, and blonde hair, but there's still a strong resemblance. Too strong to be a coincidence."

Danny cursed. "It's *always* the spouse, man. It's so obvious and yet we overlooked it because she acted her part to a T. Academy Award-winning stuff. She doesn't even have an accent. Except..." He paused. "I did hear it once or twice when she said certain words.

Couldn't place it at the time, but I remember wondering about it."

"All right, listen," Marcus said. "I'm going to have Harvard send everything he finds your way. Try to get the Bureau involved. I'll contact Quinn and see if we can set up a protective detail on Van Amee. Keep in touch."

He hung up and was in the process of changing his clothes when his phone rang again. He expected Giancarelli, but it was Harvard.

Switching the phone to speaker mode, he tugged off his dirty shirt and picked a clean one out of his dresser. "Nice timing, man. I was just about to call—"

"I checked Chloe Van Amee's financial records," Harvard said without preamble. "Her personal accounts are nearly dry, but she scraped together enough to buy a first class ticket to Costa Rica. For *tonight*. Her plane arrived in San Jose two hours ago."

• • •

Chloe blinked when Gabe slid a protective arm around Audrey's waist. If she had less Botox injected into her face, that pinched expression might have been a frown.

"Who's he?" she asked again in a voice full of suspicion and a hint of gossipy speculation.

Audrey ignored the question, instead answering with a couple of her own. "Where's Bryson? Is he okay?"

Chloe wasn't the type of sister-in-law to drop in unannounced. She wasn't even the type to drop in announced. Five minutes ago, Audrey would have bet her life savings that Chloe would never see the inside of her home, yet here she stood on the porch, staring warily at Gabe.

Jeez, was today the day for unexpected visits or what?

"I wanted to talk to you," Chloe said.

"You couldn't do it over the phone?" Gabe asked.

Her too-plump lips pressed together. "No. I couldn't." Then she looked him over with a critical eye. "You're one of the men that rescued my husband."

He inclined his head. "I am."

"What are *you* doing here?"

Audrey opened her mouth to say it was none of Chloe's business, but Gabe spoke over her. "I live here."

It gave her a little thrill to hear him say it. So what if he technically didn't have any of his belongings here yet. Just the fact that he said it with that note of finality in his voice made her go all warm and gooey inside. He lived here. With her.

Chloe harrumphed. "Aren't you going to invite me inside?"

"We're busy," Gabe said and Audrey's face heated.

Oh God. The last thing she needed was for Chloe to report to her brother that she was shacked up with some man, doing the sorts of things that keep healthy men and women busy in the middle of the night. Chloe would make the situation into the apocalypse and Gabe into Lucifer, and Bryson would go on one of his brotherly rampages before she had a chance to ease him into the idea of her having a live-in lover.

She nudged Gabe in the side with a soft, reprimanding, "Gabriel," but he didn't seem to notice.

"Unless this is an emergency," he said, "I suggest you try back in the morning."

Something flashed in Chloe's dark eyes, but she dipped her head before Audrey was able to identify the emotion. Anger, maybe. Chloe did tend to have a short fuse, and having someone so succinctly tell her off wasn't something that happened often to the overindulged woman. Certainly wasn't fear. A person had to be intelligent to be afraid of the likes of Gabe, and her sister-in-law wasn't known for her brains.

"Chloe, it *is* late and I'm tired. I'm sure you are, too, if you just arrived." Audrey tried to keep her voice soft, soothing them both. "As long as Bryson is okay, there's no need for this right now. Come back in the morning and we can talk or whatever over breakfast, okay?"

Chloe hesitated. "Alone."

"Hell no—"

Audrey cut off Gabe's protest with a finger against his lips. "Yes, alone. I'll see you in the morning."

Even after the door shut, Audrey kept her finger pressed to his lips. The expression in his gold eyes faded from pissed off to mulish, then flared with heat as he opened his mouth and sucked her finger inside.

She laughed even as sensation sparked from the tip of her finger and zinged through her blood to her belly. "Didn't you get enough earlier?"

"I'll never get enough of you, woman." After one last swirling lick, he released her finger and moved to the window, still in warrior mode, full of that deadly catlike grace. He parted the curtains. Chloe's headlights splashed over the hard angles of his face as she backed out of the driveway.

"I don't like her."

Audrey let out a huff of laughter. "C'mon, hon. She's a pain-in-the-ass, but she's harmless."

"I don't know about harmless. There's something about her…" He backed away from the window and moved his shoulders as if trying to shake off a cold chill. "It's out of the ordinary for her to visit, right?"

"I'll say. I honestly didn't think she even knew where I lived."

"Yeah, about that. I don't like out of the ordinary." After picking up the gun he'd set on the foyer table, he gave her a quick kiss. "Go on to bed. I'll check out the grounds, make sure we're secure, then be in."

She caught his face in her hands. "Careful, Gabriel, your paranoia is showing."

"Probably." His faint smile never touched his eyes. "But humor me. Lock yourself in the bedroom until I come back, okay?"

Audrey watched him slip out the front door and fade into the night. She sighed and moved toward the bedroom to follow her SEAL's orders. She supposed this was something she'd have to get used to, though she planned to ease away his constant fear of attack. That was no way for anyone, even a former SEAL, to live. Everyone needed a refuge, some place untouched by the outside world, where he can let down his guard. This was going to be Gabe Bristow's haven. She'd make sure of it.

She heard him come in the back door just as she was straightening the sex-rumpled quilt on the bed. He paused in the kitchen for so long she finally gave up waiting and opened the bedroom door.

"Gabe?"

Footsteps.

Except, no, those couldn't belong to Gabe. It sounded like a Clydesdale stomping through the kitchen and as big as he was, he never walked with heavy boots, always ghosted about even in the comfort of his own home. He'd more than once frightened her today, sneaking up behind her with his barely-there footfalls.

A shadow appeared at the end of the short hallway, backlit by the lamp she always left burning in the living room. Definitely not Gabe. Too short. Too scrawny.

Oh God.

As silently as she could, she closed and locked the bedroom door. She had no way of knowing if the intruder had seen her—the interior hallway was always dark, and the way the door was set into the wall with a slight indentation provided a little protection—but from the sounds of his footsteps, it didn't matter. He knew the layout of her house and bypassed the laundry room, the guest bath, and the extra bedroom, moving with unerring accuracy toward the master bedroom.

Toward her.

• • •

Something was not right.

Everything looked normal. The nearly full moon floating over the ocean in the inky sky provided a good view of the house and yard, and Gabe saw nothing out of place. No odd shadows that shouldn't be there, no movement except for the sway of the palms, no sound but the soft lapping of the ocean against the dock.

Still. He couldn't shake the gut feeling that something was way off, and he knew better than to argue with his gut—it had saved his ass in more near-fatal situations than any one man should survive. So he walked the grounds again, still found nothing, and his instincts still told him it didn't matter. He strode to the end of the drive and looked both ways on the narrow, empty road.

Maybe he should take Audrey to a hotel for the night. She had next-to-nil for security—something he planned to fix if he was going to live here—and the crappy system she did have had so many holes it would work better as a colander than a security system.

Actually, that sounded like a damn good idea. He'd sleep better tonight knowing they were secure. Tomorrow, he'd make some calls and pull some strings to have a security specialist out here by noon. Maybe Jean-Luc's brother-in-law would want the job.

He turned to go back to the house, and out of the corner of his eye, caught a glint of moonlight off something down the street. A car, a blue sedan, parked in the foliage alongside the road. Given that Audrey had no immediate neighbors and lived on a twisty, rarely used road that fought a constant losing battle with the encroaching jungle, it was not normal to have a car just sitting in the street. That was probably the cause of his unease. He'd bet his good foot it was Chloe's car, and he was not a betting man. People don't just pop up for random personal visits in the middle of the night unless there was a problem. Especially not wealthy, pampered people like Chloe Van Amee. He could only come up with a couple reasons why she'd leave the car here in this specific spot, hidden from view, and none of them were good.

Weapon aimed, he melted into the jungle shadows alongside the road and moved toward the car, keeping down and to the right so he'd come up in the driver's blind spot.

And what do you know, it wasn't abandoned. Chloe still sat in the driver's seat. She jumped when he opened the passenger side door and pointed his gun at her forehead.

"Hi," he said. "Mind if I join you? No? Great."

Her eyes flicked from his gun to his face then skipped away. "You shouldn't be here."

"Could say the same of you, Mrs. Van Amee."

Her hands tightened on the steering wheel until her manicured nails dug into the braided leather. "You wouldn't understand."

"What don't I understand?"

She pressed those grotesque, collagen-injected lips together, refusing to answer.

"Chloe." He made her name into the verbal equivalent of a dagger, all edges, and she flinched.

"I'm sorry." She turned in the seat, brown eyes wide and wild as tears spilled over. "God, I am so sorry. I-I love my husband, and I didn't think anyone would get hurt. Rorro—" She said his name with a Spanish inflection, rolling the Rs, and Gabe held up a hand to stop her.

Average American women from Kansas couldn't roll their Rs like that.

"Your real name isn't Chloe," he said. "Who are you?"

"Claudia." Just like that, she dropped the perfect Midwestern accent, and the lilting sounds of Colombian Spanish weaved through her words. "My name is Claudia Rivera."

"Jesus Christ. Angel and Jacinto's missing sister." How the fuck had they all missed that connection? His first instinct was to get back to Audrey as fast as his bum foot could carry him. Second was to shoot Chloe Van Amee on principle because he suddenly knew who set up Bryson's abduction and caused Audrey so much anguish. Chloe may not have been the mastermind, but she was in this shitstorm up to her liposuctioned rear end.

"I tried to get away from them," Claudia sobbed. "I didn't want any part of my family, but they dragged me back. Rorro called me a year ago and said he'd tell Bryson who I was and what I'd done in Colombia if I didn't go along with his plans. I had no choice. I didn't want to lose my husband. My house."

She said nothing about her sons, and inwardly, Gabe ached for the poor boys. He knew exactly what it was like to grow up with a mother who put on all the right appearances, but really didn't care about anyone but herself. At least Grayson and Ashton still had a loving aunt and father.

Maybe.

"What plans?" Gabe demanded.

"At first he only wanted money," Claudia said. "But he bled me dry. The allowance Bryson gave me wasn't enough, and I couldn't draw from our joint accounts without making him suspicious. When I explained that to Rorro, he said we had to come up with another way for me to pay. Then he saw a stupid action movie and it gave him an idea to kidnap Bryson for ransom and blame it on the EPC. He had me call Jacinto with the plan because he didn't want anyone to know he isn't as dumb as he pretends to be. He likes when people underestimate him."

Gabe thought back to the raid and hell, that's exactly what he'd done, even after Luis Mena warned him that Rorro was vicious and not to be underestimated.

They all thought Rorro had tossed his cousin to the wolves out of fear, but it had been a more calculated move than that. He had deemed Jacinto's usefulness tapped out and disposed of him like a rancher putting down a lame horse.

A chill shot down Gabe's spine and nailed him in the ass. "Where is he now?"

Claudia gazed over at him. In the light of the fat white moon overhead, her plasticized face took on the macabre look of a skull with sunken cheeks and a peculiar hollowness in her eyes. It was the same thousand-yard stare he'd seen in soldiers who had looked death in the face and walked away alive. The same empty, lonely stare Gabe saw every time he looked at Quinn.

"Claudia. Where. Is. He?"

"He thinks it's Audrey's fault he didn't get the ransom money because she called the FBI and ruined everything." She moistened her lips and looked away. Guilt thickened her voice. "He's going to kill her."

CHAPTER TWENTY-FIVE

Weapon. She needed a weapon.

Audrey looked around, spotted the bedside lamp. It had worked when she thought Jean-Luc was attacking her in Bryson's apartment in Bogotá, but Jean-Luc hadn't really wanted to harm her. Somehow, she didn't think the man banging against the door that she'd barricaded with her dresser felt the same way. His sole purpose was to harm.

Where was Gabe? Had this man harmed him?

Oh God.

Okay, think. There had to be something in here she could use as a weapon.

Steadying herself with a fortifying breath, she took another look around. Besides the lamp, she had framed photos of Bryson, her nephews, and her parents on the nightstand. Bottles of perfume and lotion rattled on her dresser, more falling with each heave of the man on the other side of the door. The scent from the broken bottles was cloying, flowers and fruits and spices filling her head, making her dizzy, and she promised she'd never put on another drop of the stuff if she lived through this.

Her closet. She must have something in there. She ripped open the door. Hangers. And none of them were even metal. An iron and ironing board. She grabbed the iron and plugged it in. If all else failed, she could hit him with it when it was still hot.

The banging on the bedroom door stopped. She paused for a half second and listened, didn't hear anything on the other side but didn't dare hope that he was gone. That's how people got killed in horror movies. She dived back into the closet and found a broken palette knife missing half of its wooden handle.

Better than nothing.

Up on the shelf: Plastic containers filled with all the miscellaneous junk that she had shoved out of sight, out of mind to sort on some rainy day in the future. Loose screws, plastic thingamajigs, and cords to who knows what. Old birthday cards, tax returns, random junk mail she never threw away. None of this was going to help her.

Oh, why couldn't she be in the kitchen? She had all sorts of weapons in there. Butcher knives, frying pans. Her X-Acto knives, carving sets, files, and palette knives three times the size of the one in her hand. Shards of sculpture metal and welding supplies. Primers, glues, and—

Paint thinners.

Audrey froze. Despite the overwhelming odor of the perfume, she caught the pungent, piney stench of turpentine, heard the splash of it hitting her door, saw the puddle oozing underneath.

No, no, no, no.

She scrambled backward, away from the growing puddle.

Fumes burned her nose and eyes and she curled into a ball in the farthest corner of the room, burying her nose in the edge of her shirt. Something fell behind her and hit her shoulder. Gabe's cane. She snatched it up, held it to her chest like a child held a teddy bear to fend off the boogeyman.

Gabe.

She remembered the fear and wonder in his eyes as he told her how much loving her scared him. Scared *him*, her brave SEAL. God, the thought of what he might do when she was gone frightened her more than the thought of dying.

No, she couldn't die and leave him to his own devices. He needed her.

Audrey gripped the cane like a baseball bat and stood, tiptoeing around the spreading pool of turpentine. The easiest way out was the window, but she didn't dare, too afraid the intruder was waiting for her out there. He probably didn't expect her to charge out the door, brandishing a cane like a maniac, so that's exactly what she'd do.

She listened, but didn't hear anything in the hallway. Made sense. If her intruder planned to burn her to death, he'd get out before lighting the match. Which he could be doing right this very second.

Fear threatened to freeze her. The chemical-heavy air threatened to choke her, and the room morphed into a funhouse mirror before her eyes, all stretched and wobbly. The floor surged and pitched under her feet, and the short trip to the door was a feat of equilibrium that would turn any gold medal gymnast green with envy.

Next up on the balance beam: Audrey Van Amee.

She giggled. Stopped. Shook her head. Nothing about this was funny. Stay focused. If she let the chemicals get to her, she was dead.

She shoved the dresser aside, its legs scraping loud across the wood floor. She didn't let herself think about how that might alert him and flung open the door. He was there in the hallway, tossing aside an empty can of turpentine, grinning at her as he dug in his pocket.

Flash of silver. A lighter.

She charged, brought the cane down hard on his head. He staggered but didn't collapse. With her forward momentum and the slippery turpentine covering the floor, she couldn't have stopped even if she wanted to. She slammed into him, taking him to the floor. He was small. So much smaller than an attacker bent on burning her alive should be. A boy, not a man.

He cursed in livid Spanish, jarringly foul words in a voice that was still more child's than man's. She reached for his hand, stabbing her fingers into the fleshy part, hoping he'd drop the lighter.

He did.

She snatched it up and scuttled away from him as he rose to his feet. Oh God, he had a gun. Why did she not think that he'd have a gun? He pointed the muzzle at her head.

"Get up."

She stared at the gun. Something was dripping…

Turpentine.

He was as smeared with the paint thinner as she was.

She opened her hand and stared at the silver lighter with the initials R.S.V. engraved in extravagant letters on the side. One of those fancy kinds that light when the lid flips off.

Anger surged. If he was going to kill her, then he was damn well going with her. She pressed her thumb against the lid and met his widened eyes.

"Don't make me do it," she told him in Spanish.

For a second, he looked like the boy that he really was. Then he firmed up his grip on the gun and raised it again. "You won't."

Audrey shut her eyes, flipped the lid, and threw the lighter at him. She heard his screams, felt the rush of blistering heat, heard the gun go off, its retort little more than a pop in the roar of the flames.

And she knew she was dead.

• • •

He's going to kill her.

The words echoed inside Gabe's head, a gruesome mantra that played over and over and over as he hobbled up the driveway in a ridiculous lopsided run. Earlier, when confessing to Audrey he'd screwed up because he was afraid of loving her, he'd said it terrified him more than anything else he'd ever faced as a man or a SEAL. At the time, he'd been telling the absolute truth.

Not so anymore.

This terrified him more. Knowing that she may be in trouble right now, that he could be losing her at this very second, and he couldn't get to her fast enough because he'd left his cane in the bedroom and his damn foot didn't want to hold anymore.

Bang!

A gunshot.

Gabe staggered and almost went to his knees there in the driveway. "Audrey!"

No answer.

Screw the pain in his foot. He didn't care if the fucking thing fell off.

Redoubling his speed, he leapt onto the porch and slammed through the front door. Smoke. It clogged his nose, assaulted his eyes. Flames danced in the hallway, eating their way across the floor and ceiling into the living room.

"Audrey!"

He spotted her, curled into a ball on the floor, fire raging around her, licking closer and closer.

Flames blistered his legs. He didn't notice. He scooped her into his arms and tried not to think about how limp she was, tried not to worry about whether she was breathing. He just hugged her close and got her out of that hell.

Outside, Gabe carried her to the edge of the beach and sat her down where the waves rolled up and kissed the sand. No doubt the salt would sting like a bitch in her burns, but he had to get the chemicals he smelled on her off her skin. She moaned when the ocean rolled over her and struggled against his hold.

"I got you, Aud. Shh, honey. I know it hurts, but I'm here."

Her lashes, caked with soot and ash, fluttered open. "Gabe?"

Scooping water over her singed hair, he tried to smile. "Hi, honey."

"You're okay. He didn't…hurt you. I thought…"

"No, he didn't hurt me." But he was still out there somewhere, and Gabe raised his head to scan the thick tangle of jungle abutting the beach. Shit, he could be three feet in there and Gabe wouldn't see him. "Audrey, honey, where is he? Where did Rorro go after he set the fire?"

"Rorro?" In that instant, her eyes cleared. She looked at her burning house. "He's dead. I started the fire. I threw his lighter at him and he... He's dead."

Bile surged up Gabe's throat. She lit a fire knowing she was soaked in flammable chemicals. She was lucky she hadn't gone up in flames the moment the spark flared.

"Christ." His whole body started to shake like a palsy victim's from the mix of adrenaline after-burn and gut-wrenching fear. He couldn't stop it, couldn't control it. Gathering her up, he held her tight. "Don't do that again."

"Didn't want to...first time. He was going to kill me. Why?" Her voice broke. "What did I do to him? *He* kidnapped *my* brother!"

"Later, honey. I'll explain it later." He just wanted to hold her now. And never, ever let her go.

"My house is gone," she sobbed.

"We can build another. Bigger, with a workshop for you and an office for me. Maybe a guesthouse for when your brother and nephews come visit. Or, God help us, for when Raffi comes to visit."

"But my paintings..."

"You can paint more."

"I guess so." She sounded unconvinced.

"Audrey..."

"No, no, you're right. I know you're right. Just all that work — gone." She let go a ragged breath and snuggled against his chest. "But that doesn't matter because I'm safe and you're safe and we'll build a new life together."

"Absolutely. We'll make this work, okay? I promise."

He felt her lips curve in a small smile against his shoulder. "And my SEAL never makes promises he can't keep."

As they sat there on the beach watching her house burn, Gabe heard the unmistakable beat of a helo's rotor over the crackle of flames. The bird swung in low over the treetops and hovered over the beach nearby.

Audrey squinted and raised a hand to shield her eyes against the prop-wash of sand. "Is that…?"

A rope fell from the chopper and one by one, six men slid down, armed for war.

"Yeah." Gabe grinned and helped her stand as Quinn and the others ran toward them. "Our knights in shining armor have arrived."

EPILOGUE

"I still like HORNET."

"No," Gabe told Jean-Luc for the hundredth time. But he had to raise his beer to his lips to hide a smile. He'd missed the guys and was glad they'd all made it to the housewarming party Audrey had somehow thrown together. Even Bryson and his boys had shown. Danny Giancarelli also put in an appearance with his stunning wife. And, of course, no party would be complete without Raffi.

Gabe hadn't had much time over the past month to hang out with the guys, what with them attending constant training exercises, him buying the new house, setting up the international team office, and dealing with all the incoming contracts and resumes. Not to mention the way Audrey had thrown herself into her career and constantly spirited him off to Paris or New York or Tokyo for showings. He still wasn't sure how he felt that her most popular painting was *Sunday Liberty*, a watercolor of him lying in a hammock in nothing but cargo shorts and his dog tags. Sure, the figure in the painting was faceless, but everyone *knew* it was him. It even said so on Audrey's website.

The guys had given him grief about it for weeks.

"Well," Jean-Luc said like a petulant child. "What else are we going to call ourselves? It's a great acronym. I thought all you military types like acronyms?"

"No," everyone said in unison.

"Will you drop it already?" Marcus said with an eye roll. "Nobody wants to be called HORNET."

"Oh, hey, that reminds me." Audrey jumped up from her seat on the lounger beside Gabe. "I made something for everyone."

Handing him her margarita, she left the room.

"Should I get my swim trunks?" Marcus asked.

Gabe shrugged. He couldn't begin to guess what she was up to. Last time she told them she had a present at Harvard's twenty-fourth birthday party last month, she'd bombed them with water balloons.

Gabe heard the door of her workshop off the kitchen open and close. Please, he thought, don't let her have water balloons again. Or worse, a hose.

All smiles, she came back to the patio with nothing but a box of gray T-shirts and set it on the table.

"I used to draw caricatures for a living so…" She unfolded the first and shook it out. "Here, Jean-Luc, this one's yours."

Jean-Luc grinned, yanked off his shirt, and pulled on the one she handed him. Across the shoulders in dark yellow lettering was his nickname, "Ragin' Cajun." Underneath that, in smaller lettering: "Hostage Rescue & Negotiation Team."

No wonder she wanted to know everyone's nicknames last week. The little sneak. He'd known for weeks she was up to something, but hadn't been able to figure out what.

"I kind of went with Jean-Luc's hornet theme," she explained as she passed the shirts out.

On the front was a cartoony depiction of a beehive surrounded by six hornets sporting the faces of each of the men. Marcus's hornet wore a fedora and Harvard's carried a book. Jesse's wore a stethoscope and cowboy hat. Ian's carried a bomb with a lit fuse, which made the hardass chuckle when she handed him his shirt. Even Quinn's lips twitched as he got a load of the camouflage greasepaint and bandolier his hornet wore.

Finally, she returned to Gabe's side and handed him the last folded shirt. His hornet stood inside the hive with a cane and an air of superiority.

The cane. He looked at it, propped beside the chair. Had she included the damn thing six months ago, he would've taken offense. Now—not that he'd admit it aloud—he kind of liked it. He *really* liked the crown she'd drawn on his hornet's head. Grinning, he held up the shirt and read the back. Instead of "Stonewall," the nickname his SEAL teammates had dubbed him so many years ago, it said, "King Bee."

Gabe caught her hand and drew her down onto his lap for a kiss. "It's perfect. Thank you."

"Good." She returned his kiss. "'Cuz I made myself one that says Queen Bee. Of course, we'll have to get married to make it official."

He sputtered. "Married? But—but—I thought living together

was enough."

With an indulgent smile, she patted his cheek. "It was. Now it's not. I'm flighty like that, so you'd better get me to the altar before I change my mind again." She gave him another quick kiss on the lips as Raffi strolled over and held out a hand to help her off his lap.

"I'm kidnapping your woman," Raffi said, "and holding her ransom for some girl talk."

Gabe pointed at him. "Don't even joke about that. It's not funny."

"Bro, I never joke about girl talk." With a grin, he looped his arm through Audrey's and they sidled away, laughing quietly together.

Gabe stared after them with a scowl. She wanted to get married? Okay, yeah, he'd known from the start she did. Someday. But not now. She had to know how much he loved her—he sure showed her as often as he could—so why did she need the rings, and the priest, and the cake, and the license? Couldn't they just go on like they had been? Why screw with something that wasn't broken?

"You look like my sister just beaned you upside the head with a two-by-four."

"She did," Gabe muttered and rubbed his head. "A whopper of a two-by-four."

Married?

Bryson grinned and held out a fresh bottle of beer. "Here. I've discovered this is the best cure for the headache she causes."

"Thanks." He took a swig from the bottle and eyed his possible future brother-in-law. Bryson had aged considerably over the past several months, had lost the little bit of extra weight he'd carried before the hostage situation, and had very little hair left on his head. But stress did that to a guy.

"How you holding up?"

"Actually," he said and looked toward the beach where Ian—of all people—played with Bryson's sons in the water. "I'm good. And no, I'm not just saying that. Audrey was right."

"She does have that annoying habit."

"Yes, she does. And I wish I would have listened to her a lot sooner. There's so much I've missed out on with my sons—that's all I kept thinking about when I was in that basement. That I'd never see them again, never hold them, or kiss them goodnight. No more baseball games or karate lessons or birthday parties, stuff I always took for granted. But even after I got home, I fell back into my old habits. What Chloe—Claudia—did was the wake-up call I needed." He winced, took a swallow of beer. "I can't say I'd do it all over again, because if I had known from the start about Chloe—Claudia—whatever her name is—I wouldn't have married her."

"We still haven't found her," Gabe said.

"You won't." His laugh sounded bitter and self-deprecating. "She cleaned out one of our joint accounts, and I'm sure by now she's found herself another rich husband to sponge off of. God, I was a fool, but I really did love her. Part of me still does."

A squeal of sheer excitement boomeranged up from the beach. Gabe glanced down, watched as Ian picked up Ashton and all but body slammed the kid into the next incoming wave. Laughing and splashing, Ashton surfaced like a buoy thanks to his bright red water wings. He launched himself at Ian, who pretended to stagger under both boys' weight when Grayson joined in. The three of them went under the next wave together.

Bryson chuckled. "He's good with them."

Yeah, go figure. "How about your boys? How are they coping?"

"Better than me," Bryson admitted. "They haven't asked about her once. She was never… Even though she was their mother, they were better judges of—" He broke off and took another drink, but he didn't have to finish the thought. Gabe knew what he was trying to say, because he felt the exact same way toward Catherine Bristow as the boys did about Claudia.

Just because a woman gives birth does not mean she's a mother in any but one sense of the word.

"So," Bryson said after a long moment of watching his sons play. He turned to face Gabe. "I don't suppose I have to give you that cliché speech about not hurting my sister or blah, blah, blah."

Gabe laughed. "No, you don't."

"Good, because I like you. Beyond the obvious reason that you saved my life, you're good for her. She's always marched to the beat of her own drum—"

"Marched? More like done the conga."

Bryson grinned with genuine pleasure. "See, you get her. You…ground her in a way I've never been able to, and you make her happy. Just don't let her railroad you into marriage if you're not ready. Believe me, you'll both be much happier in the long run."

Gabe managed to hold back a wince as Bryson walked away. There was that M word again.

God. Marriage.

She wanted to get married.

But then, as he sat there watching Ian play with the kids, he thought about it, really considered it. What if she did change her mind about them and kicked him to the curb? It would destroy him—he was that ridiculously in love with her. So why not make his claim to her legal?

Actually, he kind of enjoyed the idea of her wearing his ring, having his last name, and started wondering if any jewelers in San Jose were open on Sunday. Or, even better, a drive-thru chapel? The faster he tied her to him forever, the better.

Too bad they weren't closer to Las Vegas....

As a matter of fact, that was a good idea. A Vegas wedding. It was so unlike him, so wild, so spontaneous, so...*Audrey*. She'd love it.

He pushed out of the lounger, gimped through the living room to the closed doors of his office, and slipped inside. In five minutes, he had two first-class plane tickets and a suite at Caesars Palace booked for a week. They left the day after tomorrow.

Smiling, Gabe shut his laptop and picked up the printed tickets. He'd surprise her with them later tonight after everyone turned in, after he took her to bed and made slow, careful love to her for several delicious hours.

A knock sounded at the door and Jesse poked his head into the office. "Got a minute?"

"Sure." He sat behind his desk again, still grinning, and Jesse gave him a look like he was worried about Gabe's sanity, which just made him grin more. "What's up?"

"Wanted to talk to you about—" Jesse noticed the printouts and paused. Almost, Gabe thought, like he wanted the distraction.

"Whacha got there?"

"Plane tickets. I'm marrying Audrey in Vegas on Tuesday. You're all invited."

Jesse's eyes widened. Then he laughed. "Well, hell, I guess congrats are in order, then."

"Sure are. I'm a lucky guy."

"You'll get no arguments from me." He lifted his beer in a toast. "You're stupid if you don't put a ring on that lady's finger before someone else does. Luckily, I never figured you for a stupid man."

"Just don't mention it to her," Gabe said. "She doesn't know yet."

"Lips. Sealed." He even made a zipping motion across his lips.

"Thanks," Gabe said. "So what did you want to talk to me about?"

Jesse's smile faded. He set his beer on the edge of the desk, but hesitated, twirling the neck of the bottle between two fingers. "I don't know how to put this…"

"Jess," Gabe said when he trailed off. "Talk to me."

"Yeah, all right." He took off his hat and dragged a hand through his hair in that habitual way he had, then set the Stetson beside his beer. "It's about Quinn. He's not physically fit to be out in the field."

Gabe sat back, taking a long moment to absorb that news. Jesse and Quinn had their issues, but he knew better than to think this was anything other than Jesse's medical opinion. The cowboy was too good at what he did to sully his reputation with a misdiagnosis.

"Why?"

Jesse blew out a breath and slung one long jean-clad leg over the corner of the desk. He met Gabe's stare head-on. "Did he tell you why the SEALs wouldn't take him back?"

"His shoulder's fucked up, but that shouldn't factor into our job. What we do isn't nearly as physically demanding as—"

Jesse was already shaking his head. "It's because of the brain injury."

Stunned speechless, Gabe stared at him for five long seconds. "Uh, whoa, back up. The *what*?"

"Think about it," Jesse said. "When you two were in that car accident, you were traveling at what? Sixty-five, seventy miles an hour—and Quinn was thrown through the windshield. Man, he's lucky to be alive and functioning as well as he is. He sustained massive head trauma, was in a coma for a week."

Gabe recalled one night when Quinn came into his hospital room to check on him, and vaguely remembered the bandages wrapped around his friend's head. He hadn't thought much of it at the time, too muddled by the painkillers in his system from his last surgery, too focused on healing his foot so he could keep his job. He had wondered, at one time or another throughout the past year, why a messed up shoulder had gotten the best of Quinn, why the great Achilles hadn't even fought to stay a SEAL like Gabe had.

Now he understood and his throat tightened. "How bad is he?"

"Like I said, he's awesome, considering. A goddamn walking miracle, you ask me," Jesse added. "But he's not sleeping or eating like he should, and he's blacking out, losing time. I saw him do it once back in Bogotá, and I have a feeling it's happening pretty regular."

"Does he know? I mean, is he losing time and doesn't realize it, or — "

"He knows. That's why he kicked up such a fuss about me doing a physical and seeing his medical records."

Gabe sighed. "If I pull him off the team, it'll kill him."

Jesse stood. "It's your call, boss." He settled his Stetson on his head, picked up his beer. "But, fair warning. If you don't pull him, he'll black out at the wrong time. Then he'll wind up dead a whole helluva lot quicker."

Gabe sat back in his chair and stared at the office door for a long time after Jesse left.

"Oh, man, Q," he groaned and rubbed both hands over his face. "Why didn't you tell me?"

"Why didn't he tell you what?"

He looked up as Audrey slipped inside his office and shut the door behind her. He started to say, "Nothing," but closed his mouth and studied her. She wore another of her flowing dresses, her hair loose around her shoulders, her feet bare. He could tell by the way she kept curling her toes into his carpet that her feet were cold, as usual.

"C'mere." He patted the desk. She crossed the room and pulled herself up to sit in front of him. Sure enough, her foot was like an ice cube despite the humid day, and he closed his hands around it to warm it up. "I'm going to buy you a pair of slippers."

She made a face. "I won't wear them." She let him massage her foot for a moment longer, then tucked both feet under his thighs in the chair and drew him closer so that they were nose to nose. She kissed his forehead. "Everything okay?"

"No, I don't think so." He told her about Quinn's medical

condition. Her eyes glazed with tears and he pulled her down onto his lap.

"Oh, no. Poor Quinn. What are you going to do?"

"About him? I don't know." And frankly, he didn't want to think about it at the moment. He lifted her chin with the curve of his index finger and tried on a smile. "But you… I know exactly what I'm going to do about you."

"Hmm." She pressed a lingering kiss to his mouth. "Did Raffi's little ploy work?"

"What little ploy?"

"He told me if I wanted to get you to the altar, I had to be a *tad*"—she held her fingers a millimeter apart—"manipulative. Make you think there's a chance I'd leave you."

"There isn't?"

"For a smart man, you sure can be an idiot sometimes." She laughed and slapped his chest. "So? Did it work?"

Gabe thought of the last time he was asked that question by Quinn during his retirement party. Thought about how lonely he'd been back then and he hadn't even known it, how colorless his life had been without Audrey to brighten it up. He never wanted to go back to that dull, lonely existence again.

"Yeah," he admitted, "it worked." He reached into his desk drawer for the plane tickets, but had to bite the inside of his cheek to fight a smile. He'd been played beautifully, and he loved her all the more for it. "We leave tomorrow."

"Vegas?" She fanned the two tickets out and grinned at him. "So are you just carting me off like a caveman, or are you gonna ask me like a good, honorable SEAL should?"

Gabe pretended to think about it for a half second, then

scooped her into his arms and carried her through the door adjoining his office to their bedroom.

"Gabe, no. We have company!" She laughed when she hit the bed with a bounce, but the laughter soon turned to moans as he settled between her open legs and dragged his lips up her neck to her ear.

"Caveman," he said and nibbled her earlobe. "I'm not a SEAL anymore."

And for the first time, that didn't bother him in the least.

ACKNOWLEDGMENTS

First, I want to thank my editor, the lovely Heather Howland, and the rest of the amazing people in the Entangled family for putting untold hours into this book. It's been a year in the making, but seeing the guys of HORNET out in the world is still the best birthday present anyone has ever given me. Thanks for all of your encouragement and support.

A nod of thanks also goes to Seton Hill University's MFA program. Without all of the excellent critique sessions, I doubt this novel would have seen print. And a special thank you to my fellow Unteachables for putting up with my occasional lack-of-sleep-induced internet rants and random bursts of "OMG, it's really happening!" You guys rock!

I need to take a moment to show appreciation for the Western New York chapter of RWA, especially Helen Jones. If you had never told me about Entangled during lunch last March, this book would still be just another file on my computer.

I'd also be remiss if I didn't mention my eighth grade literature teacher, Ms. Hoopsick. You saw something in my writing before anyone else. By reading all of my silly stories (including that epic romance/fantasy/mystery/sci-fi concoction), you nurtured my fragile middle school writer's soul and pushed me the first steps down the path to publication. Thank you.

And to my family, thanks for always being there. I know it's not always easy having a crazy writer on the family tree. Love you!